Agatha Christie®

The Mirror Crack'd From Side to Side

HARPER

HARPER

An imprint of HarperCollins*Publishers*
1 London Bridge Street
London SE1 9GF
www.harpercollins.co.uk

This paperback edition 2016

First published in Great Britain by
Collins, The Crime Club 1962

A catalogue record for this book is available from the British Library

ISBN 978-0-00-819659-2

Set in Sabon LT Std by Palimpsest Book Production Limited,
Falkirk, Stirlingshire
Printed and bound in Great Britain

MIX
Paper from
responsible sources

FSC
www.fsc.org **FSC™ C007454**

To
Margaret Rutherford
in admiration

Out flew the web and floated wide;
  The mirror crack'd from side to side;
'The curse is come upon me,' cried
  The Lady of Shalott

Alfred Tennyson

CHAPTER 1

Miss Jane Marple was sitting by her window. The window looked over her garden, once a source of pride to her. That was no longer so. Nowadays she looked out of the window and winced. Active gardening had been forbidden her for some time now. No stooping, no digging, no planting—at most a little light pruning. Old Laycock who came three times a week, did his best, no doubt. But his best, such as it was (which was not much) was only the best according to *his* lights, and not according to those of his employer. Miss Marple knew exactly what she wanted done, and when she wanted it done, and instructed him duly. Old Laycock then displayed his particular genius which was that of enthusiastic agreement and subsequent lack of performance.

'That's right, missus. We'll have them mecosoapies there and the Canterburys along the wall and as you say it ought to be got on with first thing next week.'

Laycock's excuses were always reasonable, and strongly resembled those of Captain George's in *Three Men in a Boat* for avoiding going to sea. In the captain's case the

Agatha Christie

wind was always wrong, either blowing off shore or in
shore, or coming from the unreliable west, or the even
more treacherous east. Laycock's was the weather. Too
dry—too wet—waterlogged—a nip of frost in the air.
Or else something of great importance had to come first
(usually to do with cabbages or brussels sprouts of which
he liked to grow inordinate quantities). Laycock's own
principles of gardening were simple and no employer,
however knowledgeable, could wean him from them.

They consisted of a great many cups of tea, sweet and
strong, as an encouragement to effort, a good deal of
sweeping up of leaves in the autumn, and a certain
amount of bedding out of his own favourite plants,
mainly asters and salvias—to 'make a nice show', as he
put it, in summer. He was all in favour of syringeing
roses for green-fly, but was slow to get around to it, and
a demand for deep trenching for sweet peas was usually
countered by the remark that you ought to see his own
sweet peas! A proper treat last year, and no fancy stuff
done beforehand.

To be fair, he was attached to his employers, humoured
their fancies in horticulture (so far as no actual hard work
was involved) but vegetables he knew to be the real stuff
of life; a nice Savoy, or a bit of curly kale; flowers were
fancy stuff such as ladies liked to go in for, having nothing
better to do with their time. He showed his affection by
producing presents of the aforementioned asters, salvias,
lobelia edging, and summer chrysanthemums.

'Been doing some work at them new houses over at the
Development. Want their gardens laid out nice, they do.

2

More plants than they needed so I brought along a few, and I've put 'em in where them old-fashioned roses ain't looking so well.'

Thinking of these things, Miss Marple averted her eyes from the garden, and picked up her knitting.

One had to face the fact: St Mary Mead was *not* the place it had been. In a sense, of course, nothing was what it had been. You could blame the war (both the wars) or the younger generation, or women going out to work, or the atom bomb, or just the Government—but what one really meant was the simple fact that one was growing old. Miss Marple, who was a very sensible lady, knew that quite well. It was just that, in a queer way, she felt it more in St Mary Mead, because it had been her home for so long.

St Mary Mead, the old world core of it, was still there. The Blue Boar was there, and the church and the vicarage and the little nest of Queen Anne and Georgian houses, of which hers was one. Miss Hartnell's house was still there, and also Miss Hartnell, fighting progress to the last gasp. Miss Wetherby had passed on and her house was now inhabited by the bank manager and his family, having been given a face-lift by the painting of doors and windows a bright royal blue. There were new people in most of the other old houses, but the houses themselves were little changed in appearances since the people who had bought them had done so because they liked what the house agent called 'old world charm'. They just added another bath-room, and spent a good deal of money on plumbing, electric cookers, and dish-washers.

But though the houses looked much as before, the same could hardly be said of the village street. When shops changed hands there, it was with a view to immediate and intemperate modernization. The fishmonger was unrecognizable with new super windows behind which the refrigerated fish gleamed. The butcher had remained conservative—good meat is good meat, if you have the money to pay for it. If not, you take the cheaper cuts and the tough joints and like it! Barnes, the grocer, was still there, unchanged, for which Miss Hartnell and Miss Marple and others daily thanked Heaven. So *obliging*, comfortable chairs to sit in by the counter, and cosy discussions as to cuts of bacon, and varieties of cheese. At the end of the street, however, where Mr Toms had once had his basket shop stood a glittering new super-market—anathema to the elderly ladies of St Mary Mead.

'Packets of things one's never even *heard* of,' exclaimed Miss Hartnell. 'All these great packets of breakfast cereal instead of cooking a child a proper breakfast of bacon and eggs. *And* you're expected to take a basket *yourself* and go round looking for things—it takes a quarter of an hour sometimes to find all one wants—and usually made up in inconvenient sizes, too much or too little. And then a long queue waiting to pay as you go out. Most tiring. Of course it's all very well for the people from the Development—'

At this point she stopped.

Because, as was now usual, the sentence came to an end there. The Development, Period, as they would say in modern terms. It had an entity of its own, and a capital letter.

*

Miss Marple uttered a sharp exclamation of annoyance. She'd dropped a stitch again. Not only that, she must have dropped it some time ago. Not until now, when she had to decrease for the neck and count the stitches, had she realized the fact. She took up a spare pin, held the knitting sideways to the light and peered anxiously. Even her new spectacles didn't seem to do any good. And that, she reflected, was because obviously there came a time when oculists, in spite of their luxurious waiting-rooms, the up-to-date instruments, the bright lights they flashed into your eyes, and the very high fees they charged, couldn't do anything much more for you. Miss Marple reflected with some nostalgia on how good her eyesight had been a few (well, not perhaps a *few*) years ago. From the vantage-point of her garden, so admirably placed to see all that was going on in St Mary Mead, how little had escaped her noticing eye! And with the help of her bird glasses—(an interest in birds was *so* useful!)—she had been able to see—She broke off there and let her thoughts run back over the past. Ann Protheroe in her summer frock going along to the Vicarage garden. And Colonel Protheroe—poor man—a very tiresome and unpleasant man, to be sure—but to be murdered like that—She shook her head and went on to thoughts of Griselda, the vicar's pretty young wife. Dear Griselda—such a faithful friend—a Christmas card every year. That attractive baby of hers was a strapping young man now, and with a very good job. Engineering, was it? He always *had* enjoyed taking his mechanical trains to pieces. Beyond the Vicarage, there had been the stile and the field path with Farmer Giles's cattle beyond in the meadows where now—now . . .

The Development.

And why not? Miss Marple asked herself sternly. These things had to be. The houses were necessary, and they were very well built, or so she had been told. 'Planning', or whatever they called it. Though why everything had to be called a Close she couldn't imagine. Aubrey Close and Longwood Close, and Grandison Close and all the rest of them. Not really Closes at all. Miss Marple knew what a Close was perfectly. Her uncle had been a Canon of Chichester Cathedral. As a child she had gone to stay with him in the Close.

It was like Cherry Baker who always called Miss Marple's old-world overcrowded drawing-room the 'lounge'. Miss Marple corrected her gently, 'It's the drawing-room, Cherry.' And Cherry, because she was young and kind, endeavoured to remember, though it was obvious to her 'drawing-room' was a very funny word to use—and 'lounge' came slipping out. She had of late, however, compromised on 'living-room'. Miss Marple liked Cherry very much. Her name was Mrs Baker and she came from the Development. She was one of the detachment of young wives who shopped at the supermarket and wheeled prams about the quiet streets of St Mary Mead. They were all smart and well turned out. Their hair was crisp and curled. They laughed and talked and called to one another. They were like a happy flock of birds. Owing to the insidious snares of Hire Purchase, they were always in need of ready money, though their husbands all earned good wages; and so they came and did housework or cooking. Cherry was a quick and efficient cook, she was an intelligent girl, took telephone calls correctly and was quick to spot inaccuracies in the tradesmen's books. She was not much given to turning mattresses, and as far as washing up went Miss Marple always now passed the pantry door with her head turned away so as not to observe Cherry's method which was that of thrusting everything into the sink together and letting loose a snowstorm of detergent on it. Miss Marple had quietly removed her old Worcester teaset from daily circulation and put it in the corner cabinet whence it only emerged on special occasions. Instead she had purchased a modern service with a pattern of pale grey on white and no gilt on it whatsoever to be washed away in the sink.

How different it had been in the past . . . Faithful Florence, for instance, that grenadier of a parlourmaid—and there had been Amy and Clara and Alice, those 'nice little maids'—arriving from St Faith's Orphanage, to be 'trained', and then going on to better-paid jobs elsewhere. Rather simple, some of them had been, and frequently adenoidal, and Amy distinctly moronic. They had gossiped and chattered with the other maids in the village and walked out with the fishmonger's assistant, or the under-gardener at the Hall, or one of Mr Barnes the grocer's numerous assistants. Miss Marple's mind went back over them affectionately thinking of all the little woolly coats she had knitted for their subsequent offspring. They had not been very good with the telephone, and no good at all at arithmetic. On the other hand, they knew how to wash up, and how to make a bed. They had had skills, rather than education. It was odd that nowadays it should be the educated girls who went in for all the domestic chores. Students from abroad, girls *au pair*, university students in the vacation, young married women like Cherry Baker, who lived in spurious Closes on new building developments.

There were still, of course, people like Miss Knight. This last thought came suddenly as Miss Knight's tread overhead made the lustres on the mantelpiece tinkle warningly. Miss Knight had obviously had her afternoon rest and would now go out for her afternoon walk. In a moment she would come to ask Miss Marple if she could get her anything in the town. The thought of Miss Knight brought the usual reaction to Miss Marple's mind. Of course, it was very generous of dear Raymond (her nephew) and nobody could be kinder than Miss Knight, and of course that attack of bronchitis *had* left her very weak, and Dr Haydock had said very firmly that she must not go on sleeping alone in the house with only someone coming in daily, but—She stopped there. Because it was no use going on with the thought which was 'If only it could have been someone other than Miss Knight.' But there wasn't much choice for elderly ladies nowadays. Devoted maidservants had gone out of fashion. In real illness you could have a proper hospital nurse, at vast expense and procured with difficulty, or you could go to hospital. But after the critical phase of illness had passed, you were down to the Miss Knights.

There wasn't, Miss Marple reflected, anything wrong about the Miss Knights other than the fact that they were madly irritating. They were full of kindness, ready to feel affection towards their charges, to humour them, to be bright and cheerful with them and in general to treat them as slightly mentally afflicted children.

'But I,' said Miss Marple to herself, 'although I may be old, am *not* a mentally afflicted child.'

At this moment, breathing rather heavily, as was her custom, Miss Knight bounced brightly into the room. She was a big, rather flabby woman of fifty-six with yellowing grey hair very elaborately arranged, glasses, a long thin nose, and below it a good-natured mouth and a weak chin.

'Here we are!' she exclaimed with a kind of beaming boisterousness, meant to cheer and enliven the sad twilight of the aged. 'I hope *we*'ve had our little snooze?'

'*I* have been knitting,' Miss Marple replied, putting some emphasis on the pronoun, 'and,' she went on, confessing her weakness with distaste and shame, 'I've dropped a stitch.'

'Oh dear, dear,' said Miss Knight. 'Well, we'll soon put that right, won't we?'

'*You* will,' said Miss Marple. '*I*, alas, am unable to do so.'

The slight acerbity of her tone passed quite unnoticed. Miss Knight, as always, was eager to help.

'There,' she said after a few moments. 'There you are, dear. Quite all right now.'

Though Miss Marple was perfectly agreeable to be called 'dear' (and even 'ducks') by the woman at the greengrocer or the girl at the paper shop, it annoyed her intensely to be called 'dear' by Miss Knight. Another of those things that elderly ladies have to bear. She thanked Miss Knight politely.

'And now I'm just going out for my wee toddle,' said Miss Knight humorously. 'Shan't be long.'

'Please don't dream of hurrying back,' said Miss Marple politely and sincerely.

'Well, I don't like to leave you too long on your own, dear, in case you get moped.'

'I assure you I am quite happy,' said Miss Marple. 'I probably shall have' (she closed her eyes) 'a little nap.'

'That's right, dear. Anything I can get you?'

Miss Marple opened her eyes and considered.

'You might go into Longdon's and see if the curtains are ready. And perhaps another skein of the blue wool from Mrs Wisley. And a box of blackcurrant lozenges at the chemist's. And change my book at the library—but don't let them give you anything that isn't on my list. This last one was too terrible. I couldn't read it.' She held out *The Spring Awakens*.

'Oh dear dear! Didn't you like it? I thought you'd love it. Such a pretty story.'

'And if it isn't too far for you, perhaps you wouldn't mind going as far as Halletts and see if they have one of those up-and-down egg whisks—*not* the turn-the-handle kind.'

(She knew very well they had nothing of the kind, but Halletts was the farthest shop possible.)

'If all this isn't too much—' she murmured.

But Miss Knight replied with obvious sincerity.

'Not at all. I shall be delighted.'

Miss Knight loved shopping. It was the breath of life to her. One met acquaintances, and had the chance of a chat, one gossiped with the assistants, and had the opportunity of examining various articles in the various shops. And one could spend quite a long time engaged in these pleasant occupations without any guilty feeling that it was one's duty to hurry back.

So Miss Knight started off happily, after a last glance at the frail old lady resting so peacefully by the window.

After waiting a few minutes in case Miss Knight should return for a shopping bag, or her purse, or a handkerchief (she was a great forgetter and returner), and also to recover from the slight mental fatigue induced by thinking of so many unwanted things to ask Miss Knight to get, Miss Marple rose briskly to her feet, cast aside her knitting and strode purposefully across the room and into the hall. She took down her summer coat from its peg, a stick from the hall stand and exchanged her bedroom slippers for a pair of stout walking shoes. Then she left the house by the side door.

'It will take her at least an hour and a half,' Miss Marple estimated to herself. 'Quite that—with all the people from the Development doing their shopping.'

Miss Marple visualized Miss Knight at Longdon's making abortive inquiries re curtains. Her surmises were remarkably accurate. At this moment Miss Knight was exclaiming, 'Of course, I felt quite sure in my own mind they wouldn't be ready yet. But of course I said I'd come along and see when the old lady spoke about it. Poor old dears, they've got so little to look forward to. One must humour them. And she's a sweet old lady. Failing a little now, it's only to be expected—their faculties get dimmed. Now that's a pretty material you've got there. Do you have it in any other colours?'

A pleasant twenty minutes passed. When Miss Knight had finally departed, the senior assistant remarked with a sniff, 'Failing, is she? I'll believe that when I see it for myself. Old Miss Marple has always been as sharp as a needle, and I'd say she still is.' She then gave her attention to a young woman in tight trousers and a sail-cloth jersey who wanted plastic material with crabs on it for bathroom curtains.

'Emily Waters, that's who she reminds me of,' Miss Marple was saying to herself, with the satisfaction it always gave her to match up a human personality with one known in the past. 'Just the same bird brain. Let me see, what happened to Emily?'

Nothing much, was her conclusion. She had once nearly got engaged to a curate, but after an understanding of several years the affair had fizzled out. Miss Marple dismissed her nurse attendant from her mind and gave her attention to her surroundings. She had traversed the garden rapidly only observing as it were from the corner of her eye that Laycock had cut down the old-fashioned roses in a way more suitable to hybrid teas, but she did not allow this to distress her, or distract her from the delicious pleasure of having escaped for an outing entirely on her own. She had a happy feeling of adventure. She turned to the right, entered the Vicarage gate, took the path through the Vicarage garden and came out on the right of way. Where the stile had been there was now an iron swing gate giving on to a tarred asphalt path. This led to a neat little bridge over the stream and on the other side of the stream where once there had been meadows with cows, there was the Development.

CHAPTER 2

With the feeling of Columbus setting out to discover a new world, Miss Marple passed over the bridge, continued on to the path and within four minutes was actually in Aubrey Close.

Of course Miss Marple had seen the Development from the Market Basing Road, that is, had seen from afar its Closes and rows of neat well-built houses, with their television masts and their blue and pink and yellow and green painted doors and windows. But until now it had only had the reality of a map, as it were. She had not been in it and of it. But now she was here, observing the brave new world that was springing up, the world that by all accounts was foreign to all she had known. It was like a neat model built with child's bricks. It hardly seemed real to Miss Marple.

The people, too, looked unreal. The trousered young women, the rather sinister-looking young men and boys, the exuberant bosoms of the fifteen-year-old girls. Miss Marple couldn't help thinking that it all looked terribly depraved. Nobody noticed her much as she trudged along. She turned out of Aubrey Close and was presently in

Darlington Close. She went slowly and as she went she listened avidly to the snippets of conversation between mothers wheeling prams, to the girls addressing young men, to the sinister-looking Teds (she supposed they were Teds) exchanging dark remarks with each other. Mothers came out on doorsteps calling to their children who, as usual, were busy doing all the things they had been told not to do. Children, Miss Marple reflected gratefully, never changed. And presently she began to smile, and noted down in her mind her usual series of recognitions.

That woman is just like Carry Edwards—and the dark one is just like that Hooper girl—she'll make a mess of her marriage just like Mary Hooper did. Those boys—the dark one is just like Edward Leeke, a lot of wild talk but no harm in him—a nice boy really—the fair one is Mrs Bedwell's Josh all over again. Nice boys, both of them. The one like Gregory Binns won't do very well, I'm afraid. I expect he's got the same sort of mother . . .

She turned a corner into Walsingham Close and her spirits rose every moment.

The new world was the same as the old. The houses were different, the streets were called Closes, the clothes were different, the voices were different, but the human beings were the same as they always had been. And though using slightly different phraseology, the subjects of conversation were the same.

By dint of turning corners in her exploration, Miss Marple had rather lost her sense of direction and had arrived at the edge of the housing estate again. She was now in Carrisbrook Close, half of which was still 'under construction'. At the first-floor window of a nearly finished house a young couple were standing. Their voices floated down as they discussed the amenities.

'You must admit it's a nice position, Harry.'

'Other one was just as good.'

'This one's got two more rooms.'

'And you've got to pay for them.'

'Well, I *like* this one.'

'You would!'

'Ow, don't be such a spoil-sport. You know what Mum said.'

'Your Mum never stops saying.'

'Don't you say nothing against Mum. Where'd I have been without her? And she might have cut up nastier than she did. She could have taken you to court.'

'Oh, come off it, Lily.'

'It's a good view of the hills. You can almost see—' She leaned far out, twisting her body to the left. 'You can almost see the reservoir—'

She leant farther still, not realizing that she was resting her weight on loose boards that had been laid across the sill. They slipped under the pressure of her body, sliding outwards, carrying her with them. She screamed, trying to regain her balance.

'Harry—'

The young man stood motionless—a foot or two behind her. He took one step backwards—

Desperately, clawing at the wall, the girl righted herself. 'Oo!' She let out a frightened breath. 'I near as nothing fell out. Why didn't you get hold of me?'

'It was all so quick. Anyway you're all right.'

'That's all you know about it. I nearly went, I tell you. And look at the front of my jumper, it's all mussed.'

Miss Marple went on a little way, then on impulse, she turned back.

Lily was outside in the road waiting for the young man to lock up the house.

Miss Marple went up to her and spoke rapidly in a low voice.

'If I were you, my dear, I shouldn't marry that young man. You want someone whom you can rely upon if you're in danger. You must excuse me for saying this to you—but I feel you ought to be warned.'

She turned away and Lily stared after her.

'Well, of all the—'

Her young man approached.

'What was she saying to you, Lil?'

Lily opened her mouth—then shut it again.

'Giving me the gipsy's warning, if you want to know.'

She eyed him in a thoughtful manner.

Miss Marple in her anxiety to get away quickly, turned a corner, stumbled over some loose stones and fell.

A woman came running out of one of the houses.

'Oh dear, what a nasty spill! I hope you haven't hurt yourself?'

With almost excessive goodwill she put her arms round Miss Marple and tugged her to her feet.

'No bones broken, I hope? There we are. I expect you feel rather shaken.'

Her voice was loud and friendly. She was a plump

16

squarely built woman of about forty, brown hair just turning grey, blue eyes, and a big generous mouth that seemed to Miss Marple's rather shaken gaze to be far too full of white shining teeth.

'You'd better come inside and sit down and rest a bit. I'll make you a cup of tea.'

Miss Marple thanked her. She allowed herself to be led through the blue-painted door and into a small room full of bright cretonne-covered chairs and sofas.

'There you are,' said her rescuer, establishing her on a cushioned arm-chair. 'You sit quiet and I'll put the kettle on.'

She hurried out of the room which seemed rather restfully quiet after her departure. Miss Marple took a deep breath. She was not really hurt, but the fall had shaken her. Falls at her age were not to be encouraged. With luck, however, she thought guiltily, Miss Knight need never know. She moved her arms and legs gingerly. Nothing broken. If she could only get home all right. Perhaps, after a cup of tea—

The cup of tea arrived almost as the thought came to her. Brought on a tray with four sweet biscuits on a little plate.

'There you are.' It was placed on a small table in front of her. 'Shall I pour it out for you? Better have plenty of sugar.'

'No sugar, thank you.'

'You must have sugar. Shock, you know. I was abroad with ambulances during the war. Sugar's wonderful for shock.' She put four lumps in the cup and stirred vigorously. 'Now you get that down, and you'll feel as right as rain.'

Miss Marple accepted the dictum.

'A kind woman,' she thought. 'She reminds me of someone—now who is it?'

'You've been very kind to me,' she said, smiling.

'Oh, that's nothing. The little ministering angel, that's me. I love helping people.' She looked out of the window as the latch of the outer gate clicked. 'Here's my husband home. Arthur—we've got a visitor.'

She went out into the hall and returned with Arthur who looked rather bewildered. He was a thin pale man, rather slow in speech.

'This lady fell down—right outside our gate, so of course I brought her in.'

'Your wife is very kind, Mr—'

'Badcock's the name.'

'Mr Badcock, I'm afraid I've given her a lot of trouble.'

'Oh, no trouble to Heather. Heather enjoys doing things for people.' He looked at her curiously. 'Were you on your way anywhere in particular?'

'No, I was just taking a walk. I live in St Mary Mead, the house beyond the Vicarage. My name is Marple.'

'Well, I never!' exclaimed Heather. 'So *you're* Miss Marple. I've heard about you. You're the one who does all the murders.'

'Heather! What *do* you—'

'Oh, you know what I mean. Not actually *do* murders— find out about them. That's right, isn't it?'

Miss Marple murmured modestly that she *had* been mixed up in murders once or twice.

'I heard there have been murders here, in this village.

They were talking about it the other night at the Bingo Club. There was one at Gossington Hall. I wouldn't buy a place where there'd been a murder. I'd be sure it was haunted.'

'The murder wasn't committed in Gossington Hall. A dead body was brought there.'

'Found in the library on the hearthrug, that's what they said?'

Miss Marple nodded.

'Did you ever? Perhaps they're going to make a film of it. Perhaps that's why Marina Gregg has bought Gossington Hall.'

'Marina Gregg?'

'Yes. She and her husband. I forget his name—he's a producer, I think, or a director—Jason something. But Marina Gregg, she's lovely, isn't she? Of course she hasn't been in so many pictures of late years—she was ill for a long time. But I still think there's never anybody like her. Did you see her in *Carmanella*? And *The Price of Love*, and *Mary of Scotland*? She's not so young any more, but she'll always be a wonderful actress. I've always been a terrific fan of hers. When I was a teenager I used to dream about her. The big thrill of my life was when there was a big show in aid of the St John Ambulance in Bermuda, and Marina Gregg came to open it. I was mad with excitement, and then on the very day I went down with a temperature and the doctor said I couldn't go. But I wasn't going to be beaten. I didn't actually feel too bad. So I got up and put a lot of make-up on my face and went along. I was introduced to her and she talked to me for quite

three minutes and gave me her autograph. It was wonderful.
I've never forgotten that day.'

Miss Marple stared at her.

'I hope there were no—unfortunate after-effects?' she
said anxiously.

Heather Badcock laughed.

'None at all. Never felt better. What I say is, if you want
a thing you've got to take risks. I always do.'

She laughed again, a happy strident laugh.

Arthur Badcock said admiringly, 'There's never any
holding Heather. She always gets away with things.'

'Alison Wilde,' murmured Miss Marple, with a nod of
satisfaction.

'Pardon?' said Mr Badcock.

'Nothing. Just someone I used to know.'

Heather looked at her inquiringly.

'You reminded me of her, that is all.'

'Did I? I hope she was nice.'

'She was very nice indeed,' said Miss Marple slowly.
'Kind, healthy, full of life.'

'But she had her faults, I suppose?' laughed Heather. 'I
have.'

'Well, Alison always saw her own point of view so clearly
that she didn't always see how things might appear to, or
affect, other people.'

'Like the time you took in that evacuated family from
a condemned cottage and they went off with all our
teaspoons,' Arthur said.

'But Arthur!—I couldn't have turned them away. It
wouldn't have been kind.'

'They were family spoons,' said Mr Badcock sadly. 'Georgian. Belonged to my mother's grandmother.'

'Oh, do forget those old spoons, Arthur. You do harp so.'

'I'm not very good at forgetting, I'm afraid.'

Miss Marple looked at him thoughtfully.

'What's your friend doing now?' asked Heather of Miss Marple with kindly interest.

Miss Marple paused a moment before answering.

'Alison Wilde? Oh—she died.'

CHAPTER 3

'I'm glad to be back,' said Mrs Bantry. 'Although, of course, I've had a wonderful time.'

Miss Marple nodded appreciatively, and accepted a cup of tea from her friend's hand.

When her husband, Colonel Bantry, had died some years ago, Mrs Bantry had sold Gossington Hall and the considerable amount of land attached to it, retaining for herself what had been the East Lodge, a charming porticoed little building replete with inconvenience, where even a gardener had refused to live. Mrs Bantry had added to it the essentials of modern life, a built-on kitchen of the latest type, a new water supply from the main, electricity, and a bathroom. This had all cost her a great deal, but not nearly so much as an attempt to live at Gossington Hall would have done. She had also retained the essentials of privacy, about three quarters of an acre of garden nicely ringed with trees, so that, as she explained, 'Whatever they do with Gossington I shan't really see it or worry.'

For the last few years she had spent a good deal of the year travelling about, visiting children and grandchildren in various parts of the globe, and coming back from time to time to enjoy the privacies of her own home. Gossington Hall itself had changed hands once or twice. It had been run as a guest house, failed, and been bought by four people who had shared it as four roughly divided flats and subsequently quarrelled. Finally the Ministry of Health had bought it for some obscure purpose for which they eventually did not want it. The Ministry had now resold it—and it was this sale which the two friends were discussing.

'I have heard rumours, of course,' said Miss Marple.

'Naturally,' said Mrs Bantry. 'It was even said that Charlie Chaplin and all his children were coming to live here. That would have been wonderful fun; unfortunately there isn't a word of truth in it. No, it's definitely Marina Gregg.'

'How very lovely she was,' said Miss Marple with a sigh. 'I always remember those early films of hers. *Bird of Passage* with that handsome Joel Roberts. And the Mary, Queen of Scots film. And of course it was very sentimental, but I *did* enjoy *Comin' Thru the Rye*. Oh dear, that was a long time ago.'

'Yes,' said Mrs Bantry. 'She must be—what do you think? Forty-five? Fifty?'

Miss Marple thought nearer fifty.

'Has she been in anything lately? Of course I don't go very often to the cinema nowadays.'

'Only small parts, I think,' said Mrs Bantry. 'She hasn't been a star for quite a long time. She had that bad nervous breakdown. After one of her divorces.'

'Such a lot of husbands they all have,' said Miss Marple. 'It must really be very tiring.'

'It wouldn't suit *me*,' said Mrs Bantry. 'After you've fallen in love with a man and married him and got used to his ways and settled down comfortably—to go and throw it all up and start again! It seems to me madness.'

'I can't presume to speak,' said Miss Marple with a little spinsterish cough, 'never having married. But it seems, you know, a *pity*.'

'I suppose they can't help it really,' said Mrs Bantry vaguely. 'With the kind of lives they have to live. So public, you know. I met her,' she added. 'Marina Gregg, I mean, when I was in California.'

'What was she like?' Miss Marple asked with interest.

'Charming,' said Mrs Bantry. 'So natural and unspoiled.' She added thoughtfully, 'It's like a kind of livery really.'

'What is?'

'Being unspoiled and natural. You learn how to do it, and then you have to go on being it all the time. Just think of the hell of it—never to be able to chuck something, and say, "Oh, for the Lord's sake stop bothering me." I dare say that in sheer self-defence you have to have drunken parties or orgies.'

'She's had five husbands, hasn't she?' Miss Marple asked.

'At least. An early one that didn't count, and then a foreign Prince or Count, and then another film star, Robert Truscott, wasn't it? That was built up as a great romance. But it only lasted four years. And then Isidore Wright, the playwright. That was rather serious and quiet, and she had a baby—apparently she'd always longed to have a child— she's even half-adopted a few strays—anyway this was the real thing. Very much built up. Motherhood with a capital

M. And then, I believe, it was an imbecile, or queer or something—and it was after that, that she had this breakdown and started to take drugs and all that, and threw up her parts.'

'You seem to know a lot about her,' said Miss Marple.

'Well, naturally,' said Mrs Bantry. 'When she bought Gossington I was interested. She married the present man about two years ago, and they say she's quite all right again now. He's a producer—or do I mean a director? I always get mixed. He was in love with her when they were quite young, but he didn't amount to very much in those days. But now, I believe, he's got quite famous. What's his name now? Jason—Jason something—Jason Hudd, no, Rudd, that's it. They've bought Gossington because it's handy for'—she hesitated—'Elstree?' she hazarded.

Miss Marple shook her head.

'I don't think so,' she said. 'Elstree's in North London.'

'It's the fairly new studios. Hellingforth—that's it. Sounds so Finnish, I always think. About six miles from Market Basing. She's going to do a film on Elizabeth of Austria, I believe.'

'What a lot you know,' said Miss Marple. 'About the private lives of film stars. Did you learn it all in California?'

'Not really,' said Mrs Bantry. 'Actually I get it from the extraordinary magazines I read at my hairdresser's. Most of the stars I don't even know by name, but as I said because Marina Gregg and her husband have bought Gossington, I was interested. Really the things those magazines say! I don't suppose half of it is true—probably not a quarter. I *don't* believe Marina Gregg is a nymphomaniac,

25

I *don't* think she drinks, pobably she doesn't even take drugs, and quite likely she just went away to have a nice rest and didn't have a nervous breakdown at all!—but it's true that she is coming here to live.'

'Next week, I heard,' said Miss Marple.

'As soon as that? I know she's lending Gossington for a big fête on the twenty-third in aid of the St John Ambulance Corps. I suppose they've done a lot to the house?'

'Practically everything,' said Miss Marple. 'Really it would have been much simpler, and probably cheaper, to have pulled it down and built a new house.'

'Bathrooms, I suppose?'

'Six new ones, I hear. And a palm court. And a pool. And what I believe they call picture windows, and they've knocked your husband's study and the library into one to make a music room.'

'Arthur will turn in his grave. You know how he hated music. Tone deaf, poor dear. His face, when some kind friend took us to the opera! He'll probably come back and haunt them.' She stopped and then said abruptly, 'Does anyone ever hint that Gossington might be haunted?'

Miss Marple shook her head.

'It isn't,' she said with certainty.

'That wouldn't prevent people saying it was,' Mrs Bantry pointed out.

'Nobody ever has said so.' Miss Marple paused and then said, 'People aren't really foolish, you know. Not in villages.'

Mrs Bantry shot her a quick look. 'You've always stuck to that, Jane. And I won't say that you're not right.'

She suddenly smiled.

'Marina Gregg asked me, very sweetly and delicately, if I wouldn't find it very painful to see my old home occupied by strangers. I assured her that it wouldn't hurt me at all. I don't think she quite believed me. But after all, as you know, Jane, Gossington wasn't our home. We weren't brought up there as children—that's what really counts. It was just a house with a nice bit of shooting and fishing attached, that we bought when Arthur retired. We thought of it, I remember, as a house that would be nice and easy to run! How we can ever have thought that, I can't imagine! All those staircases and passages. Only four servants! *Only*! Those were the days, ha ha!' She added suddenly: 'What's all this about your falling down? That Knight woman ought not to let you go out by yourself.'

'It wasn't poor Miss Knight's fault. I gave her a lot of shopping to do and then I—'

'Deliberately gave her the slip? I see. Well, you shouldn't do it, Jane. Not at your age.'

'How did you hear about it?'

Mrs Bantry grinned.

'You can't keep any secrets in St Mary Mead. You've often told me so. Mrs Meavy told me.'

'Mrs Meavy?' Miss Marple looked at sea.

'She comes in daily. She's from the Development.'

'Oh, the Development.' The usual pause happened.

'What were you doing in the Development?' asked Mrs Bantry, curiously.

'I just wanted to see it. To see what the people were like.'

'And what did you think they were like?'

'Just the same as everyone else. I don't quite know if that was disappointing or reassuring.'

'Disappointing, I should think.'

'No. I think it's reassuring. It makes you—well—recognize certain types—so that when anything occurs—one will understand quite well why and for what reason.'

'Murder, do you mean?'

Miss Marple looked shocked.

'I don't know why you should assume that I think of murder *all* the time.'

'Nonsense, Jane. Why don't you come out boldly and call yourself a criminologist and have done with it?'

'Because I am nothing of the sort,' said Miss Marple with spirit. 'It is simply that I have a certain knowledge of human nature—that is only natural after having lived in a small village all my life.'

'You probably have something there,' said Mrs Bantry thoughtfully, 'though most people wouldn't agree, of course. Your nephew Raymond always used to say this place was a complete backwater.'

'Dear Raymond,' said Miss Marple indulgently. She added: 'He's always been so kind. He's paying for Miss Knight, you know.'

The thought of Miss Knight induced a new train of thought and she arose and said: 'I'd better be going back now, I suppose.'

'You didn't walk all the way here, did you?'

'Of course not. I came in Inch.'

This somewhat enigmatic pronouncement was received

28

with complete understanding. In days very long past, Mr Inch had been the proprietor of two cabs, which met trains at the local station and which were also hired by the local ladies to take them 'calling', out to tea parties, and occasionally, with their daughters, to such frivolous entertainments as dances. In the fullness of time Inch, a cheery red-faced man of seventy odd, gave place to his son—known as 'young Inch' (he was then aged forty-five) though old Inch still continued to drive such elderly ladies as considered his son too young and irresponsible. To keep up with the times, young Inch abandoned horse vehicles for motor cars. He was not very good with machinery and in due course a certain Mr Bardwell took over from him. The name Inch persisted. Mr Bardwell in due course sold out to Mr Roberts, but in the telephone book *Inch's Taxi Service* was still the official name, and the older ladies of the community continued to refer to their journeys as going somewhere 'in Inch', as though they were Jonah and Inch was a whale.

'Dr Haydock called,' said Miss Knight reproachfully. 'I told him you'd gone to tea with Mrs Bantry. He said he'd call in again tomorrow.'

She helped Miss Marple off with her wraps.

'And now, I expect, we're tired out,' she said accusingly.

'*You* may be,' said Miss Marple. '*I* am not.'

'You come and sit cosy by the fire,' said Miss Knight, as usual paying no attention. ('You don't need to take much notice of what the old dears say. I just humour them.')

Agatha Christie

'And how would we fancy a nice cup of Ovaltine? Or Horlicks for a change?'

Miss Marple thanked her and said she would like a small glass of dry sherry. Miss Knight looked disapproving.

'I don't know what the doctor would say to that, I'm sure,' she said, when she returned with the glass.

'We will make a point of asking him tomorrow morning,' said Miss Marple.

On the following morning Miss Knight met Dr Haydock in the hall, and did some agitated whispering.

The elderly doctor came into the room rubbing his hands, for it was a chilly morning.

'Here's our doctor to see us,' said Miss Knight gaily. 'Can I take your gloves, Doctor?'

'They'll be all right here,' said Haydock, casting them carelessly on a table. 'Quite a nippy morning.'

'A little glass of sherry perhaps?' suggested Miss Marple.

'I heard you were taking to drink. Well, you should never drink alone.'

The decanter and the glasses were already on a small table by Miss Marple. Miss Knight left the room.

Dr Haydock was a very old friend. He had semi-retired, but came to attend certain of his old patients.

'I hear you've been falling about,' he said as he finished his glass. 'It won't do, you know, not at your age. I'm warning you. And I hear you didn't want to send for Sandford.'

Sandford was Haydock's partner.

'That Miss Knight of yours sent for him anyway—and she was quite right.'

30

'I was only bruised and shaken a little. Dr Sandford said so. I could have waited quite well until you were back.'

'Now look here, my dear. I can't go on for ever. And Sandford, let me tell you, has better qualifications than I have. He's a first class man.'

'The young doctors are all the same,' said Miss Marple. 'They take your blood pressure, and whatever's the matter with you, you get some kind of mass produced variety of new pills. Pink ones, yellow ones, brown ones. Medicine nowadays is just like a supermarket—all packaged up.'

'Serve you right if I prescribed leeches, and black draught, and rubbed your chest with camphorated oil.'

'I do that myself when I've got a cough,' said Miss Marple with spirit, 'and very comforting it is.'

'We don't like getting old, that's what it is,' said Haydock gently. 'I hate it.'

'You're quite a young man compared to me,' said Miss Marple. 'And I don't really mind getting old—not that in itself. It's the lesser indignities.'

'I think I know what you mean.'

'Never being alone! The difficulty of getting out for a few minutes by oneself. And even my knitting—such a comfort that has always been, and I really am a good knitter. Now I drop stitches all the time—and quite often I don't even know I've dropped them.'

Haydock looked at her thoughtfully.

Then his eyes twinkled.

'There's always the opposite.'

'Now what do you mean by that?'

'If you can't knit, what about unravelling for a change? Penelope did.'

'I'm hardly in her position.'

'But unravelling's rather in your line, isn't it?'

He rose to his feet.

'I must be getting along. What I'd prescribe for you is a nice juicy murder.'

'That's an outrageous thing to say!'

'Isn't it? However, you can always make do with the depth the parsley sank into the butter on a summer's day. I always wondered about that. Good old Holmes. A period piece, nowadays, I suppose. But he'll never be forgotten.'

Miss Knight bustled in after the doctor had gone.

'There,' he said, 'we look *much* more cheerful. Did the doctor recommend a tonic?'

'He recommended me to take an interest in murder.'

'A nice detective story?'

'No,' said Miss Marple. 'Real life.'

'Goodness,' exclaimed Miss Knight. 'But there's not likely to be a murder in this quiet spot.'

'Murders,' said Miss Marple, 'can happen anywhere. And do.'

'At the Development, perhaps?' mused Miss Knight. 'A lot of those Teddy-looking boys carry knives.'

But the murder, when it came, was not at the Development.

CHAPTER 4

Mrs Bantry stepped back a foot or two, surveyed herself in the glass, made a slight adjustment to her hat (she was not used to wearing hats), drew on a pair of good quality leather gloves and left the lodge, closing the door carefully behind her. She had the most pleasurable anticipations of what lay in front of her. Some three weeks had passed since her talk with Miss Marple. Marina Gregg and her husband had arrived at Gossington Hall and were now more or less installed there.

There was to be a meeting there this afternoon of the main persons involved in the arrangements for the fête in aid of the St John Ambulance. Mrs Bantry was not among those on the committee, but she had received a note from Marina Gregg asking her to come and have tea beforehand. It had recalled their meeting in California and had been signed, 'Cordially, Marina Gregg.' It had been handwritten, not typewritten. There is no denying that Mrs Bantry was both pleased and flattered. After all, a celebrated film star is a celebrated film star and elderly ladies, though they may be of local importance, are aware of their complete

Agatha Christie

unimportance in the world of celebrities. So Mrs Bantry had the pleased feeling of a child for whom a special treat had been arranged.

As she walked up the drive Mrs Bantry's keen eyes went from side to side registering her impressions. The place had been smartened up since the days when it had passed from hand to hand. 'No expense spared,' said Mrs Bantry to herself, nodding in satisfaction. The drive afforded no view of the flower garden and for that Mrs Bantry was just as pleased. The flower garden and its special herbaceous border had been her own particular delight in the far-off days when she had lived at Gossington Hall. She permitted regretful and nostalgic memories of her irises. The best iris garden of any in the country, she told herself with a fierce pride.

Faced by a new front door in a blaze of new paint she pressed the bell. The door was opened with gratifying prompt-ness by what was undeniably an Italian butler. She was ushered by him straight to the room which had been Colonel Bantry's library. This, as she had already heard, had been thrown into one with the study. The result was impressive. The walls were panelled, the floor was parquet. At one end was a grand piano and halfway along the wall was a superb record player. At the other end of the room was a small island, as it were, which comprised Persian rugs, a tea-table and some chairs. By the tea-table sat Marina Gregg, and leaning against the mantelpiece was what Mrs Bantry at first thought to be the ugliest man she had ever seen.

Just a few moments previously when Mrs Bantry's hand had been advanced to press the bell, Marina Gregg had been saying in a soft, enthusiastic voice, to her husband:

'This place is right for me, Jinks, just right. It's what I've always wanted. *Quiet*. English quiet and the English countryside. I can see myself living here, living here all my life if need be. And we'll adopt the English way of life. We'll have afternoon tea every afternoon with China tea and my lovely Georgian tea service. And we'll look out of the window on those lawns and that English herbaceous border. I've come *home* at last, that's what I feel. I feel that I can settle down here, that I can be quiet and happy. It's going to be home, this place. That's what I feel. *Home.*'

And Jason Rudd (known to his wife as Jinks) had smiled at her. It was an acquiescent smile, indulgent, but it held its reserve because, after all, he had heard it very often before. Perhaps this time it would be true. Perhaps this *was* the place that Marina Gregg might feel at home. But he knew her early enthusiasms so well. She was always so sure that at last she had found exactly what she wanted. He said in his deep voice:

'That's grand, honey. That's just grand. I'm glad you like it.'

'Like it? I adore it. Don't you adore it too?'

'Sure,' said Jason Rudd. 'Sure.'

It wasn't too bad, he reflected to himself. Good, solidly built, rather ugly Victorian. It had, he admitted, a feeling of solidity and security. Now that the worst of its fantastic inconveniences had been ironed out, it would be quite reasonably comfortable to live in. Not a bad place to come back to from time to time. With luck, he thought, Marina wouldn't start taking a dislike to it for perhaps two years to two years and a half. It all depended.

Marina said, sighing softly:

'It's so wonderful to feel well again. Well and strong. Able to cope with things.'

And he said again: 'Sure, honey, sure.'

And it was at that moment that the door opened and the Italian butler had ushered in Mrs Bantry.

Marina Gregg's welcome was all that was charming. She came forward, hands outstretched, saying how delightful it was to meet Mrs Bantry again. And what a coincidence that they should have met that time in San Francisco and that two years later she and Jinks should actually buy the house that had once belonged to Mrs Bantry. And she did hope, she really did hope that Mrs Bantry wouldn't mind terribly the way they'd pulled the house about and done things to it and she hoped she wouldn't feel that they were terrible intruders living here.

'Your coming to live here is one of the most exciting things that has ever happened to this place,' said Mrs Bantry cheerfully and she looked towards the mantelpiece. Whereupon, almost as an afterthought, Marina Gregg said:

'You don't know my husband, do you? Jason, this is Mrs Bantry.'

Mrs Bantry looked at Jason Rudd with some interest. Her first impression that this was one of the ugliest men she had ever seen became qualified. He had interesting eyes. They were, she thought, more deeply sunk in his head than any eyes she had seen. Deep quiet pools, said Mrs Bantry to herself, and felt like a romantic lady novelist. The rest of his face was distinctly craggy, almost ludicrously out of proportion. His nose jutted upwards and a little red paint would have transformed it into the nose of a clown very easily. He had, too, a clown's big sad mouth. Whether he was at this moment in a furious temper or whether he always looked as though he were in a furious temper she did not quite know. His voice when he spoke was unexpectedly pleasant. Deep and slow.

'A husband,' he said, 'is always an afterthought. But let me say with my wife that we're very glad to welcome you here. I hope you don't feel that it ought to be the other way about.'

'You must get it out of your head,' said Mrs Bantry, 'that I've been driven forth from my old home. It never *was* my old home. I've been congratulating myself ever since I sold it. It was a most inconvenient house to run. I liked the garden but the house became more and more of a worry. I've had a perfectly splendid time ever since, travelling abroad and going and seeing my married daughters and my grandchildren and my friends in all different parts of the world.'

'Daughters,' said Marina Gregg, 'you have daughters and sons?'

'Two sons and two daughters,' said Mrs Bantry, 'and pretty widely spaced. One in Kenya, one in South Africa. One near Texas and the other, thank goodness, in London.'

'Four,' said Marina Gregg. 'Four—and grandchildren?'

'Nine up to date,' said Mrs Bantry. 'It's great fun being a grandmother. You don't have any of the worry of parental responsibility. You can spoil them in the most unbridled way—'

Jason Rudd interrupted her. 'I'm afraid the sun catches your eyes,' he said, and went to a window to adjust the blind. 'You must tell us all about this delightful village,' he said as he came back.

He handed her a cup of tea.

'Will you have a hot scone or a sandwich, or this cake? We have an Italian cook and she makes quite good pastry and cakes. You see we have quite taken to your English afternoon tea.'

'Delicious tea too,' said Mrs Bantry, sipping the fragrant beverage.

Marina Gregg smiled and looked pleased. The sudden nervous movement of her fingers which Jason Rudd's eyes had noticed a minute or two previously, was stilled again. Mrs Bantry looked at her hostess with great admiration. Marina Gregg's heyday had been before the rise to supreme importance of vital statistics. She could not have been described as Sex Incarnate, or 'The Bust' or 'The Torso'. She had been long and slim and willowy. The bones of her face and head had had some of the beauty associated with those of Garbo. She had brought personality to her pictures rather than mere sex. The sudden turn of her head, the opening of the deep lovely eyes, the faint quiver of her mouth, all these were what brought to one suddenly that feeling of breath-taking loveliness that comes not from regularity of feature but from some sudden magic of the flesh that catches the onlooker unawares. She still had this quality though it was not now so easily apparent. Like many film and stage actresses she had what seemed to be a habit of turning off personality at will. She could retire into herself, be quiet, gentle, aloof, disappointing to an eager fan. And then suddenly the turn of the head, the movement of the hands, the sudden smile and the magic was there.

One of her greatest pictures had been *Mary, Queen of Scots*, and it was of her performance in that picture that Mrs Bantry was reminded now as she watched her. Mrs Bantry's eye switched to the husband. He too was watching Marina. Off guard for a moment, his face expressed clearly his feelings. 'Good Lord,' said Mrs Bantry to herself, 'the man adores her.'

She didn't know why she should feel so surprised. Perhaps because film stars and their love affairs and their devotion were so written up in the Press that one never expected to see the real thing with one's own eyes. On an impulse she said:

'I do hope you'll enjoy it here and that you'll be able to stay here some time. Do you expect to have the house for long?'

Marina opened wide surprised eyes as she turned her head. 'I want to stay here always,' she said. 'Oh, I don't mean that I shan't have to go away a lot. I shall, of course. There's a possibility of making a film in North Africa next year although nothing's settled yet. No, but this will be my home. I shall come back here. I shall always be able to come back here.' She sighed. 'That's what's so wonderful. To have found a *home* at last.'

'I see,' said Mrs Bantry, but at the same time she thought to herself, 'All the same I don't believe for a moment that it *will* be like that. I don't believe you're the kind that can ever settle down.'

Again she shot a quick surreptitious glance at Jason

Rudd. He was not scowling now. Instead he was smiling, a sudden very sweet and unexpected smile, but it was a sad smile. 'He knows it too,' thought Mrs Bantry.

The door opened and a woman came in. 'Bartletts want you on the telephone, Jason,' she said.

'Tell them to call back.'

'They said it was urgent.'

He sighed and rose. 'Let me introduce you to Mrs Bantry,' he said. 'Ella Zielinsky, my secretary.'

'Have a cup of tea, Ella,' said Marina as Ella Zielinsky acknowledged the introduction with a smiling 'Pleased to meet you.'

'I'll have a sandwich,' said Ella. 'I don't go for China tea.'

Ella Zielinsky was at a guess thirty-five. She wore a well cut suit, a ruffled blouse and appeared to breathe self-confidence. She had short-cut black hair and a wide forehead.

'You used to live here, so they tell me,' she said to Mrs Bantry.

'It's a good many years ago now,' said Mrs Bantry. 'After my husband's death I sold it and it's passed through several hands since then.'

'Mrs Bantry really says she doesn't hate the things we've done to it,' said Marina.

'I should be frightfully disappointed if you hadn't,' said Mrs Bantry. 'I came up here all agog. I can tell you the most splendid rumours have been going around the village.'

'Never knew how difficult it was to get hold of plumbers in this country,' said Miss Zielinsky, champing a sandwich in a businesslike way. 'Not that that's been really my job,' she went on.

'Everything is your job,' said Marina, 'and you know it is, Ella. The domestic staff and the plumbing and arguing with the builders.'

'They don't seem ever to have heard of a picture window in this country.'

Ella looked towards the window. 'It's a nice view, I must admit.'

'A lovely old-fashioned rural English scene,' said Marina. 'This house has got *atmosphere*.'

'It wouldn't look so rural if it wasn't for the trees,' said Ella Zielinsky. 'That housing estate down there grows while you look at it.'

'That's new since my time,' said Mrs Bantry.

'You mean there was nothing but the village when you lived here?'

Mrs Bantry nodded.

'It must have been hard to do your shopping.'

'I don't think so,' said Mrs Bantry. 'I think it was frightfully easy.'

'I understand having a flower garden,' said Ella Zielinsky, 'but you folk over here seem to grow all your vegetables as well. Wouldn't it be much easier to buy them—there's a supermarket?'

'It's probably coming to that,' said Mrs Bantry, with a sigh. 'They don't taste the same, though.'

'Don't spoil the atmosphere, Ella,' said Marina.

The door opened and Jason looked in. 'Darling,' he said to Marina, 'I hate to bother you but would you mind? They just want your private view about this.'

Marina sighed and rose. She trailed languidly towards

the door. 'Always something,' she murmured. 'I'm so sorry, Mrs Bantry. I don't really think that this will take longer than a minute or two.'

'Atmosphere,' said Ella Zielinsky, as Marina went out and closed the door. 'Do you think the house has got atmosphere?'

'I can't say I ever thought of it that way,' said Mrs Bantry. 'It was just a house. Rather inconvenient in some ways and very nice and cosy in other ways.'

'That's what I should have thought,' said Ella Zielinsky. She cast a quick direct look at Mrs Bantry. 'Talking of atmosphere, when did the murder take place here?'

'No murder ever took place here,' said Mrs Bantry.

'Oh come now. The stories I've heard. There are always stories, Mrs Bantry. On the hearthrug, right there, wasn't it?' said Miss Zielinsky nodding towards the fireplace.

'Yes,' said Mrs Bantry. 'That was the place.'

'So there *was* a murder?'

Mrs Bantry shook her head. 'The murder didn't take place here. The girl who had been killed was brought here and planted in this room. She'd nothing to do with us.'

Miss Zielinsky looked interested.

'Possibly you had a bit of difficulty making people believe that?' she remarked.

'You're quite right there,' said Mrs Bantry.

'When did you find it?'

'The housemaid came in in the morning,' said Mrs Bantry, 'with early morning tea. We had housemaids then, you know.'

'I know,' said Miss Zielinksy, 'wearing print dresses that rustled.'

'I'm not sure about the print dress,' said Mrs Bantry, 'it may have been overalls by then. At any rate, she burst in and said there was a body in the library. I said "nonsense", then I woke up my husband and we came down to see.'

'And there it was,' said Miss Zielinsky. 'My, the way things happen.' She turned her head sharply towards the door and then back again. 'Don't talk about it to Miss Gregg, if you don't mind,' she said. 'It's not good for her, that sort of thing.'

'Of course. I won't say a word,' said Mrs Bantry. 'I never do talk about it, as a matter of fact. It all happened so long ago. But won't she—Miss Gregg I mean—won't she hear it anyway?'

'She doesn't come very much in contact with reality,' said Ella Zielinsky. 'Film stars can lead a fairly insulated life, you know. In fact very often one has to take care that they do. Things upset them. Things upset *her*. She's been seriously ill the last year or two, you know. She only started making a comeback a year ago.'

'She seems to like the house,' said Mrs Bantry, 'and to feel she will be happy here.'

'I expect it'll last a year or two,' said Ella Zielinsky.

'Not longer than that?'

'Well, I rather doubt it. Marina is one of those people, you know, who are always thinking they've found their heart's desire. But life isn't as easy as that, is it?'

'No,' said Mrs Bantry forcefully, 'it isn't.'

'It'll mean a lot to him if she's happy here,' said Miss Zielinsky. She ate two more sandwiches in an absorbed, rather gobbling fashion in the manner of one who crams food into themselves as though they had an important train to catch. 'He's a genius, you know,' she went on. 'Have you seen any of the pictures he's directed?'

Mrs Bantry felt slightly embarrassed. She was of the type of woman who when she went to the cinema went entirely for the picture. The long lists of casts, directors, producers, photography and the rest of it passed her by. Very frequently, indeed, she did not even notice the names of the stars. She was not, however, anxious to call attention to this failing on her part.

'I get mixed up,' she said.

'Of course he's got a lot to contend with,' said Ella Zielinsky. 'He's got her as well as everything else and she's not easy. You've got to keep her happy, you see; and it's not really easy, I suppose, to keep people happy. Unless— that is—they—they are—' she hesitated.

'Unless they're the happy kind,' suggested Mrs Bantry. 'Some people,' she added thoughtfully, 'enjoy being miserable.'

'Oh, Marina isn't like that,' said Ella Zielinsky, shaking her head. 'It's more that her ups and downs are so violent. You know—far too happy one moment, far too pleased with everything and delighted with everything and how wonderful she feels. Then of course some little thing happens and down she goes to the opposite extreme.'

'I suppose that's temperament,' said Mrs Bantry vaguely.

'That's right,' said Ella Zielinsky. 'Temperament. They've all got it, more or less, but Marina Gregg has got it more than most people. Don't we know it! The stories I could tell you!' She ate the last sandwich. 'Thank God I'm only the social secretary.'

CHAPTER 5

The throwing open of the grounds of Gossington Hall for the benefit of the St John Ambulance Association was attended by a quite unprecedented number of people. Shilling admission fees mounted up in a highly satisfactory fashion. For one thing, the weather was good, a clear sunny day. But the preponderant attraction was undoubtedly the enormous local curiosity to know exactly what these 'film people' had done to Gossington Hall. The most extravagant assumptions were entertained. The swimming pool in particular caused immense satisfaction. Most people's ideas of Hollywood stars were of sun-bathing by a pool in exotic surroundings and in exotic company. That the climate of Hollywood might be more suited to swimming pools than that of St Mary Mead failed to be considered. After all, England always has one fine hot week in the summer and there is always one day that the Sunday papers publish articles on How to Keep Cool, How to Have Cool Suppers and How to Make Cool Drinks. The pool was almost exactly what everyone had imagined it might be. It was large, its waters were blue, it had a kind of exotic pavilion for changing and was surrounded with a highly artificial plantation of hedges and shrubs. The reactions of the multitude were exactly as might have been expected and hovered over a wide range of remarks.

'O-oh, isn't it lovely!'

'Two penn'orth of splash here, all right!'

'Reminds me of that holiday camp I went to.'

'Wicked luxury *I* call it. It oughtn't to be allowed.'

'Look at all that fancy marble. It must have cost the earth!'

'Don't see why these people think they can come over here and spend all the money they like.'

'Perhaps this'll be on the telly sometime. That'll be fun.'

Even Mr Sampson, the oldest man in St Mary Mead, boasting proudly of being ninety-six though his relations insisted firmly that he was only eighty-six, had staggered along supporting his rheumatic legs with a stick, to see this excitement. He gave it his highest praise: 'Wicked, this!' He smacked his lips hopefully. 'Ah, there'll be a lot of wickedness here, I don't doubt. Naked men and women drinking and smoking what they call in the papers them reefers. There'll be all that, I expect. Ah yes,' said Mr Sampson with enormous pleasure, 'there'll be a lot of wickedness.'

It was felt that the final seal of approval had been set on the afternoon's entertainment. For an extra shilling people were allowed to go into the house, and study the new music room, the drawing-room, the completely unrecognizable dining-room, now done in dark oak and Spanish leather, and a few other joys.

'Never think this was Gossington Hall, would you, now?' said Mr Sampson's daughter-in-law.

Mrs Bantry strolled up fairly late and observed with pleasure that the money was coming in well and that the attendance was phenomenal.

The large marquee in which tea was being served was jammed with people. Mrs Bantry hoped the buns were going to go round. There seemed some very competent women, however, in charge. She herself made a bee-line for the herbaceous border and regarded it with a jealous eye. No expense had been spared on the herbaceous border, she was glad to note, and it was a proper herbaceous border, well planned and arranged and expensively stocked. No personal labours had gone into it, she was sure of that. Some good gardening firm had been given the contract, no doubt. But aided by *carte blanche* and the weather, they had turned out a very good job.

Looking round her, she felt there was a faint flavour of a Buckingham Palace garden party about the scene. Everybody was craning to see all they could see, and from time to time a chosen few were led into one of the more secret recesses of the house. She herself was presently approached by a willowy young man with long wavy hair.

'Mrs Bantry? You *are* Mrs Bantry?'

'I'm Mrs Bantry, yes.'

'Hailey Preston.' He shook hands with her. 'I work for Mr Rudd. Will you come up to the second floor? Mr and Mrs Rudd are asking a few special friends up there.'

Duly honoured Mrs Bantry followed him. They went in through what had been called in her time the garden door.

Agatha Christie

A red cord cordoned off the bottom of the main stairs. Hailey Preston unhooked it and she passed through. Just in front of her Mrs Bantry observed Councillor and Mrs Allcock. The latter who was stout was breathing heavily.

'Wonderful what they've done, isn't it, Mrs Bantry?' panted Mrs Allcock. 'I'd like to have a look at the bathrooms, I must say, but I suppose I shan't get the chance.' Her voice was wistful.

At the top of the stairs Marina Gregg and Jason Rudd were receiving this specially chosen élite. What had once been a spare bedroom had been thrown into the landing so as to make a wide lounge-like effect. Giuseppe the butler was officiating with drinks.

A stout man in livery was announcing guests.

'Councillor and Mrs Allcock,' he boomed.

Marina Gregg was being, as Mrs Bantry had described her to Miss Marple, completely natural and charming. She could already hear Mrs Allcock saying later: '—and so *unspoiled*, you know, in spite of being so famous.'

How very nice of Mrs Allcock to come, *and* the Councillor, and she did hope they'd enjoy their afternoon. 'Jason, please look after Mrs Allcock.'

Councillor and Mrs Allcock were passed on to Jason and drinks.

'Oh, Mrs Bantry, it *is* nice of you to come.'

'I wouldn't have missed it for the world,' said Mrs Bantry and moved on purposefully towards the Martinis.

The young man called Hailey Preston ministered to her in a tender manner and then made off, consulting a little list in his hand, to fetch, no doubt, more of the Chosen to the Presence. It was all being managed very well, Mrs Bantry thought, turning, Martini in hand, to watch the next arrivals. The vicar, a lean, ascetic man, was looking vague and slightly bewildered. He said earnestly to Marina Gregg:

'Very nice of you to ask me. I'm afraid, you know, I haven't got a television set myself, but of course I—er—I—well, of course my young people keep me up to the mark.'

Nobody knew what he meant. Miss Zielinsky, who was also on duty, administered a lemonade to him with a kindly smile. Mr and Mrs Badcock were next up the stairs. Heather Badcock, flushed and triumphant, came a little ahead of her husband.

'Mr and Mrs Badcock,' boomed the man in livery.

'Mrs Badcock,' said the vicar, turning back, lemonade in his hand, 'the indefatigable secretary of the association. She's one of our hardest workers. In fact I don't know what the St John would do without her.'

'I'm sure you've been wonderful,' said Marina.

'You don't remember me?' said Heather, in an arch manner. 'How should you, with all the hundreds of people you meet. And anyway, it was years ago. In Bermuda of all places in the world. I was there with one of our ambulance units. Oh, it's a long time ago now.'

'Of course,' said Marina Gregg, once more all charm and smiles.

'I remember it all so well,' said Mrs Badcock. 'I was thrilled, you know, absolutely thrilled. I was only a girl at the time. To think there was a chance of seeing Marina Gregg in the flesh—oh! I was a mad fan of yours always.'

'It's too kind of you, really too kind of you,' said Marina sweetly, her eyes beginning to hover faintly over Heather's shoulder towards the next arrivals.

'I'm not going to detain you,' said Heather—'but I must—'

'Poor Marina Gregg,' said Mrs Bantry to herself. 'I suppose this kind of thing is always happening to her! The patience they need!'

Heather was continuing in a determined manner with her story.

Mrs Allcock breathed heavily at Mrs Bantry's shoulder.

'The changes they've made here! You wouldn't believe till you saw for yourself. What it must have *cost* . . .'

'I—didn't feel really ill—and I thought I just must—'

'This is vodka,' Mrs Allcock regarded her glass suspiciously. 'Mr Rudd asked if I'd like to try it. Sounds very Russian. I don't think I like it very much . . .'

'—I said to myself: I won't be beaten! I put a lot of make-up on my face—'

'I suppose it would be rude if I just put it down somewhere.' Mrs Allcock sounded desperate.

Mrs Bantry reassured her gently.

'Not at all. Vodka ought really to be thrown straight down the throat'—Mrs Allcock looked startled—'but that needs practice. Put it down on the table and get yourself a Martini from that tray the butler's carrying.'

She turned back to hear Heather Badcock's triumphant peroration.

'I've never forgotten how wonderful you were that day. It was a hundred times worth it.'

Marina's response was this time not so automatic. Her eyes which had wavered over Heather Badcock's shoulder, now seemed to be fixed on the wall midway up the stairs. She was staring and there was something so ghastly in her expression that Mrs Bantry half took a step forward. Was the woman going to faint? What on earth could she be seeing that gave her that basilisk look? But before she could reach Marina's side the latter had recovered herself. Her eyes, vague and unfocussed, returned to Heather and the charm of manner was turned on once more, albeit a shade mechanically.

'What a nice little story. Now, what will you have to drink? Jason! A cocktail?'

'Well, really I usually have lemonade or orange juice.'

'You must have something better than that,' said Marina. 'This is a feast day, remember.'

'Let me persuade you to an American daiquiri,' said Jason, appearing with a couple in his hand. 'They're Marina's favourites, too.'

He handed one to his wife.

'I shouldn't drink any more,' said Marina, 'I've had three already.' But she accepted the glass.

Heather took her drink from Jason. Marina turned away to meet the next person who was arriving.

Mrs Bantry said to Mrs Allcock, 'Let's go and see the bathrooms.'

'Oh, do you think we can? Wouldn't it look rather rude?'

'I'm sure it wouldn't,' said Mrs Bantry. She spoke to Jason Rudd. 'We want to explore your wonderful new bathrooms, Mr Rudd. May we satisfy this purely domestic curiosity?'

'Sure,' said Jason, grinning. 'Go and enjoy yourselves, girls. Draw yourselves baths if you like.'

Mrs Allcock followed Mrs Bantry along the passage.

'That was ever so kind of you, Mrs Bantry. I must say I wouldn't have dared myself.'

'One has to dare if one wants to get anywhere,' said Mrs Bantry.

They went along the passage, opening various doors. Presently 'Ahs' and 'Ohs' began to escape Mrs Allcock and two other women who had joined the party.

'I do like the pink one,' said Mrs Allcock. 'Oh, I like the pink one a lot.'

'I like the one with the dolphin tiles,' said one of the other women.

Mrs Bantry acted the part of hostess with complete enjoyment. For a moment she had really forgotten that the house no longer belonged to her.

'All those showers!' said Mrs Allcock with awe. 'Not that I really *like* showers. I never know how you keep your head dry.'

'It'd be nice to have a peep into the bedrooms,' said one of the other women, wistfully, 'but I suppose it'd be a bit *too* nosy. What do *you* think?'

'Oh, I don't think we could do *that*,' said Mrs Allcock. They both looked hopefully at Mrs Bantry.

'Well,' said Mrs Bantry, 'no, I suppose we oughtn't to—' then she took pity on them, 'but—I don't think anyone would know if we have one peep.' She put her hand on a door-handle.

But that had been attended to. The bedrooms were locked. Everyone was very disappointed.

'I suppose they've got to have some privacy,' said Mrs Bantry kindly.

They retraced their steps along the corridors. Mrs Bantry looked out of one of the landing windows. She noted below her Mrs Meavy (from the Development) looking incredibly smart in a ruffled organdie dress. With Mrs Meavy, she noticed, was Miss Marple's Cherry, whose last name for the moment Mrs Bantry could not remember. They seemed to be enjoying themselves and were laughing and talking.

Suddenly the house felt to Mrs Bantry old, worn-out and highly artificial. In spite of its new gleaming paint, its alterations, it was in essence a tired old Victorian mansion. 'I was wise to go,' thought Mrs Bantry. 'Houses are like everything else. There comes a time when they've just had their day. This has had its day. It's been given a face lift, but I don't really think it's done it any good.'

Suddenly a slight rise in the hum of voices reached her. The two women with her started forward.

'What's happening?' said one. 'It sounds as though something's happening.'

They stepped back along the corridor towards the stairs. Ella Zielinksy came rapidly along and passed them. She tried a bedroom door and said quickly, 'Oh, damn. Of course they've locked them all.'

'Is anything the matter?' asked Mrs Bantry.

'Someone's taken ill,' said Miss Zielinsky shortly.

'Oh dear, I'm sorry. Can I do anything?'

'I suppose there's a doctor here somewhere?'

'I haven't seen any of our local doctors,' said Mrs Bantry, 'but there's almost sure to be one here.'

'Jason's telephoning,' said Ella Zielinsky, 'but she seems pretty bad.'

'Who is it?' asked Mrs Bantry.

'A Mrs Badcock, I think.'

'Heather Badcock? But she looked so well just now.'

Ella Zielinksy said impatiently, 'She's had a seizure, or a fit, or something. Do you know if there's anything wrong with her heart or anything like that?'

'I don't really know anything about her,' said Mrs Bantry. 'She's new since my day. She comes from the Development.'

'The Development? Oh, you mean that housing estate. I don't even know where her husband is or what he looks like.'

'Middle-aged, fair, unobtrusive,' said Mrs Bantry. 'He came with her so he must be about somewhere.'

Ella Zielinsky went into a bathroom. 'I don't know really what to give her,' she said. 'Sal volatile, do you think, something like that?'

'Is she faint?' said Mrs Bantry.

'It's more than that,' said Ella Zielinsky.

'I'll see if there's anything I can do,' said Mrs Bantry. She turned away and walked rapidly back towards the head of the stairs. Turning a corner she cannoned into Jason Rudd.

'Have you seen Ella?' he said. 'Ella Zielinsky?'

'She went along there into one of the bathrooms. She was looking for something. Sal volatile—something like that.'

'She needn't bother,' said Jason Rudd.

Something in his tone struck Mrs Bantry. She looked up sharply. 'Is it bad?' she said, 'really bad?'

'You could call it that,' said Jason Rudd. 'The poor woman's dead.'

'Dead!' Mrs Bantry was really shocked. She said, as she had said before, 'But she looked so well just now.'

'I know. I know,' said Jason. He stood there, scowling. 'What a thing to happen!'

CHAPTER 6

'Here we are,' said Miss Knight, settling a breakfast tray on the bed-table beside Miss Marple. 'And how are we this morning? I see we've got our curtains pulled back,' she added with a slight note of disapproval in her voice.

'I wake early,' said Miss Marple. 'You probably will, when you're my age,' she added.

'Mrs Bantry rang up,' said Miss Knight, 'about half an hour ago. She wanted to talk to you but I said she'd better ring up again after you'd had your breakfast. I wasn't going to disturb you at that hour, before you'd even had a cup of tea or anything to eat.'

'When my friends ring up,' said Miss Marple, 'I prefer to be told.'

'I'm sorry, I'm sure,' said Miss Knight, 'but it seemed to me very inconsiderate. When you've had your nice tea and your boiled egg and your toast and butter, we'll see.'

'Half an hour ago,' said Miss Marple, thoughtfully, 'that would have been—let me see—eight o'clock.'

'Much too early,' reiterated Miss Knight.

'I don't believe Mrs Bantry would have rung me up then

unless it was for some particular reason,' said Miss Marple thoughtfully. 'She doesn't usually ring up in the early morning.'

'Oh well, dear, don't fuss your head about it,' said Miss Knight soothingly. 'I expect she'll be ringing up again very shortly. Or would you like me to get her for you?'

'No, thank you,' said Miss Marple. 'I prefer to eat my breakfast while it's hot.'

'Hope I haven't forgotten anything,' said Miss Knight, cheerfully.

But nothing had been forgotten. The tea had been properly made with boiling water, the egg had been boiled exactly three and three-quarter minutes, the toast was evenly browned, the butter was arranged in a nice little pat and the small jar of honey stood beside it. In many ways undeniably Miss Knight was a treasure. Miss Marple ate her breakfast and enjoyed it. Presently the whirr of a vacuum cleaner began below. Cherry had arrived.

Competing with the whirr of the vacuum cleaner was a fresh tuneful voice singing one of the latest popular tunes of the day. Miss Knight, coming in for the breakfast tray, shook her head.

'I really wish that young woman wouldn't go singing all over the house,' she said. 'It's not what I call respectful.'

Miss Marple smiled a little. 'It would never enter Cherry's head that she would have to be respectful,' she remarked. 'Why should she?'

Miss Knight sniffed and said, 'Very different to what things used to be.'

'Naturally,' said Miss Marple. 'Times change. That is a

thing which has to be accepted.' She added, 'Perhaps you'll ring up Mrs Bantry now and find out what it was she wanted.'

Miss Knight bustled away. A minute or two later there was a rap on the door and Cherry entered. She was looking bright and excited and extremely pretty. A plastic overall rakishly patterned with sailors and naval emblems was tied round her dark blue dress.

'Your hair looks nice,' said Miss Marple.

'Went for a perm yesterday,' said Cherry. 'A bit stiff still, but it's going to be all right. I came up to see if you'd heard the news.'

'What news?' said Miss Marple.

'About what happened at Gossington Hall yesterday. You know there was a big do there for the St John Ambulance?'

Miss Marple nodded. 'What happened?' she asked.

'Somebody died in the middle of it. A Mrs Badcock. Lives round the corner from us. I don't suppose you'd know her.'

'Mrs Badcock?' Miss Marple sounded alert. 'But I do know her. I think—yes, that was the name—she came out and picked me up when I fell down the other day. She was very kind.'

'Oh, Heather Badcock's kind all right,' said Cherry. 'Over-kind, some people say. They call it interfering. Well, anyway, she up and died. Just like that.'

'Died! But what of?'

'Search me,' said Cherry. 'She'd been taken into the house because of her being the secretary of the St John Ambulance, I suppose. She and the mayor and a lot of others. As far as I heard, she had a glass of something and about five minutes later she was took bad and died before you could snap your fingers.'

'What a shocking occurrence,' said Miss Marple. 'Did she suffer from heart trouble?'

'Sound as a bell, so they say,' Cherry said. 'Of course, you never know, do you? I suppose you can have something wrong with your heart and nobody knowing about it. Anyway, I can tell you this. They've not sent her home.'

Miss Marple looked puzzled. 'What do you mean, not sent her home?'

'The body,' said Cherry, her cheerfulness unimpaired. 'The doctor said there'd have to be an autopsy. Post-mortem—whatever you call it. He said he hadn't attended her for anything and there was nothing to show the cause of death. Looks funny to me,' she added.

'Now what do you mean by funny?' said Miss Marple.

'Well.' Cherry considered. 'Funny. As though there was something behind it.'

'Is her husband terribly upset?'

'Looks as white as a sheet. Never saw a man as badly hit, to look at—that is to say.'

Miss Marple's ears, long attuned to delicate nuances, led her to cock her head slightly on one side like an inquisitive bird.

'Was he so very devoted to her?'

'He did what she told him and gave her her own way,' said Cherry, 'but that doesn't always mean you're devoted, does it? It may mean you haven't got the courage to stick up for yourself.'

Agatha Christie

'You didn't like her?' asked Miss Marple.

'I hardly know her really,' said Cherry. 'Knew her, I mean. I don't—didn't—dislike her. But she's just not my type. Too interfering.'

'You mean inquisitive, nosy?'

'No, I don't,' said Cherry. 'I don't mean that at all. She was a very kind woman and she was always doing things for people. And she was always quite sure she knew the best thing to do. What they thought about it wouldn't have mattered. I had an aunt like that. Very fond of seed cake herself and she used to bake seed cakes for people and take them to them, and she never troubled to find out whether they liked seed cake or not. There are people can't bear it, just can't stand the flavour of caraway. Well, Heather Badcock was a bit like that.'

'Yes,' said Miss Marple thoughtfully, 'yes, she would have been. I knew someone a little like that. Such people,' she added, 'live dangerously—though they don't know it themselves.'

Cherry stared at her. 'That's a funny thing to say. I don't quite get what you mean.'

Miss Knight bustled in. 'Mrs Bantry seems to have gone out,' she said. 'She didn't say where she was going.'

'I can guess where she's going,' said Miss Marple. 'She's coming here. I shall get up now,' she added.

Miss Marple had just ensconced herself in her favourite chair by the window when Mrs Bantry arrived. She was slightly out of breath.

'I've got plenty to tell you, Jane,' she said.

'About the fête?' asked Miss Knight. 'You went to the fête yesterday, didn't you? I was there myself for a short time early in the afternoon. The tea tent was very crowded. An astonishing lot of people seemed to be there. I didn't catch a glimpse of Marina Gregg, though, which was rather disappointing.'

She flicked a little dust off a table and said brightly, 'Now I'm sure you two want to have a nice little chat together,' and went out of the room.

'She doesn't seem to know anything about it,' said Mrs Bantry. She fixed her friend with a keen glance. 'Jane, I believe you *do* know.'

'You mean about the death yesterday?'

'You always know everything,' said Mrs Bantry. 'I cannot think how.'

'Well, really dear,' said Miss Marple, 'in the same way one always has known everything. My daily helper, Cherry Baker, brought the news. I expect the butcher will be telling Miss Knight presently.'

'And what do you think of it?' said Mrs Bantry.

'What do I think of what?' said Miss Marple.

'Now don't be aggravating, Jane, you know perfectly what I mean. There's this woman—whatever her name is—'

'Heather Badcock,' said Miss Marple.

'She arrives full of life and spirit. I was there when she came. And about a quarter of an hour later she sits down in a chair, says she doesn't feel well, gasps a bit and dies. What do you think of *that*?'

'One mustn't jump to conclusions,' said Miss Marple.

'The point is, of course, what did a medical man think of it?'

Mrs Bantry nodded. 'There's to be an inquest and a post-mortem,' she said. 'That shows what they think of it, doesn't it?'

'Not necessarily,' said Miss Marple. 'Anyone may be taken ill and die suddenly and they have to have a post-mortem to find out the cause.'

'It's more than that,' said Mrs Bantry.

'How do you know?' said Miss Marple.

'Dr Sandford went home and rang up the police.'

'Who told you that?' said Miss Marple, with great interest.

'Old Briggs,' said Mrs Bantry. 'At least, he didn't tell me. You know he goes down after hours in the evening to see to Dr Sandford's garden, and he was clipping something quite close to the study and he heard the doctor ringing up the police station in Much Benham. Briggs told his daughter and his daughter mentioned it to the postwoman and she told me,' said Mrs Bantry.

Miss Marple smiled. 'I see,' she said, 'that St Mary Mead has not changed very much from what it used to be.'

'The grape-vine is much the same,' agreed Mrs Bantry. 'Well, now, Jane, tell me what you think.'

'One thinks, of course, of the husband,' said Miss Marple reflectively. 'Was he there?'

'Yes, he was there. You don't think it would be suicide,' said Mrs Bantry.

'Certainly not suicide,' said Miss Marple decisively. 'She wasn't the type.'

'How did you come across her, Jane?'

'It was the day I went for a walk to the Development, and fell down near her house. She was kindness itself. She was a very kind woman.'

'Did you see the husband? Did he look as though he'd like to poison her?

'You know what I mean,' Mrs Bantry went on as Miss Marple showed some slight signs of protesting. 'Did he remind you of Major Smith or Bertie Jones or someone you've known years ago who did poison a wife, or tried to?'

'No,' said Miss Marple, 'he didn't remind me of anyone I know.' She added, 'But she did.'

'Who—Mrs Badcock?'

'Yes,' said Miss Marple, 'she reminded me of someone called Alison Wilde.'

'And what was Alison Wilde like?'

'She didn't know at all,' said Miss Marple slowly, 'what the world was like. She didn't know what people were like. She'd never thought about them. And so, you see, she couldn't guard against things happening to her.'

'I don't really think I understand a word of what you're saying,' said Mrs Bantry.

'It's very difficult to explain exactly,' said Miss Marple, apologetically. 'It comes really from being self-centred, and I don't mean selfish by that,' she added. 'You can be kind and unselfish and even thoughtful. But if you're like Alison Wilde, you never really know what you may be doing. And so you never know what may happen to you.'

'Can't you make that a little clearer?' said Mrs Bantry.

'Well, I suppose I could give you a sort of figurative example. This isn't anything that actually happened, it's just something I'm inventing.'

'Go on,' said Mrs Bantry.

'Well, supposing you went into a shop, say, and you knew the proprietress had a son who was the spivvy young juvenile delinquent type. He was there listening while you told his mother about some money you had in the house, or some silver or a piece of jewellery. It was something you were excited and pleased about and you wanted to talk about it. And you also perhaps mention an evening that you were going out. You even say that you never lock the house. You're interested in what you're saying, what you're telling her, because it's so very much in your mind. And then, say, on that particular evening you come home because you've forgotten something and there's this bad lot of a boy in the house, caught in the act, and he turns round and coshes you.'

'That might happen to almost anybody nowadays,' said Mrs Bantry.

'Not quite,' said Miss Marple, 'most people have a sense of protection. They realise when it's unwise to say or do something because of the person or persons who are taking in what you say, and because of the kind of character that those people have. But as I say, Alison Wilde never thought of anybody else but herself—She was the sort of person who tells you what they've done and what they've seen and what they've felt and what they've heard. They never mention what any other people said or did. Life is a kind of one-way track—just their own progress through it. Other

people seem to them just like—like wall-paper in a room.'
She paused and then said, 'I think Heather Badcock was
that kind of person.'

Mrs Bantry said, 'You think she was the sort of person
who might have butted into something without knowing
what she was doing?'

'And without realising that it was a dangerous thing to
do,' said Miss Marple. She added, 'It's the only reason I
can possibly think of why she should have been killed. If,
of course,' added Miss Marple, 'we are right in assuming
that murder *has* been committed.'

'You don't think she was blackmailing someone?' Mrs
Bantry suggested.

'Oh, no,' Miss Marple assured her. 'She was a kind, good
woman. She'd never have done anything of *that* kind.' She
added vexedly, 'The whole thing seems to me very unlikely.
I suppose it can't have been—'

'Well?' Mrs Bantry urged her.

'I just wondered if it might have been the wrong murder,'
said Miss Marple thoughtfully.

The door opened and Dr Haydock breezed in, Miss
Knight twittering behind him.

'Ah, at it already, I see,' said Dr Haydock, looking at
the two ladies. 'I came in to see how your health was,' he
said to Miss Marple, 'but I needn't ask. I see you've begun
to adopt the treatment that I suggested.'

'Treatment, Doctor?'

Dr Haydock pointed a finger at the knitting that lay
on the table beside her. 'Unravelling,' he said. 'I'm right,
aren't I?'

Miss Marple twinkled very slightly in a discreet, old-ladyish kind of way.

'You will have your joke, Doctor Haydock,' she said.

'You can't pull the wool over my eyes, my dear lady. I've known you too many years. Sudden death at Gossington Hall and all the tongues of St Mary Mead are wagging. Isn't that so? Murder suggested long before anybody even knows the result of the inquest.'

'When is the inquest to be held?' asked Miss Marple.

'The day after tomorrow,' said Dr Haydock, 'and by that time,' he said, 'you ladies will have reviewed the whole story, decided on the verdict and decided on a good many other points too, I expect. Well,' he added, 'I shan't waste my time here. It's no good wasting time on a patient that doesn't need my ministrations. Your cheeks are pink, your eyes are bright, you've begun to enjoy yourself. Nothing like having an interest in life. I'll be on my way.' He stomped out again.

'I'd rather have him than Sandford any day,' said Mrs Bantry.

'So would I,' said Miss Marple. 'He's a good friend, too,' she added thoughtfully. 'He came, I think, to give me the go-ahead sign.'

'Then it *was* murder,' said Mrs Bantry. They looked at each other. 'At any rate, the doctors think so.'

Miss Knight brought in cups of coffee. For once in their lives, both ladies were too impatient to welcome this interruption. When Miss Knight had gone Miss Marple started immediately.

'Now then, Dolly, you were there—'

'I practically saw it happen,' said Mrs Bantry, with modest pride.

'Splendid,' said Miss Marple. 'I mean—well, you know what I mean. So you can tell me just exactly what happened from the moment she arrived.'

'I'd been taken into the house,' said Mrs Bantry. 'Snob status.'

'Who took you in?'

'Oh, a willowy-looking young man. I think he's Marina Gregg's secretary or something like that. He took me in, up the staircase. They were having a kind of reunion reception committee at the top of the stairs.'

'On the landing?' said Miss Marple, surprised.

'Oh, they've altered all that. They've knocked the dressing-room and bedroom down so that you've got a big sort of alcove, practically a room. It's very attractive looking.'

'I see. And who was there?'

'Marina Gregg, being natural and charming, looking lovely in a sort of willowy grey-green dress. And the husband, of course, and that woman, Ella Zielinsky I told you about. She's their social secretary. And there were about—oh, eight or ten people I should think. Some of them I knew, some of them I didn't. Some I think were from the studios—the ones I didn't know. There was the vicar and Doctor Sandford's wife. He wasn't there himself until later, and Colonel and Mrs Clittering and the High Sheriff. And I think there was someone from the press there. And a young woman with a big camera taking photographs.'

Agatha Christie

Miss Marple nodded.

'Go on.'

'Heather Badcock and her husband arrived just after me. Marina Gregg said nice things to me, then to somebody else, oh yes,—the vicar—and then Heather Badcock and her husband came. She's the secretary, you know, of the St John Ambulance. Somebody said something about that and how hard she worked and how valuable she was. And Marina Gregg said some pretty things. Then Mrs Badcock, who struck me, I must say, Jane, as rather a tiresome sort of woman, began some long rigmarole of how years before she'd met Marina Gregg somewhere. She wasn't awfully tactful about it since she urged exactly how long ago and the year it was and everything like that. I'm sure that actresses and film stars and people don't really like being reminded of the exact age they are. Still, she wouldn't think of that I suppose.'

'No,' said Miss Marple, 'she wasn't the kind of woman who would have thought of that. Well?'

'Well, there was nothing particular in that except for the fact that Marina Gregg didn't do her usual stuff.'

'You mean she was annoyed?'

'No, no, I don't mean that. As a matter of fact I'm not at all sure that she heard a word of it. She was staring, you know, over Mrs Badcock's shoulder and when Mrs Badcock had finished her rather silly story of how she got out of a bed of sickness and sneaked out of the house to go and meet Marina and get her autograph, there was a sort of odd silence. Then I saw her face.'

'Whose face? Mrs Badcock's?'

'No. Marina Gregg's. It was as though she hadn't heard a word the Badcock woman was saying. She was staring over her shoulder right at the wall opposite. Staring with—I can't explain it to you—'

'But do try, Dolly,' said Miss Marple, 'because I think perhaps that this might be important.'

'She had a kind of frozen look,' said Mrs Bantry, struggling with words, 'as though she'd seen something that—oh dear me, how hard it is to describe things. Do you remember the Lady of Shalott? *The mirror crack'd from side to side: "The doom has come upon me," cried the Lady of Shalott.* Well, that's what she looked like. People laugh at Tennyson nowadays, but the Lady of Shalott always thrilled me when I was young and it still does.'

'She had a frozen look,' repeated Miss Marple thoughtfully. 'And she was looking *over* Mrs Badcock's shoulder at the wall. What was on the wall?'

'Oh! A picture of some kind, I think,' said Mrs Bantry. 'You know, Italian. I think it was a copy of a Bellini Madonna, but I'm not sure. A picture where the Virgin is holding up a laughing child.'

Miss Marple frowned. 'I can't see that a *picture* could give her that expression.'

'Especially as she must see it every day,' agreed Mrs Bantry.

'There were people coming up the stairs still, I suppose?'

'Oh yes, there were.'

'Who were they, do you remember?'

'You mean she might have been looking at one of the people coming up the stairs?'

'Well, it's possible, isn't it?' said Miss Marple.

'Yes—of course—now let me see. There was the mayor, all dressed up too with his chains and all, and his wife, and there was a man with long hair and one of those funny beards they wear nowadays. Quite a young man. And there was the girl with the camera. She'd taken her position on the stairs so as to get photos of people coming up and having their hands shaken by Marina, and—let me see, two people I didn't know. Studio people, I think, and the Grices from Lower Farm. There may have been others, but that's all I can remember now.'

'Doesn't sound very promising,' said Miss Marple. 'What happened next?'

'I think Jason Rudd nudged her or something because all of a sudden she seemed to pull herself together and she smiled at Mrs Badcock, and she began to say all the usual things. You know, sweet, unspoilt, natural, charming, the usual bag of tricks.'

'And then?'

'And then Jason Rudd gave them drinks.'

'What kind of drinks?'

'Daiquiris, I think. He said they were his wife's favourites. He gave one to her and one to the Badcock woman.'

'That's very interesting,' said Miss Marple. 'Very interesting indeed. And what happened after that?'

'I don't know, because I took a gaggle of women to look at the bathrooms. The next thing I knew was when the secretary woman came rushing along and said someone had been taken ill.'

CHAPTER 7

The inquest, when it was held, was short and disappointing. Evidence of identification was given by the husband, and the only other evidence was medical. Heather Badcock had died as a result of four grains of hy-ethyl-dexyl-barbo-quindelorytate, or, let us be frank, some such name. There was no evidence to show how the drug was administered.

The inquest was adjourned for a fortnight.

After it was concluded, Detective-Inspector Frank Cornish joined Arthur Badcock.

'Could I have a word with you, Mr Badcock?'

'Of course, of course.'

Arthur Badcock looked more like a chewed-out bit of string than ever. 'I can't understand it,' he muttered. 'I simply can't understand it.'

'I've got a car here,' said Cornish. 'We'll drive back to your house, shall we? Nicer and more private there.'

'Thank you, sir. Yes, yes, I'm sure that would be much better.'

They drew up at the neat little blue-painted gate of No. 3 Arlington Close. Arthur Badcock led the way and the inspector followed him. He drew out his latch-key but before he had inserted it into the door, it was opened from inside. The woman who opened it stood back looking slightly embarrassed. Arthur Badcock looked startled.

'Mary,' he said.

'I was just getting you ready some tea, Arthur. I thought you'd need it when you came back from the inquest.'

'That's very kind of you, I'm sure,' said Arthur Badcock gratefully. Er—' he hesitated. 'This is Inspector Cornish, Mrs Bain. She's a neighbour of mine.'

'I see,' said Inspector Cornish.

'I'll get another cup,' said Mrs Bain.

She disappeared and rather doubtfully Arthur Badcock showed the inspector into the bright cretonne-covered sitting-room to the right of the hall.

'She's very kind,' said Arthur Badcock. 'Very kind always.'

'You've known her a long time?'

'Oh, no. Only since we came here.'

'You've been here two years, I believe, or is it three?'

'Just about three now,' said Arthur. 'Mrs Bain only got here six months ago,' he explained. 'Her son works near here and so, after her husband's death, she came down to live here and he boards with her.'

Mrs Bain appeared at this point bringing the tray from the kitchen. She was a dark, rather intense-looking woman of about forty years of age. She had gipsy colouring that went with her dark hair and eyes. There was something a little odd about her eyes. They had a watchful look. She put down the tray on the table and Inspector Cornish said something pleasant and non-committal. Something in him, some professional instinct, was on the alert. The watchful look in the woman's eyes, the slight start she had given when Arthur introduced him had not passed unnoticed. He was familiar with that slight uneasiness in the presence of the police. There were two kinds of uneasiness. One was the kind of natural alarm and distrust as of those who might have offended unwittingly against the majesty of the law, but there was a second kind. And it was the second kind that he felt sure was present here. Mrs Bain, he thought, had had at some time some connection with the police, something that had left her wary and ill at ease. He made a mental note to find out a little more about Mary Bain. Having set down the tea tray, and refused to partake herself saying she had to get home, she departed.

'Seems a nice woman,' said Inspector Cornish.

'Yes, indeed. She's very kind, a very good neighbour, a very sympathetic woman,' said Arthur Badcock.

'Was she a great friend of your wife?'

'No. No, I wouldn't say that. They were neighbourly and on pleasant terms. Nothing special about it though.'

'I see. Now, Mr Badcock, we want as much information as we can from you. The findings of the inquest have been a shock to you, I expect?'

'Oh, they have, Inspector. Of course I realized that you must think something was wrong and I almost thought so myself because Heather has always been such a healthy woman. Practically never a day's illness. I said to myself, "There *must* be something wrong." But it seems so incredible, if you understand what I mean, Inspector. Really quite incredible. What is this stuff—this Bi-ethyl-hex—' He came to a stop.

'There is an easier name for it,' said the inspector. 'It's sold under a trade name, the trade name of Calmo. Ever come across it?'

Arthur Badcock shook his head, perplexed.

'It's more used in America than here,' said the inspector. 'They prescribe it very freely over there, I understand.'

'What's it for?'

'It induces, or so I understand, a happy and tranquil state of mind,' said Cornish. 'It's prescribed for those under strain; suffering anxiety, depression, melancholy, sleeplessness and a good many other things. The properly prescribed dose is not dangerous, but overdoses are not to be advised. It would seem that your wife took something like six times the ordinary dose.'

Badcock stared. 'Heather never took anything like that in her life,' he said. 'I'm sure of it. She wasn't one for taking medicines anyway. She was never depressed or worried. She was one of the most cheerful women you could possibly imagine.'

The inspector nodded. 'I see. And no doctor had prescribed anything of this kind for her?'

'No. Certainly not. I'm sure of that.'

'Who was her doctor?'

'She was on Dr Sims's panel, but I don't think she's been to him once since we've been here.'

Inspector Cornish said thoughtfully, 'So she doesn't seem the kind of woman to have been likely to need such a thing, or to have taken it?'

'She didn't, Inspector, I'm sure she didn't. She must have taken it by a mistake of some kind.'

'It's a very difficult mistake to imagine,' said Inspector Cornish. 'What did she have to eat and drink that afternoon?'

'Well, let me see. For lunch—'

'You needn't go back as far as lunch,' said Cornish. 'Given in such quantity the drug would act quickly and suddenly. Tea. Go back to tea.'

'Well, we went into the marquee in the grounds. It was a terrible scrum in there, but we managed in the end to get a bun each and a cup of tea. We finished it as quickly as possible because it was very hot in the marquee and we came out again.'

'And that's all she had, a bun and a cup of tea there?'

'That's right, sir.'

'And after that you went into the house. Is that right?'

'Yes. The young lady came and said that Miss Marina Gregg would be very pleased to see my wife if she would like to come into the house. Of course my wife was delighted. She had been talking about Marina Gregg for days. Everybody was excited. Oh well, you know that, Inspector, as well as anyone does.'

'Yes, indeed,' said Cornish. 'My wife was excited, too. Why, from all around people were paying their shilling to go in and see Gossington Hall and what had been done there, and hoped to catch a glimpse of Marina Gregg herself.'

'The young lady took us into the house,' said Arthur Badcock, 'and up the stairs. That's where the party was. On the landing up there. But it looked quite different from what it used to look like, so I understand. It was more like a room, a sort of big hollowed out place with chairs and tables with drinks on them. There were about ten or twelve people there, I suppose.'

Inspector Cornish nodded. 'And you were received there—by whom?'

'By Miss Marina Gregg herself. Her husband was with her. I've forgotten his name now.'

'Jason Rudd,' said Inspector Cornish.

'Oh, yes, not that I noticed him at first. Well, anyway, Miss Gregg greeted Heather very nicely and seemed very pleased to see her, and Heather was talking and telling a story of how she'd once met Miss Gregg years ago in the West Indies and everything seemed as right as rain.'

'Everything seemed as right as rain,' echoed the inspector. 'And then?'

'And then Miss Gregg said what would we have? And Miss Gregg's husband, Mr Rudd, got Heather a kind of cocktail, a dickery or something like that.'

'A daiquiri.'

'That's right, sir. He brought two. One for her and one for Miss Gregg.'

'And you, what did you have?'

'I had a sherry.'

'I see. And you three stood there drinking your drinks together?'

'Well, not quite like that. You see there were more people coming up the stairs. There was the mayor, for one, and some other people—an American gentleman and lady, I think—so we moved off a bit.'

'And your wife drank her daiquiri then?'

'Well, no, not then, she didn't.'

'Well, if she didn't drink it then, when did she drink it?'

Arthur Badcock stood frowning in remembrance. 'I think—she set it down on one of the tables. She saw some friends there. I think it was someone to do with the St John Ambulance who'd driven over from Much Benham or somewhere like that. Anyway they got to talking together.'

'And when did she drink her drink?'

Arthur Badcock again frowned. 'It was a little after that,' he said. 'It was getting rather more crowded by then. Somebody jogged Heather's elbow and her glass got spilt.'

'What's that?' Inspector Cornish looked up sharply. 'Her glass was spilt?'

'Yes, that's how I remember it . . . She'd picked it up and I think she took a little sip and made rather a face. She didn't really like cocktails, you know, but all the same she wasn't going to be downed by that. Anyway, as she stood there, somebody jogged her elbow and the glass spilled over. It went down her dress and I think it went on Miss Gregg's dress too. Miss Gregg couldn't have been nicer. She said it didn't matter at all and it would make no stain and she gave Heather her handkerchief to wipe up Heather's dress, and then she passed over the drink she was holding and said, "Have this, I haven't touched it yet."'

'She handed over her own drink, did she?' said the inspector. 'You're sure of that?'

Arthur Badcock paused a moment while he thought. 'Yes, I'm quite sure of that,' he said.

'And your wife took the drink?'

'Well, she didn't want to at first, sir. She said, "Oh no,

Agatha Christie

I couldn't do that" and Miss Gregg laughed and said, "I've had far too much to drink already."'

'And so your wife took that glass and did what with it?'

'She turned away a little and drank it, rather quickly, I think. And then we walked a little way along the corridor looking at some of the pictures and the curtains. Lovely curtain stuff it was, like nothing we'd seen before. Then I met a pal of mine, Councillor Allcock, and I was just passing the time of day with him when I looked round and saw Heather was sitting on a chair looking rather odd, so I came to her and said, "What's the matter?" She said she felt a little queer.'

'What kind of queerness?'

'I don't know, sir. I didn't have time. Her voice sounded very queer and thick and her head was rolling a little. All of a sudden she made a great half gasp and her head fell forward. She was dead, sir, dead.'

CHAPTER 8

'St Mary Mead, you say?' Chief-Inspector Craddock looked up sharply.

The assistant commissioner was a little surprised.

'Yes,' he said, 'St Mary Mead. Why? Does it—'

'Nothing really,' said Dermot Craddock.

'It's quite a small place, I understand,' went on the other. 'Though of course there's a great deal of building development going on there now. Practically all the way from St Mary Mead to Much Benham, I understand. Hellingforth Studios,' he added, 'are on the other side of St Mary Mead, towards Market Basing.' He was still looking slightly inquiring. Dermot Craddock felt that he should perhaps explain.

'I know someone living there,' he said. 'At St Mary Mead. An old lady. A very old lady by now. Perhaps she's dead, I don't know. But if not—'

The assistant commissioner took his subordinate's point, or at any rate he thought he did.

'Yes,' he said, 'it would give you an "in" in a way. One needs a bit of local gossip. The whole thing is a curious business.'

'The County have called us in?' Dermot asked.

'Yes. I've got the chief constable's letter here. They don't seem to feel that it's necessarily a local affair. The largest house in the neighbourhood, Gossington Hall, was recently sold as a residence for Marina Gregg, the film star, and her husband. They're shooting a film at their new studios, at Hellingforth, in which she is starring. A fête was held in the grounds in aid of the St John Ambulance. The dead woman—her name is Mrs Heather Badcock—was the local secretary of this and had done most of the administrative work for the fête. She seems to have been a competent, sensible person, well liked locally.'

'One of those bossy women?' suggested Craddock.

'Very possibly,' said the assistant commissioner. 'Still in my experience, bossy women seldom get themselves murdered. I can't think why not. When you come to think of it, it's rather a pity. There was a record attendance at the fête, it seems, good weather, everything running to plan. Marina Gregg and her husband held a kind of small private reception in Gossington Hall. About thirty or forty people attended this. The local notables, various people connected with the St John Ambulance Association, several friends of Marina Gregg herself, and a few people connected with the studios. All very peaceful, nice and happy. But, fantastically and improbably, Heather Badcock was poisoned there.'

Dermot Craddock said thoughtfully, 'An odd place to choose.'

'That's the chief constable's point of view. If anyone wanted to poison Heather Badcock, why choose that particular afternoon and circumstances? Hundreds of much simpler ways of doing it. A risky business anyway, you know, to slip a dose of deadly poison into a cocktail in the middle of twenty or thirty people milling about. Somebody ought to have seen something.'

'It definitely was in the drink?'

'Yes, it was definitely in the drink. We have the particulars here. One of those inexplicable names that doctors delight in, but actually a fairly common prescription in America.'

'In America. I see.'

'Oh, this country too. But these things are handed out much more freely on the other side of the Atlantic. Taken in small doses, beneficial.'

'Supplied on prescription or can it be bought freely?'

'No. You have to have a prescription.'

'Yes, it's odd,' said Dermot. 'Heather Badcock have any connection with these film people?'

'None whatever.'

'Any member of her own family at this do?'

'Her husband.'

'Her husband,' said Dermot thoughtfully.

'Yes, one always thinks that way,' agreed his superior officer, 'but the local man—Cornish, I think his name is—doesn't seem to think there's anything in that, although he does report that Badcock seemed ill at ease and nervous, but he agrees that respectable people often are like that when interviewed by the police. They appear to have been quite a devoted couple.'

'In other words, the police there don't think it's their

pigeon. Well, it ought to be interesting. I take it I'm going down there, sir?'

'Yes. Better get there as soon as possible, Dermot. Who do you want with you?'

Dermot considered for a moment or two.

'Tiddler, I think,' he said thoughtfully. 'He's a good man and, what's more, he's a film fan. That might come in useful.'

The assistant commissioner nodded. 'Good luck to you,' he said.

'Well!' exclaimed Miss Marple, going pink with pleasure and surprise. 'This *is* a surprise. How are you, my dear boy—though you're hardly a boy now. What are you—a Chief-Inspector or this new thing they call a Commander?'

Dermot explained his present rank.

'I suppose I need hardly ask what you are doing down here,' said Miss Marple. 'Our local murder is considered worthy of the attention of Scotland Yard.'

'They handed it over to us,' said Dermot, 'and so, naturally, as soon as I got down here I came to headquarters.'

'Do you mean—' Miss Marple fluttered a little.

'Yes, Aunty,' said Dermot disrespectfully. 'I mean you.'

'I'm afraid,' said Miss Marple regretfully, 'I'm very much out of things nowadays. I don't get out much.'

'You get out enough to fall down and be picked up by a woman who's going to be murdered ten days later,' said Dermot Craddock.

Miss Marple made the kind of noise that would once have been written down as 'tut-tut'.

'I don't know where you hear these things,' she said.

'You should know,' said Dermot Craddock. 'You told me yourself that in a village everybody knows everything.

'And just off the record,' he added, 'did you think she was going to be murdered as soon as you looked at her?'

'Of course not, of course not,' exclaimed Miss Marple. 'What an idea!'

'You didn't see that look in her husband's eye that reminded you of Harry Simpson or David Jones or somebody you've known years ago, and subsequently pushed his wife off a precipice.'

'No, I did *not*!' said Miss Marple. 'I'm sure Mr Badcock would never do a wicked thing of that kind. At least,' she added thoughtfully, 'I'm nearly sure.'

'But human nature being what it is—' murmured Craddock, wickedly.

'Exactly,' said Miss Marple. She added, 'I dare say, after the first natural grief, he won't miss her very much . . .'

'Why? Did she bully him?'

'Oh no,' said Miss Marple, 'but I don't think that she— well, she wasn't a considerate woman. Kind, yes. Considerate—no. She would be fond of him and look after him when he was ill and see to his meals and be a good housekeeper, but I don't think she would ever—well, that she would ever even know what he might be feeling or thinking. That makes rather a lonely life for a man.'

'Ah,' said Dermot, 'and is his life less likely to be lonely in future?'

'I expect he'll marry again,' said Miss Marple. 'Perhaps quite soon. And probably, which is such a pity, a woman of much the same type. I mean he'll marry someone with a stronger personality than his own.'

'Anyone in view?' asked Dermot.

'Not that I know of,' said Miss Marple. She added regretfully, 'But I know so little.'

'Well, what do you *think*?' urged Dermot Craddock. 'You've never been backward in thinking things.'

'I think,' said Miss Marple, unexpectedly, 'that you ought to go and see Mrs Bantry.'

'Mrs Bantry? Who is she? One of the film lot?'

'No,' said Miss Marple, 'she lives in the East Lodge at Gossington. She was at the party that day. She used to own Gossington at one time. She and her husband, Colonel Bantry.'

'She was at the party. And she saw something?'

'I think she must tell you herself what it was she saw. You mayn't think it has any bearing on the matter, but I think it might be—just might be—suggestive. Tell her I sent you to her and—ah yes, perhaps you'd better just mention the Lady of Shalott.'

Dermot Craddock looked at her with his head just slightly on one side.

'The Lady of Shalott,' he said. 'Those are the code words, are they?'

'I don't know that I should put it that way,' said Miss Marple, 'but it will remind her of what I mean.'

Dermot Craddock got up. 'I shall be back,' he warned her.

'That is very nice of you,' said Miss Marple. 'Perhaps if you have time, you would come and have tea with me one

84

day. If you still drink tea,' she added rather wistfully. 'I know that so many young people nowadays only go out to drinks and things. They think that afternoon tea is a very outmoded affair.'

'I'm not as young as all that,' said Dermot Craddock. 'Yes, I'll come and have tea with you one day. We'll have tea and gossip and talk about the village. Do you know any of the film stars, by the way, or any of the studio lot?'

'Not a thing,' said Miss Marple, 'except what I hear,' she added.

'Well, you usually hear a good deal,' said Dermot Craddock. 'Goodbye. It's been very nice to see you.'

'Oh, how do you do?' said Mrs Bantry, looking slightly taken aback when Dermot Craddock had introduced himself and explained who he was. 'How very exciting to see you. Don't you always have sergeants with you?'

'I've got a sergeant down here, yes,' said Craddock. 'But he's busy.'

'On routine inquiries?' asked Mrs Bantry, hopefully.

'Something of the kind,' said Dermot gravely.

'And Jane Marple sent you to me,' said Mrs Bantry, as she ushered him into her small sitting-room. 'I was just arranging some flowers,' she explained. 'It's one of those days when flowers won't do anything you want them to. They fall out, or stick up where they shouldn't stick up or won't lie down where you want them to lie down. So I'm thankful to have a distraction, and especially such an exciting one. So it really was murder, was it?'

'Did you think it was murder?'

'Well, it could have been an accident, I suppose,' said Mrs Bantry. 'Nobody's said anything definite, officially, that is. Just that rather silly piece about no evidence to show by whom or in what way the poison was administered. But, of course, we all talk about it as murder.'

'And about who did it?'

'That's the odd part of it,' said Mrs Bantry. 'We don't. Because I really don't see who *can* have done it.'

'You mean as a matter of definite physical fact you don't see who could have done it?'

'Well, no, not that. I suppose it would have been difficult but not impossible. No, I mean, I don't see who could have *wanted* to do it.'

'Nobody, you think, could have wanted to kill Heather Badcock?'

'Well, frankly,' said Mrs Bantry, 'I can't imagine *anybody* wanting to kill Heather Badcock. I've seen her quite a few times, on local things, you know. Girl guides and the St John Ambulance, and various parish things. I found her a rather trying sort of woman. Very enthusiastic about everything and a bit given to over-statement, and just a little bit of a gusher. But you don't want to murder people for that. She was the kind of woman who in the old days if you'd seen her approaching the front door, you'd have hurried out to say to your parlourmaid—which was an institution we had in those days, and very useful too—and told her to say "not at home" or "not at home to visitors", if she had conscientious scruples about the truth.'

'You mean that one might take pains to avoid Mrs

Badcock, but one would have no urge to remove her permanently.'

'Very well put,' said Mrs Bantry, nodding approval.

'She had no money to speak of,' mused Dermot, 'so nobody stood to gain by her death. Nobody seems to have disliked her to the point of hatred. I don't suppose she was blackmailing anybody?'

'She wouldn't have dreamed of doing such a thing, I'm sure,' said Mrs Bantry. 'She was the conscientious and high-principled kind.'

'And her husband wasn't having an affair with someone else?'

'I shouldn't think so,' said Mrs Bantry. 'I only saw him at the party. He looked like a bit of chewed string. Nice but wet.'

'Doesn't leave much, does it?' said Dermot Craddock. 'One falls back on the assumption she knew something.'

'Knew something?'

'To the detriment of somebody else.'

Mrs Bantry shook her head again. 'I doubt it,' she said. 'I doubt it very much. She struck me as the kind of woman who if she had known anything about anyone, couldn't have helped talking about it.'

'Well, that washes that out,' said Dermot Craddock, 'so we'll come, if we may, to my reasons for coming to see you. Miss Marple, for whom I have the greatest admiration and respect, told me that I was to say to you the Lady of Shalott.'

'Oh, *that*!' said Mrs Bantry.

'Yes,' said Craddock. '*That*! Whatever it is.'

'People don't read much Tennyson nowadays,' said Mrs Bantry.

'A few echoes come back to me,' said Dermot Craddock. 'She looked out to Camelot, didn't she?

Out flew the web and floated wide;
The Mirror crack'd from side to side;
'The curse has come upon me,' cried
The Lady of Shalott.'

'Exactly. She did,' said Mrs Bantry.

'I beg your pardon. Who did? Did what?'

'Looked like that,' said Mrs Bantry.

'Who looked like what?'

'Marina Gregg.'

'Ah, Marina Gregg. When was this?'

'Didn't Jane Marple tell you?'

'She didn't tell me anything. She sent me to you.'

'That's tiresome of her,' said Mrs Bantry, 'because she can always tell things better than I can. My husband always used to say that I was so abrupt that he didn't know what I was talking about. Anyway, it may have been only my fancy. But when you see anyone looking like that you can't help remembering it.'

'Please tell me,' said Dermot Craddock.

'Well, it was at the party. I call it a party because what can one call things? But it was just a sort of reception up at the top of the stairs where they've made a kind of recess. Marina Gregg was there and her husband. They fetched some of us in. They fetched me, I suppose, because I once owned the house, and they fetched Heather Badcock and her husband because she'd done all the running of the fête, and the arrangements. And we happened to go up the stairs at about the same time, so I was standing there, you see, when I noticed it.'

'Quite. When you noticed what?'

'Well, Mrs Badcock went into a long spiel as people do when they meet celebrities. You know, how wonderful it was, and what a thrill and they'd always hoped to see them. And she went into a long story of how she'd once met her years ago and how exciting it had been. And I thought, in my own mind, you know, what a bore it must be for these poor celebrities to have to say all the right things. And then I noticed that Marina Gregg wasn't saying the right things. She was just staring.'

'Staring—at Mrs Badcock?'

'No—no, it looked as though she'd forgotten Mrs Badcock altogether. I mean, I don't believe she'd even heard what Mrs Badcock was saying. She was just staring with what I call this Lady of Shalott look, as though she'd seen something awful. Something frightening, something that she could hardly believe she saw and couldn't bear to see.'

'"The curse has come upon me"?' suggested Dermot Craddock.

'Yes, just that. That's why I call it the Lady of Shalott look.'

'But what was she looking *at*, Mrs Bantry?'

'Well, I wish I knew,' said Mrs Bantry.

'She was at the top of the stairs, you say?'

'She was looking over Mrs Badcock's head—no, more over one shoulder, I think.'

'Straight at the middle of the staircase?'

'It might have been a little to one side.'

'And there were people coming up the staircase?'

'Oh yes, I should think about five or six people.'

'Was she looking at one of these people in particular?'

'I can't possibly tell,' said Mrs Bantry. 'You see, I wasn't facing that way. I was looking at *her*. My back was to the stairs. I thought perhaps she was looking at one of the pictures.'

'But she must know the pictures quite well if she's living in the house.'

'Yes, yes, of course. No, I suppose she must have been looking at one of the people. I wonder which.'

'We have to try and find out,' said Dermot Craddock. 'Can you remember at all who the people were?'

'Well, I know the mayor was one of them and his wife. There was someone who I think was a reporter, with red hair, because I was introduced to him later, but I can't remember his name. I never hear names. Galbraith— something like that. Then there was a big black man. I don't mean a negro—I just mean very dark, forceful looking. And an actress with him. A bit over-blonde and the minky kind. And old General Barnstaple from Much Benham. He's practically ga-ga now, poor old boy. I don't think *he* could have been anybody's doom. Oh! and the Grices from the farm.'

'Those are all the people you can remember?'

'Well, there may have been others. But you see I

wasn't—well, I mean I wasn't noticing particularly. I know that the mayor and General Barnstaple and the Americans did arrive about that time. And there were people taking photographs. One I think was a local man, and there was a girl from London, an arty-looking girl with long hair and a rather large camera.'

'And you think it was one of those people who brought that look to Marina Gregg's face?'

'I didn't really think anything,' said Mrs Bantry with complete frankness. 'I just wondered what on earth made her look like that and then I didn't think of it any more. But afterwards one remembers about these things. But of course,' added Mrs Bantry with honesty, 'I *may* have imagined it. After all, she may have had a sudden toothache or a safety pin run into her or a sudden violent colic. The sort of thing where you try to go on as usual and not to show anything, but your face can't help looking awful.'

Dermot Craddock laughed. 'I'm glad to see you're a realist, Mrs Bantry,' he said. 'As you say, it may have been something of that kind. But it's certainly just one interesting little fact that might be a pointer.'

He shook his head and departed to present his official credentials in Much Benham.

CHAPTER 9

'So locally you've drawn a blank?' said Craddock, offering his cigarette case to Frank Cornish.

'Completely,' said Cornish. 'No enemies, no quarrels, on good terms with her husband.'

'No question of another woman or another man?'

The other shook his head. 'Nothing of that kind. No hint of scandal anywhere. She wasn't what you'd call the sexy kind. She was on a lot of committees and things like that and there were some small local rivalries, but nothing beyond that.'

'There wasn't anyone else the husband wanted to marry? No one in the office where he worked?'

'He's in Biddle & Russell, the estate agents and valuers. There's Florrie West with adenoids, and Miss Grundle, who is at least fifty and as plain as a haystack—nothing much there to excite a man. Though for all that I shouldn't be surprised if he *did* marry again soon.'

Craddock looked interested.

'A neighbour,' explained Cornish. 'A widow. When I went back with him from the inquest she'd gone in and was making him tea and looking after him generally. He seemed surprised and grateful. If you ask me, she's made up her mind to marry him, but he doesn't know it yet, poor chap.'

'What sort of a woman is she?'

'Good looking,' admitted the other. 'Not young but handsome in a gipsyish sort of way. High colour. Dark eyes.'

'What's her name?'

'Bain. Mrs Bain. Mary Bain. She's a widow.'

'What'd her husband do?'

'No idea. She's got a son working near here who lives with her. She seems a quiet, respectable woman. All the same, I've a feeling I've seen her before.' He looked at his watch. 'Ten to twelve. I've made an appointment for you at Gossington Hall at twelve o'clock. We'd best be going.'

Dermot Craddock's eyes, which always looked gently inattentive, were in actuality making a close mental note of the features of Gossington Hall. Inspector Cornish had taken him there, had delivered him over to a young man called Hailey Preston, and had then taken a tactful leave. Since then, Dermot Craddock had been gently nodding at Mr Preston. Hailey Preston, he gathered, was a kind of public relations or personal assistant, or private secretary, or more likely, a mixture of all three, to Jason Rudd. He talked. He talked freely and at length without much modulation and managing miraculously not to repeat himself too often. He was a pleasant young man, anxious that his own views, reminiscent of those of Dr Pangloss that all was for the best in the best of all possible worlds, should be shared by anyone in whose company he happened to be. He said several times and in different ways what a terrible shame this had been, how worried everyone had been, how Marina was absolutely prostrated, how Mr Rudd was more upset than he could possibly say, how it absolutely beat anything that a thing like that should happen, didn't it? Possibly there might have been some kind of allergy to some particular kind of substance? He just put that forward as an idea—allergies were extraordinary things. Chief-Inspector Craddock was to count on every possible co-operation that Hellingforth Studios or any of their staff could give. He was to ask any questions he wanted, go anywhere he liked. If they could help in any way they would do so. They all had had the greatest respect for Mrs Badcock and appreciated her strong social sense and the valuable work she had done for the St John Ambulance Association.

He then started again, not in the same words but using the same motifs. No one could have been more eagerly co-operative. At the same time he endeavoured to convey how very far this was from the cellophane world of studios; and Mr Jason Rudd and Miss Marina Gregg, or any of the people in the house who surely were going to do their utmost to help in any way they possibly could. Then he nodded gently some forty-four times. Dermot Craddock took advantage of the pause to say:

'Thank you very much.'

It was said quietly but with a kind of finality that brought Mr Hailey Preston up with a jerk. He said:

'Well—' and paused inquiringly.

'You said I might ask questions?'

'Sure. Sure. Fire ahead.'

'Is this the place where she died?'

'Mrs Badcock?'

'Mrs Badcock. Is this the place?'

'Yes, sure. Right here. At least, well actually I can show you the chair.'

They were standing on the landing recess. Hailey Preston walked a short way along the corridor and pointed out a rather phony-looking oak arm-chair.

'She was sitting right there,' he said. 'She said she didn't feel well. Someone went to get her something, and then she just died, right there.'

'I see.'

'I don't know if she'd seen a physician lately. If she'd been warned that she had anything wrong with her heart—'

'She had nothing wrong with her heart,' said Dermot Craddock. 'She was a healthy woman. She died of six times the maximum dose of a substance whose official name I will not try to pronounce but which I understand is generally known as Calmo.'

'I know, I know,' said Hailey Preston. 'I take it myself sometimes.'

'Indeed? That's very interesting. You find it has a good effect?'

'Marvellous. Marvellous. It bucks you up *and* it soothes you down, if you understand what I mean. Naturally,' he added, 'you would have to take it in the proper dosage.'

'Would there be supplies of this substance in the house?'

He knew the answer to the question, but he put it as

though he did not. Hailey Preston's answer was frankness itself.

'Loads of it, I should say. There'll be a bottle of it in most of the bathroom cupboards here.'

'Which doesn't make our task easier.'

'Of course,' said Hailey Preston, 'she might have used the stuff herself and taken a dose, and as I say, had an allergy.'

Craddock looked unconvinced—Hailey Preston sighed and said:

'You're quite definite about the dosage?'

'Oh yes. It was a lethal dose and Mrs Badcock did not take any such things herself. As far as we can make out the only things she ever took were bicarbonate of soda or aspirin.'

Hailey Preston shook his head and said, 'That sure gives us a problem. Yes, it sure does.'

'Where did Mr Rudd and Miss Gregg receive their guests?'

'Right here.' Hailey Preston went to the spot at the top of the stairs.

Chief-Inspector Craddock stood beside him. He looked at the wall opposite him. In the centre was an Italian Madonna and child. A good copy, he presumed, of some well-known picture. The blue-robed Madonna held aloft the infant Jesus and both child and mother were laughing. Little groups of people stood on either side, their eyes upraised to the child. One of the more pleasing Madonnas, Dermot Craddock thought. To the right and left of this picture were two narrow windows. The whole effect was very charming but it seemed to him that there was emphatically nothing there that would cause a woman to look like the Lady of Shalott whose doom had come upon her.

'People, of course, were coming up the stairs?' he asked.

'Yes. They came in driblets, you know. Not too many at once. I shepherded up some, Ella Zielinsky, that's Mr Rudd's secretary, brought some of the others. We wanted to make it all pleasant and informal.'

'Were you here yourself at the time Mrs Badcock came up?'

'I'm ashamed to tell you, Chief-Inspector Craddock, that I just can't remember. I had a list of names, I went out and I shepherded people in. I introduced them, saw to drinks, then I'd go out and come up with the next batch. At the time I didn't know this Mrs Badcock by sight, and she wasn't one of the ones on my list to bring up.'

'What about a Mrs Bantry?'

'Ah yes, she's the former owner of this place, isn't she? I believe she, and Mrs Badcock and her husband, *did* come up about the same time.' He paused. 'And the mayor came just about then. He had a big chain on and a wife with yellow hair, wearing royal blue with frills. I remember all of them. I didn't pour drinks for any of them because I had to go down and bring up the next lot.'

'Who did pour drinks for them?'

'Why, I can't exactly say. There were three or four of us on duty. I know I went down the stairs just as the mayor was coming up.'

'Who else was on the stairs as you went down, if you can remember?'

97

'Jim Galbraith, one of the newspaper boys who was covering this, three or four others whom I didn't know. There were a couple of photographers, one of the locals, I don't remember his name, and an arty girl from London, who rather specialises in queer angle shots. Her camera was set right up in that corner so that she could get a view of Miss Gregg receiving. Ah, now let me think, I rather fancy that that was when Ardwyck Fenn arrived.'

'And who is Ardwyck Fenn?'

Hailey Preston looked shocked. 'He's a big shot, Chief-Inspector. A very big shot in the television and moving picture world. We didn't even know he was in this country.'

'His turning up was a surprise?'

'I'll say it was,' said Preston. 'Nice of him to come and quite unexpected.'

'Was he an old friend of Miss Gregg's and Mr Rudd's?'

'He was an old friend of Marina's a good many years ago when she was married to her second husband. I don't know how well Jason knew him.'

'Anyway, it was a pleasant surprise when he arrived?'

'Sure it was. We were all delighted.'

Craddock nodded and passed from that to other subjects. He made meticulous inquiries about the drinks, their ingredients, how they were served, who served them, what servants and hired servants were on duty. The answers seemed to be, as Inspector Cornish had already hinted was the case that, although any one of thirty people *could* have poisoned Heather Badcock with the utmost ease, yet at the same time any one of the thirty might have been seen doing so! It was, Craddock reflected, a big chance to take.

'Thank you,' he said at last. 'Now I would like, if I may, to speak to Miss Marina Gregg.'

Hailey Preston shook his head.

'I'm sorry,' he said. 'I really am sorry but that's right out of the question.'

Craddock's eyebrows rose.

'Surely!'

'She's prostrated. She's absolutely prostrated. She's got her own physician here looking after her. He wrote out a certificate. I've got it here. I'll show it to you.'

Craddock took it and read it.

'I see,' he said. He asked, 'Does Marina Gregg always have a physician in attendance?'

'They're very high strung, all these actors and actresses. It's a big strain, this life. It's usually considered desirable in the case of the big shots that they should have a physician who understands their constitution and their nerves. Maurice Gilchrist has a very big reputation. He's looked after Miss Gregg for many years now. She's had a great deal of illness, as you may have read, in the last few years. She was hospitalized for a very long time. It's only about a year ago that she got her strength and health back.'

'I see.'

Hailey Preston seemed relieved that Craddock was not making any more protests.

'You'll want to see Mr Rudd?' he suggested. 'He'll be—' he looked at his watch, '—he'll be back from the studios in about ten minutes if that's all right for you.'

'That'll do admirably,' said Craddock. 'In the meantime is Dr Gilchrist actually here in the house?'

Agatha Christie

'He is.'

'Then I'd like to talk to him.'

'Why, certainly. I'll fetch him right away.'

The young man bustled away. Dermot Craddock stood thoughtfully at the top of the stairs. Of course this frozen look that Mrs Bantry had described might have been entirely Mrs Bantry's imagination. She was, he thought, a woman who would jump to conclusions. At the same time he thought it quite likely that the conclusion to which she had jumped was a just one. Without going so far as to look like the Lady of Shalott seeing doom coming down upon her, Marina Gregg might have seen something that vexed or annoyed her. Something that had caused her to have been negligent to a guest to whom she was talking. Somebody had come up those stairs, perhaps, who could be described as an unexpected guest—an unwelcome guest?

He turned at the sound of footsteps. Hailey Preston was back and with him was Dr Maurice Gilchrist. Dr Gilchrist was not at all as Dermot Craddock had imagined him. He had no suave bedside manner, neither was he theatrical in appearance. He seemed on the face of it a blunt, hearty, matter-of-fact man. He was dressed in tweeds, slightly florid tweeds to the English idea. He had a thatch of brown hair and observant, keen dark eyes.

'Doctor Gilchrist? I am Chief-Inspector Dermot Craddock. May I have a word or two with you in private?'

The doctor nodded. He turned along the corridor and went along it almost to the end, then he pushed the door open and invited Craddock to enter.

'No one will disturb us here,' he said.

It was obviously the doctor's own bedroom, a very comfortably appointed one. Dr Gilchrist indicated a chair and then sat down himself.

'I understand,' said Craddock, 'that Miss Marina Gregg, according to you, is unable to be interviewed. What's the matter with her, Doctor?'

Gilchrist shrugged his shoulders very slightly.

'Nerves,' he said. 'If you were to ask her questions now she'd be in a state bordering on hysteria within ten minutes. I can't permit that. If you like to send your police doctor to see me, I'd be willing to give him my views. She was unable to be present at the inquest for the same reason.'

'How long,' asked Craddock, 'is such a state of things likely to continue?'

Dr Gilchrist looked at him and smiled. It was a likeable smile.

'If you want my opinion,' he said, 'a human opinion, that is, not a medical one, any time within the next forty-eight hours, and she'll be not only willing, but asking to see you! She'll be wanting to ask questions. She'll be wanting to answer your questions. They're like that!' He leaned forward. 'I'd like to try and make you understand if I can, Chief-Inspector, a little bit what makes these people act the way they do. The motion picture life is a life of continuous strain, and the more successful you are, the greater the strain. You live always, all day, in the public eye. When you're on location, when you're working, it's hard monotonous work with long hours. You're there in the morning, you sit and you wait. You do your small bit, the bit that's being shot over and over again. If you're rehearsing on the stage you'd be rehearsing as likely as not a whole act, or at any rate a part of an act. The thing would be in sequence, it would be more or less human and credible. But when you're shooting a picture everything's taken out of sequence. It's a monotonous, grinding business. It's exhausting. You live in luxury, of course, you have soothing drugs, you have baths and creams and powders and medical attention, you have relaxations and parties and people, but you're always in the public eye. You can't enjoy yourself quietly. You can't really—*ever relax.*'

'I can understand that,' said Dermot. 'Yes, I can understand.'

'And there's another thing,' went on Gilchrist. 'If you adopt this career, and especially if you're any good at it, you are a certain kind of person. You're a person—or so I've found in my experience—with a skin too few—a person who is plagued the whole time with diffidence. A terrible feeling of inadequacy, of apprehension that you can't do what's required of you. People say that actors and actresses are vain. That isn't true. They're not *conceited* about themselves; they're *obsessed* with themselves, yes, but they need reassurance the whole time. They *must* be continually reassured. Ask Jason Rudd. He'll tell you the same. You have to make them feel they can do it, to assure them they can do it, take them over and over again over the same thing encouraging them the whole time until you get the effect you want. But they are always doubtful of themselves. And that makes them, in an ordinary human, unprofessional word: nervy. Damned nervy! A mass of nerves. And the worse their nerves are the better they are at the job.'

'That's interesting,' said Craddock. 'Very interesting.' He paused, adding: 'Though I don't see quite why you—'

'I'm trying to make you understand Marina Gregg,' said Maurice Gilchrist. 'You've seen her pictures, no doubt.'

'She's a wonderful actress,' said Dermot, 'wonderful. She has a personality, a beauty, a sympathy.'

'Yes,' said Gilchrist, 'she has all those, and she's had to work like the devil to produce the effects that she has produced. In the process her nerves get shot to pieces, and she's not actually a strong woman physically. Not as strong as you need to be. She's got one of those temperaments that swing to and fro between despair and rapture. She can't help it. She's made that way. She's suffered a great deal in her life. A large part of the suffering has been her own fault, but some of it hasn't. None of her marriages has been happy, except, I'd say, this last one. She's married to a man now who loves her dearly and who's loved her for years. She's sheltering in that love and she's happy in it. At least, at the moment she's happy in it. One can't say how long all that will last. The trouble with her is that either she thinks that at last she's got to that spot or place or that moment in her life where everything's like a fairy tale come true, that nothing can go wrong, that she'll never be unhappy again; or else she's down in the dumps, a woman whose life is ruined, who's never known love and happiness and who never will again.' He added dryly, 'If she could only stop half-way between the two it'd be wonderful for her; and the world would lose a fine actress.'

He paused, but Dermot Craddock did not speak. He was wondering why Maurice Gilchrist was saying what he did. Why this close detailed analysis of Marina Gregg? Gilchrist was looking at him. It was as though he was urging Dermot to ask one particular question. Dermot wondered very much what the question was that he ought to ask. He said at last slowly, with the air of one feeling his way:

'She's been very much upset by this tragedy happening here?'

'Yes,' said Gilchrist, 'she has.'

'Almost unnaturally so?'

'That depends,' said Dr Gilchrist.

'On what does it depend?'

'On her reason for being so upset.'

'I suppose,' said Dermot, feeling his way, 'that it was a shock, a sudden death happening like that in the midst of a party.'

He saw very little response in the face opposite him 'Or might it,' he said, 'be something more than that?'

'You can't tell, of course,' said Dr Gilchrist, 'how people are going to react. You can't tell however well you know them. They can always surprise you. Marina might have taken this in her stride. She's a soft-hearted creature. She might say, "Oh, poor, poor woman, how tragic. I wonder how it could have happened." She could have been sympathetic without really caring. After all deaths do occasionally occur at studio parties. Or she might, if there wasn't anything very interesting going on, choose—choose unconsciously, mind you—to dramatize herself over it. She might decide to throw a scene. Or there might be some quite different reason.'

Dermot decided to take the bull by the horns. 'I wish,' he said, 'you would tell me what you really think?'

'I don't know,' said Dr Gilchrist. 'I can't be sure.' He paused and then said, 'There's professional etiquette, you know. There's the relationship between doctor and patient.'

'She has told you something?'

'I don't think I could go as far as that.'

'Did Marina Gregg know this woman, Heather Badcock? Had she met her before?'

'I don't think she knew her from Adam,' said Dr Gilchrist. 'No. That's not the trouble. If you ask me it's nothing to do with Heather Badcock.'

Dermot said, 'This stuff, this Calmo. Does Marina Gregg ever use it herself?'

'Lives on it, pretty well,' said Dr Gilchrist. 'So does everyone else around here,' he added. 'Ella Zielinsky takes it, Hailey Preston takes it, half the boiling takes it—it's the fashion at this moment. They're all much the same, these things. People get tired of one and they try a new one that comes out and they think it's wonderful, and that it makes all the difference.'

'And does it make all the difference?'

'Well,' said Gilchrist, 'it makes *a* difference. It does its work. It calms you or it peps you up, makes you feel you could do things which otherwise you might fancy that you couldn't. I don't prescribe them more than I can help, but they're not dangerous taken properly. They help people who can't help themselves.'

'I wish I knew,' said Dermot Craddock, 'what it is that you are trying to tell me.'

'I'm trying to decide,' said Gilchrist, 'what is my duty. There are two duties. There's the duty of a doctor to his patient. What his patient says to him is confidential and must be kept so. But there's another point of view. You can fancy that there is a danger to a patient. You have to take steps to avoid that danger.'

He stopped. Craddock looked at him and waited.

'Yes,' said Dr Gilchrist. 'I think I know what I must do. I must ask you, Chief-Inspector Craddock, to keep what I am telling you confidential. Not from your colleagues, of course. But as far as regards the outer world, particularly in the house here. Do you agree?'

'I can't bind myself,' said Craddock. 'I don't know what will arise. In general terms, yes, I agree. That is to say, I imagine that any piece of information you gave me I should prefer to keep to myself and my colleagues.'

'Now listen,' said Gilchrist, 'this mayn't mean anything at all. Women say anything when they're in the state of nerves Marina Gregg is now. I'm telling you something which she said to me. There may be nothing in it at all.'

'What did she say?' asked Craddock.

'She broke down after this thing happened. She sent for me. I gave her a sedative. I stayed there beside her, holding her hand, telling her to calm down, telling her things were going to be all right. Then, just before she went off into unconsciousness she said, "It was meant for *me*, Doctor."'

Craddock stared. 'She said that, did she? And afterwards—the next day?'

'She never alluded to it again. I raised the point once. She evaded it. She said, "Oh, you must have made a mistake.

I'm sure I never said anything like that. I expect I was half doped at the time."'

'But you think she meant it?'

'She meant it all right,' said Gilchrist. 'That's not to say that it is so,' he added warningly. 'Whether someone meant to poison her or meant to poison Heather Badcock I don't know. You'd probably know better than I would. All I do say is that Marina Gregg definitely thought and believed that that dose was meant for her.'

Craddock was silent for some moments. Then he said, 'Thank you, Doctor Gilchrist. I appreciate what you have told me and I realize your motive. If what Marina Gregg said to you was founded on fact it may mean, may it not, that there is still danger to her?'

'That's the point,' said Gilchrist. 'That's the whole point.'

'Have you any reason to believe that that might be so?'

'No, I haven't.'

'No idea what her reason for thinking so was?'

'No.'

'Thank you.'

Craddock got up. 'Just one thing more, Doctor. Do you know if she said the same thing to her husband?'

Slowly Gilchrist shook his head. 'No,' he said, 'I'm quite sure of that. She didn't tell her husband.'

His eyes met Dermot's for a few moments then he gave a brief nod of his head and said, 'You don't want me any more? All right. I'll go back and have a look at the patient. You shall talk to her as soon as it's possible.'

He left the room and Craddock remained, pursing his lips up and whistling very softly beneath his breath.

CHAPTER 10

'Jason's back now,' said Hailey Preston. 'Will you come with me, Chief-Inspector, I'll take you to his room.'

The room which Jason Rudd used partly for office and partly for a sitting-room, was on the first floor. It was comfortably but not luxuriously furnished. It was a room which had little personality and no indication of the private tastes or predilection of its user. Jason Rudd rose from the desk at which he was sitting, and came forward to meet Dermot. It was wholly unnecessary, Dermot thought, for the room to have a personality; the user of it had so much. Hailey Preston had been an efficient and voluble gasbag. Gilchrist had force and magnetism. But here was a man whom, as Dermot immediately admitted to himself, it would not be easy to read. In the course of his career, Craddock had met and summed up many people. By now he was fully adept in realizing the potentialities and very often reading the thoughts of most of the people with whom he came in contact. But he felt at once that one would be able to gauge only as much of Jason Rudd's thoughts as Jason Rudd himself permitted. The eyes, deepset and thoughtful, perceived but would not easily reveal. The ugly, rugged head spoke of an excellent intellect. The clown's face could repel you or attract you. Here, thought Dermot Craddock to himself, is where I sit and listen and take very careful notes.

'Sorry, Chief-Inspector, if you've had to wait for me. I was held up by some small complication over at the studios. Can I offer you a drink?'

'Not just now, thank you, Mr Rudd.'

The clown's face suddenly crinkled into a kind of ironic amusement.

'Not the house to take a drink in, is that what you're thinking?'

'As a matter of fact it wasn't what I was thinking.'

'No, no I suppose not. Well, Chief-Inspector, what do you want to know? What can I tell you?'

'Mr Preston has answered very adequately all the questions I have put to him.'

'And that has been helpful to you?'

'Not as helpful as I could wish.'

Jason Rudd looked inquiring.

'I've also seen Dr Gilchrist. He informs me that your wife is not yet strong enough to be asked questions.'

'Marina,' said Jason Rudd, 'is very sensitive. She's subject, frankly, to nerve storms. And murder at such close quarters is, as you will admit, likely to produce a nerve storm.'

'It is not a pleasant experience,' Dermot Craddock agreed, dryly.

'In any case I doubt if there is anything my wife could tell you that you could not learn equally well from me. I was standing beside her when the thing happened, and frankly I would say that I am a better observer than my wife.'

'The first question I would like to ask,' said Dermot, '(and it is a question that you have probably answered already but for all that I would like to ask again), had you or your wife any previous acquaintance with Heather Badcock?'

Jason Rudd shook his head.

'None whatever. I certainly have never seen the woman before in my life. I had two letters from her on behalf of the St John Ambulance Association, but I had not met her personally until about five minutes before her death.'

'But she claimed to have met your wife?'

Jason Rudd nodded.

'Yes, some twelve or thirteen years ago, I gather. In Bermuda. Some big garden party in aid of ambulances, which Marina opened for them, I think, and Mrs Badcock, as soon as she was introduced, burst into some long rigma-role of how although she was in bed with 'flu, she had got up and had managed to come to this affair and had asked for and got my wife's autograph.'

Again the ironical smile crinkled his face.

'That, I may say, is a very common occurrence, Chief-Inspector. Large mobs of people are usually lined up to obtain my wife's autograph and it is a moment that they treasure and remember. Quite understandably, it is an event in their lives. Equally naturally it is not likely that my wife would remember one out of a thousand or so autograph hunters. She had, quite frankly, no recollection of ever having seen Mrs Badcock before.'

'That I can well understand,' said Craddock. 'Now I

have been told, Mr Rudd, by an onlooker that your wife was slightly *distraite* during the few moments that Heather Badcock was speaking to her. Would you agree that such was the case?'

'Very possibly,' said Jason Rudd. 'Marina is not particularly strong. She was, of course, used to what I may describe as her public social work, and could carry out her duties in that line almost automatically. But towards the end of a long day she was inclined occasionally to flag. This may have been such a moment. I did not, I may say, observe anything of the kind myself. No, wait a minute, that is not quite true. I do remember that she was a little slow in making her reply to Mrs Badcock. In fact I think I nudged her very gently in the ribs.'

'Something had perhaps distracted her attention?' said Dermot.

'Possibly, but it may have been just a momentary lapse through fatigue.'

Dermot Craddock was silent for a few minutes. He looked out of the window where the view was the somewhat sombre one over the woods surrounding Gossington Hall. He looked at the pictures on the walls, and finally he looked at Jason Rudd. Jason Rudd's face was attentive but nothing more. There was no guide to his feelings. He appeared courteous and completely at ease, but he might, Craddock thought, be actually nothing of the kind. This was a man of very high mental calibre. One would not, Dermot thought, get anything out of him that he was not prepared to say unless one put one's cards on the table. Dermot took his decision. He would do just that.

'Has it occurred to you, Mr Rudd, that the poisoning of Heather Badcock may have been entirely accidental? That the real intended victim was your wife?'

There was a silence. Jason Rudd's face did not change its expression. Dermot waited. Finally Jason Rudd gave a deep sigh and appeared to relax.

'Yes,' he said quietly, 'you're quite right, Chief-Inspector. I have been sure of it all along.'

'But you have said nothing to that effect, not to Inspector Cornish, not at the inquest?'

'No.'

'Why not, Mr Rudd?'

'I could answer you very adequately by saying that it was merely a belief on my part unsupported by any kind of evidence. The facts that led me to deduce it, were facts equally accessible to the law which was probably better qualified to decide than I was. I knew nothing about Mrs Badcock personally. She might have enemies, someone might have decided to administer a fatal dose to her on this particular occasion, though it would seem a very curious and far-fetched decision. But it might have been chosen conceivably for the reason that at a public occasion of this kind the issues would be more confused, the number of strangers present would be considerable and just for that reason it would be more difficult to bring home to the person in question the commission of such a crime. All that is true, but I am going to be frank with you, Chief-Inspector. That was *not* my reason for keeping silent. I will tell you what that reason was. I didn't want my wife to suspect for one moment that it was she who had narrowly escaped dying by poison.'

112

'Thank you for your frankness,' said Dermot. 'Not that I quite understand your motive in keeping silent.'

'No? Perhaps it is a little difficult to explain. You would have to know Marina to understand. She is a person who badly needs happiness and security. Her life has been highly successful in the material sense. She has won renown artistically but her personal life has been one of deep unhappiness. Again and again she has thought that she has found happiness and was wildly and unduly elated thereby, and has had her hopes dashed to the ground. She is incapable, Mr Craddock, of taking a rational, prudent view of life. In her previous marriages she has expected, like a child reading a fairy story, to live happy ever afterwards.'

Again the ironic smile changed the ugliness of the clown's face into a strange, sudden sweetness.

'But marriage is not like that, Chief-Inspector. There can be no rapture continued indefinitely. We are fortunate indeed if we can achieve a life of quiet content, affection, and serene and sober happiness.' He added. 'Perhaps you are married, Chief-Inspector?'

Dermot Craddock shook his head.

'I have not so far that good, or bad, fortune,' he murmured.

'In our world, the moving picture world, marriage is a fully occupational hazard. Film stars marry often. Sometimes happily, sometimes disastrously, but seldom permanently. In that respect I should not say that Marina has had any undue cause to complain, but to one of her temperament things of that kind matter very deeply. She imbued herself with the idea that she was unlucky, that nothing would

113

ever go right for her. She has always been looking desperately for the same things, love, happiness, affection, security. She was wildly anxious to have children. According to some medical opinion, the very strength of that anxiety frustrated its object. One very celebrated physician advised the adoption of a child. He said it is often the case that when an intense desire for maternity is assuaged by having adopted a baby, a child is born naturally shortly afterwards. Marina adopted no less than three children. For a time she got a certain amount of happiness and serenity, but it was not the real thing. You can imagine her delight when eleven years ago she found she was going to have a child. Her pleasure and delight were quite indescribable. She was in good health and the doctors assured her that there was every reason to believe that everything would go well. As you may or may not know, the result was tragedy. The child, a boy, was born mentally deficient, imbecile. The result was disastrous. Marina had a complete breakdown and was severely ill for years, confined to a sanatorium. Though her recovery was slow she did recover. Shortly after that we married and she began once more to take an interest in life and to feel that perhaps she could be happy. It was difficult at first for her to get a worthwhile contract for a picture. Everyone was inclined to doubt whether her health would stand the strain. I had to battle for that.' Jason Rudd's lips set firmly together. 'Well, the battle was successful. We have started shooting the picture. In the meantime we bought this house and set about altering it. Only about a fortnight ago Marina was saying to me how happy she was, and how she felt at last she was going to be able to settle down to a happy home life, her troubles behind her. I was a little nervous because, as usual, her expectations were too optimistic. But there was no doubt that she was happy. Her nervous symptoms disappeared, there was a calmness and a quietness about her that I had never seen before. Everything was going well until—' He paused. His voice became suddenly bitter. 'Until this happened! That woman had to die—*here*! That in itself was shock enough. I couldn't risk—I was determined not to risk—Marina's knowing that an attempt had been made on *her* life. That would have been a second, perhaps fatal, shock. It might have precipitated another mental collapse.'

He looked directly at Dermot.

'Do you understand—now?'

'I see your point of view,' said Craddock, 'but forgive me, isn't there one aspect that you are neglecting? You give me your conviction that an attempt was made to poison your wife. Doesn't that danger still remain? If a poisoner does not succeed, isn't it likely that the attempt may be repeated?'

'Naturally I've considered that,' said Jason Rudd, 'but I am confident that, being forewarned so to speak, I can take all reasonable precautions for my wife's safety. I shall watch over her and arrange that others shall watch over her. The great thing, I feel, is that she herself should not know that any danger threatened her.'

'And you think,' said Dermot cautiously, 'that she does *not* know?'

'Of course not. She has no idea.'

'You're sure of that?'

'Certain. Such an idea would never occur to her.'

'But it occurred to you,' Dermot pointed out.

'That's very different,' said Jason Rudd. 'Logically it was the only solution. But my wife isn't logical, and to begin with she could not possibly imagine that anyone would want to do away with her. Such a possibility would simply not occur to her mind.'

'You may be right,' said Dermot slowly, 'but that leaves us now with several other questions. Again, let me put this bluntly. Whom do you suspect?'

'I can't tell you.'

'Excuse me, Mr Rudd, do you mean by that you can't or that you won't?'

Jason Rudd spoke quickly. 'Can't. Can't every time. It seems to me just as impossible as it would seem to her that anyone would dislike her enough—should have a sufficient grudge against her—to do such a thing. On the other hand, on the sheer, downright evidence of the facts, that is exactly what must have occurred.'

'Will you outline the facts to me as you see them?'

'If you like. The circumstances are quite clear. I poured out two daiquiri cocktails from an already prepared jug. I took them to Marina and Mrs Badcock. What Mrs Badcock did I do not know. She moved on, I presume, to speak to someone she knew. My wife had her drink in her hand. At that moment the mayor and his wife were approaching. She put down her glass, as yet untouched, and greeted them. Then there were more greetings. An old friend we'd not seen for years, some other locals and one or two people from the studios. During that time the glass containing the cocktail stood on the table which was situated at that time behind us since we had both moved forward a little to the top of the stairs. One or two photographs were taken of my wife talking to the mayor, which we hoped would please the local population, at the special request of the representatives of the local newspaper. While this was being done I brought some fresh drinks to a few of the last arrivals. During that time my wife's glass must have been poisoned. Don't ask me *how* it was done, it cannot have been easy to do. On the other hand, it is startling, if anyone has the nerve to do an action openly and unconcernedly, how little people are likely to notice it! You ask me if I have suspicions; all I can say is that at least one of about twenty people *might* have done it. People, you see, were moving about in little groups, talking, occasionally going off to have a look at the alterations which had been done to the house. There was movement, continual movement. I've thought and I've thought, I've racked my brains but there is nothing, absolutely *nothing* to direct my suspicions to any particular person.'

He paused and gave an exasperated sigh.

'I understand,' said Dermot. 'Go on, please.'

'I dare say you've heard the next part before.'

'I should like to hear it again from you.'

'Well, I had come back towards the head of the stairs. My wife had turned towards the table and was just picking up her glass. There was a slight exclamation from Mrs Badcock. Somebody must have jogged her arm and the glass slipped out of her fingers and was broken on the floor. Marina did the natural hostess's act. Her own skirt had been slightly touched with the liquid. She insisted no harm was done, used her own handkerchief to wipe Mrs Badcock's skirt and insisted on her having her own drink. If I remember she said, "I've had far too much already." So that was that. But I can assure you of this. The fatal dose could not have been added *after* that for Mrs Badcock immediately began to drink from the glass. As you know, four or five minutes later she was dead. I wonder—how I wonder—what the poisoner must have felt when he realised how badly his scheme had failed . . .'

'All this occurred to you at the time?'

'Of course not. At the time I concluded, naturally enough, this woman had had some kind of a seizure. Perhaps heart, coronary thrombosis, something of that sort. It never occurred to me that *poisoning* was involved. Would it occur to you—would it occur to anybody?'

'Probably not,' said Dermot. 'Well your account is clear enough and you seem sure of your facts. You say you have no suspicion of any particular person. I can't quite accept that, you know.'

'I assure you it's the truth.'

'Let us approach it from another angle. Who is there who could wish to harm your wife? It all sounds melodramatic if you put it this way, but what enemies has she got?'

Jason Rudd made an expressive gesture.

'Enemies? Enemies? It's so hard to define what one means by an enemy. There's plenty of envy and jealousy in the world my wife and I occupy. There are always people who say malicious things, who'll start a whispering campaign, who will do someone they are jealous of a bad turn if the opportunity occurs. But that doesn't mean that any of those people is a murderer, or indeed even a likely murderer. Don't you agree?'

'Yes, I agree. There must be something beyond petty dislikes or envies. Is there anyone whom your wife has injured, say, in the past?'

Jason Rudd did not rebut this easily. Instead he frowned.

'Honestly, I don't think so,' he said at last, 'and I may say I've given a lot of thought to that point.'

'Anything in the nature of a love affair, an association with some man?'

'There have of course been affairs of that kind. It may be considered, I suppose, that Marina has occasionally treated some man badly. But there is nothing to cause any lasting ill-will. I'm sure of it.'

'What about women? Any woman who has had a lasting grudge against Miss Gregg?'

'Well,' said Jason Rudd, 'you can never tell with women. I can't think of any particular one offhand.'

'Who'd benefit financially by your wife's death?'

'Her will benefits various people but not to any large extent. I suppose the people who'd benefit, as you put it, financially, would be myself as her husband and from another angle, possibly the star who might replace her in this film. Though, of course, the film might be abandoned altogether. These things are very uncertain.'

'Well, we need not go into all that now,' said Dermot.

'And I have your assurance that Marina will not be told that she is in possible danger?'

'We shall have to go into that matter,' said Dermot. 'I

want to impress upon you that you are taking quite a considerable risk there. However, the matter will not arise for some days since your wife is still under medical care. Now there is one more thing I would like you to do. I would like you to write down for me as accurately as you can every single person who was in that recess at the top of the stairs, or whom you saw coming up the stairs at the time of the murder.'

'I'll do my best, but I'm rather doubtful. You'd do far better to consult my secretary, Ella Zielinsky. She has a most accurate memory and also lists of the local people who were there. If you'd like to see her now—'

'I would like to talk to Miss Ella Zielinsky very much,' said Dermot.

CHAPTER 11

Surveying Dermot Craddock unemotionally through her large horn-rimmed spectacles, Ella Zielinsky seemed to him almost too good to be true. With quiet businesslike alacrity she whipped out of a drawer a typewritten sheet and passed it across to him.

'I think I can be fairly sure that there are no omissions,' she said. 'But it is just possible that I may have included one or two names—local names they will be—who were not actually there. That is to say who may have left earlier or who may not have been found and brought up. Actually, I'm pretty sure that it is correct.'

'A very efficient piece of work if I may say so,' said Dermot. 'Thank you.'

'I suppose—I am quite an ignoramus in such things—that you have to attain a high standard of efficiency in your job?'

'One has to have things pretty well taped, yes.'

'What else does your job comprise? Are you a kind of liaison officer, so to speak, between the studios and Gossington Hall?'

'No. I've nothing to do with the studios, actually, though of course I naturally take messages from there on the telephone or send them. My job is to look after Miss Gregg's social life, her public and private engagements, and to supervise in some degree the running of the house.'

'You like the job?'

'It's extremely well paid and I find it reasonably interesting. I didn't however bargain for murder,' she added dryly.

'Did it seem very incredible to you?'

'So much so that I am going to ask you if you are really sure it *is* murder?'

'Six times the dose of di-ethyl-mexine etc. etc., could hardly be anything else.'

'It might have been an accident of some kind.'

'And how would you suggest such an accident could have occurred?'

'More easily than you'd imagine, since you don't know the set-up. This house is simply full of drugs of all kinds. I don't mean dope when I say drugs. I mean properly prescribed remedies, but, like most of these things, what they call, I understand, the lethal dose is not very far removed from the therapeutic dose.'

Dermot nodded.

'These theatrical and picture people have the most curious lapses in their intelligence. Sometimes it seems to me that the more of an artistic genius you are, the less common sense you have in everyday life.'

'That may well be.'

'What with all the bottles, cachets, powders, capsules,

and little boxes that they carry about with them; what with popping in a tranquillizer here and a tonic there and a pep pill somewhere else, don't you think it would be easy enough that the whole thing might get mixed up?'

'I don't see how it could apply in this case.'

'Well, I think it could. Somebody, one of the guests, may have wanted a sedative, or a reviver, and whipped out his or her little container which they carry around and possibly because they hadn't remembered the dose because they hadn't had one for some time, might have put too much in a glass. Then their mind was distracted and they went off somewhere, and let's say this Mrs What's-her-name comes along, thinks it's her glass, picks it up and drinks it. That's surely a more feasible idea than anything else?'

'You don't think that all those possibilities haven't been gone into, do you?'

'No, I suppose not. But there were a lot of people there and a lot of glasses standing about with drinks in them. It happens often enough, you know, that you pick up the wrong glass and drink out of it.'

'Then you don't think that Heather Badcock was deliberately poisoned? You think that she drank out of somebody else's glass?'

'I can't imagine anything more likely to happen.'

'In that case,' said Dermot speaking carefully, 'it would have had to be Marina Gregg's glass. You realise that? Marina handed her her own glass.'

'Or what she thought was her own glass,' Ella Zielinsky corrected him. 'You haven't talked to Marina yet, have you? She's extremely vague. She'd pick up any glass that looked as though it were hers, and drink it. I've seen her do it again and again.'

'She takes Calmo?'

'Oh yes, we all do.'

'You too, Miss Zielinsky?'

'I'm driven to it sometimes,' said Ella Zielinsky. 'These things are rather imitative, you know.'

'I shall be glad,' said Dermot, 'when I am able to talk to Miss Gregg. She—er—seems to be prostrated for a very long time.'

'That's just throwing a temperament,' said Ella Zielinsky. 'She just dramatizes herself a good deal, you know. She'd never take murder in her stride.'

'As you manage to do, Miss Zielinsky?'

'When everybody about you is in a continual state of agitation,' said Ella dryly, 'it develops in you a desire to go to the opposite extreme.'

'You learn to take a pride in not turning a hair when some shocking tragedy occurs?'

She considered. 'It's not a really nice trait, perhaps. But I think if you didn't develop that sense you'd probably go round the bend yourself.'

'Was Miss Gregg—is Miss Gregg a difficult person to work for?'

It was something of a personal question but Dermot Craddock regarded it as a kind of test. If Ella Zielinsky raised her eyebrows and tacitly demanded what this had to do with the murder of Mrs Badcock, he would be forced to admit that it had nothing to do with it. But he wondered if Ella Zielinsky might perhaps enjoy telling him what she thought of Marina Gregg.

'She's a great artist. She's got a personal magnetism that comes over on the screen in the most extraordinary way. Because of that one feels it's rather a privilege to work with her. Taken purely personally, of course, she's hell!'

'Ah,' said Dermot.

'She's no kind of moderation, you see. She's up in the air or down in the dumps and everything is always terrifically exaggerated, and she changes her mind and there are an enormous lot of things that one must never mention or allude to because they upset her.'

'Such as?'

'Well, naturally, mental breakdown, or sanatoriums for mental cases. I think it is quite to be understood that she should be sensitive about that. And anything to do with children.'

'Children? In what way?'

'Well, it upsets her to see children, or to hear of people being happy with children. If she hears someone is going to have a baby or has just had a baby, it throws her into a state of misery at once. She can never have another child herself, you see, and the only one she did have is batty. I don't know if you knew that?'

'I had heard it, yes. It's all very sad and unfortunate. But after a good many years you'd think she'd forget about it a little.'

'She doesn't. It's an obsession with her. She broods on it.'

'What does Mr Rudd feel about it?'

'Oh, it wasn't his child. It was her last husband's, Isidore Wright's.'

'Ah yes, her last husband. Where is he now?'

'He married again and lives in Florida,' said Ella Zielinsky promptly.

'Would you say that Marina Gregg had made many enemies in her life?'

'Not unduly so. Not more than most, that is to say. There are always rows over other women or other men or over contracts or jealousy—all of those things.'

'She wasn't as far as you know afraid of anyone?'

'Marina? *Afraid* of anyone? I don't think so. Why? Should she be?'

'I don't know,' said Dermot. He picked up the list of names. 'Thank you very much, Miss Zielinsky. If there's anything else I want to know I'll come back. May I?'

'Certainly. I'm only too anxious—we're all only too anxious—to do anything we can to help.'

'Well, Tom, what have you got for me?'

Detective-Sergeant Tiddler grinned appreciatively. His name was not Tom, it was William, but the combination of Tom Tiddler had always been too much for his colleagues.

'What gold and silver have you picked up for me?' continued Dermot Craddock.

The two were staying at the Blue Boar and Tiddler had just come back from a day spent at the studios.

'The proportion of gold is very small,' said Tiddler. 'Not

126

much gossip. No startling rumours. One or two suggestions of suicide.'

'Why suicide?'

'They thought she might have had a row with her husband and be trying to make him sorry. That line of country. But that she didn't really mean to go so far as doing herself in.'

'I can't see that that's a very helpful line,' said Dermot.

'No, of course it isn't. They know nothing about it, you see. They don't know anything except what they're busy on. It's all highly technical and there's an atmosphere of "the show must go on", or as I suppose one ought to say the picture must go on, or the shooting must go on. I don't know any of the right terms. All they're concerned about is when Marina Gregg will get back to the set. She's mucked up a picture once or twice before by staging a nervous breakdown.'

'Do they like her on the whole?'

'I should say they consider her the devil of a nuisance but for all that they can't help being fascinated by her when she's in the mood to fascinate them. Her husband's besotted about her, by the way.'

'What do they think of him?'

'They think he's the finest director or producer or whatever it is that there's ever been.'

'No rumours of his being mixed up with some other star or some woman of some kind?'

Tom Tiddler stared. 'No,' he said, 'no. Not a hint of such a thing. Why, do you think there might be?'

'I wondered,' said Dermot. 'Marina Gregg is convinced that that lethal dose was meant for her.'

Agatha Christie

'Is she now? Is she right?'

'Almost certainly, I should say,' Dermot replied. 'But that's not the point. The point is that she hasn't told her husband so, only her doctor.'

'Do you think she would have told him if—'

'I just wondered,' said Craddock, 'whether she might have had at the back of her mind an idea that her husband had been responsible. The doctor's manner was a little peculiar. I may have imagined it but I don't think I did.'

'Well, there were no such rumours going about at the studios,' said Tom. 'You hear that sort of thing soon enough.'

'She herself is not embroiled with any other man?'

'No, she seems to be devoted to Rudd.'

'No interesting snippets about her past?'

Tiddler grinned. 'Nothing to what you can read in a film magazine any day of the week.'

'I think I'll have to read a few,' said Dermot, 'to get the atmosphere.'

'The things they say and hint!' said Tiddler.

'I wonder,' said Dermot thoughtfully, 'if my Miss Marple reads film magazines.'

'Is that the old lady who lives in the house by the church?'

'That's right.'

'They say she's sharp,' said Tiddler. 'They say there's nothing goes on here that Miss Marple doesn't hear about. She may not know much about the film people, but she ought to be able to give you the low-down on the Badcocks all right.'

'It's not as simple as it used to be,' said Dermot. 'There's a new social life springing up here. A housing estate, big building development. The Badcocks are fairly new and come from there.'

'I didn't hear much about the locals, of course,' said Tiddler. 'I concentrated on the sex life of film stars and such things.'

'You haven't brought back very much,' grumbled Dermot. 'What about Marina Gregg's past, anything about that?'

'Done a bit of marrying in her time but not more than most. Her first husband didn't like getting the chuck, so they said, but he was a very ordinary sort of bloke. He was a realtor or something like that. What is a realtor, by the way?'

'I think it means in the real estate business.'

'Oh well, anyway, he didn't line up as very glamorous so she got rid of him and married a foreign count or prince. That lasted hardly any time at all but there don't seem to be any bones broken. She just shook him off and teamed up with number three. Film star Robert Truscott. That was said to be a passionate love match. His wife didn't much like letting go of him, but she had to take it in the end. Big alimony. As far as I can make out everybody's hard up because they've got to pay so much alimony to all their ex-wives.'

'But it went wrong?'

'Yes. She was the broken-hearted one, I gather. But another big romance came along a year or two later. Isidore Somebody—a playwright.'

'It's an exotic life,' said Dermot. 'Well, we'll call it a day now. Tomorrow we've got to get down to a bit of hard work.'

'Such as?'

'Such as checking a list I've got here. Out of twenty-odd names we ought to be able to do *some* elimination and out of what's left we'll have to look for X.'

'Any idea who X is?'

'Not in the least. If it isn't Jason Rudd, that is.' He added with a wry and ironic smile, 'I shall have to go to Miss Marple and get briefed on local matters.'

CHAPTER 12

Miss Marple was pursuing her own methods of research.

'It's very kind, Mrs Jameson, very kind of you indeed. I can't tell you how grateful I am.'

'Oh, don't mention it, Miss Marple. I'm sure I'm glad to oblige you. I suppose you'll want the latest ones?'

'No, no, not particularly,' said Miss Marple. 'In fact I think I'd rather have some of the old numbers.'

'Well, here you are then,' said Mrs Jameson, 'there's a nice armful and I can assure you we shan't miss them. Keep them as long as you like. Now it's too heavy for you to carry. Jenny, how's your perm doing?'

'She's all right, Mrs Jameson. She's had her rinse and now she's having a good dry-out.'

'In that case, dear, you might just run along with Miss Marple here, and carry these magazines for her. No, really, Miss Marple, it's no trouble at all. Always pleased to do anything we can for you.'

How kind people were, Miss Marple thought, especially when they'd known you practically all their lives. Mrs Jameson, after long years of running a hairdressing parlour had steeled herself to going as far in the cause of progress as to repaint her sign and call herself

'DIANE. *Hair Stylist.*'

Otherwise the shop remained much as before and catered in much the same way to the needs of its clients. It turned you out with a nice firm perm: it accepted the task of shaping and cutting for the younger generation and the resultant mess was accepted without too much recrimination. But the bulk of Mrs Jameson's clientele was a bunch of solid, stick in the mud middle-aged ladies who found it extremely hard to get their hair done the way they wanted it anywhere else.

'Well, I never,' said Cherry the next morning, as she prepared to run a virulent Hoover round the lounge as she still called it in her mind. 'What's all this?'

'I am trying,' said Miss Marple, 'to instruct myself a little in the moving picture world.'

She laid aside *Movie News* and picked up *Amongst the Stars*.

'It's really very interesting. It reminds one so much of so many things.'

'Fantastic lives they must lead,' said Cherry.

'Specialized lives,' said Miss Marple. 'Highly specialized. It reminds me very much of the things a friend of mine used to tell me. She was a hospital nurse. The same simplicity of outlook and all the gossip and the rumours. And good-looking doctors causing any amount of havoc.'

'Rather sudden, isn't it, this interest of yours?' said Cherry.

'I'm finding it difficult to knit nowadays,' said Miss Marple. 'Of course the print of these *is* rather small, but I can always use a magnifying glass.'

Cherry looked on curiously.

'You're always surprising me,' she said. 'The things you take an interest in.'

'I take an interest in everything,' said Miss Marple.

'I mean taking up new subjects at your age.'

Miss Marple shook her head.

'They aren't really new subjects. It's human nature I'm interested in, you know, and human nature is much the same whether it's film stars or hospital nurses or people in St Mary Mead or,' she added thoughtfully, 'people who live in the Development.'

'Can't see much likeness between me and a film star,' said Cherry laughing, 'more's the pity. I suppose it's Marina Gregg and her husband coming to live at Gossington Hall that set you off on this.'

'That and the very sad event that occurred there,' said Miss Marple.

'Mrs Badcock, you mean? It was bad luck that.'

'What do you think of it in the—' Miss Marple paused with the 'D' hovering on her lips. 'What do you and your friends think about it?' she amended the question.

'It's a queer do,' said Cherry. 'Looks as though it were murder, doesn't it, though of course the police are too cagey to say so outright. Still, that's what it looks like.'

'I don't see what else it could be,' said Miss Marple.

'It couldn't be suicide,' agreed Cherry, 'not with Heather Badcock.'

'Did you know her well?'

'No, not really. Hardly at all. She was a bit of a nosy parker, you know. Always wanting you to join this, join that, turn up for meetings at so-and-so. Too much energy. Her husband got a bit sick of it sometimes, I think.'

'She doesn't seem to have had any real enemies.'

'People used to get a bit fed up with her sometimes. The point is, I don't see who could have murdered her unless it was her husband. And he's a very meek type. Still, the worm will turn, or so they say. I've always heard that Crippen was ever so nice a man and that man, Haigh, who pickled them all in acid—they say he couldn't have been more charming! So one never knows, does one?'

'Poor Mr Badcock,' said Miss Marple.

'And people say he was upset and nervy at the fête that day—before it happened, I mean—but people always say that kind of thing afterwards. If you ask me, he's looking better now than he's looked for years. Seems to have got a bit more spirit and go in him.'

'Indeed?' said Miss Marple.

'Nobody *really* thinks he did it,' said Cherry. 'Only if he didn't, who did? I can't help thinking myself it must have been an accident of some kind. Accidents do happen. You think you know all about mushrooms and go out and pick some. One fungus gets in among them and there you are, rolling about in agony and lucky if the doctor gets to you in time.'

'Cocktails and glasses of sherry don't seem to lend themselves to accident,' said Miss Marple.

'Oh, I don't know,' said Cherry. 'A bottle of something

or other could have got in by mistake. Somebody I knew took a dose of concentrated DDT once. Horribly ill they were.'

'Accident,' said Miss Marple thoughtfully. 'Yes, it certainly seems the best solution. I must say I can't believe that in the case of Heather Badcock it *could* have been deliberate murder. I won't say it's impossible. Nothing is impossible, but it doesn't seem like it. No, I think the truth lies somewhere here.' She rustled her magazines and picked up another one.

'You mean you're looking for some special story about someone?'

'No,' said Miss Marple. 'I'm just looking for odd mentions of people and a way of life and something—some little something that might help.' She returned to her perusal of the magazines and Cherry removed her vacuum cleaner to the upper floor. Miss Marple's face was pink and interested, and being slightly deaf now, she did not hear the footsteps that came along the garden path towards the drawing-room window. It was only when a slight shadow fell on the page that she looked up. Dermot Craddock was standing smiling at her.

'Doing your homework, I see,' he remarked.

'Inspector Craddock, how very nice to see you. And how kind to spare time to come and see me. Would you like a cup of coffee, or possibly a glass of sherry?'

'A glass of sherry would be splendid,' said Dermot. 'Don't you move,' he added. 'I'll ask for it as I come in.'

He went round by the side door and presently joined Miss Marple.

'Well,' he said, 'is all that bumph giving you ideas?'

'Rather too many ideas,' said Miss Marple. 'I'm not often shocked, you know, but this does shock me a little.'

'What, the private lives of film stars?'

'Oh no,' said Miss Marple, 'not *that*! That all seems to be *most* natural, given the circumstances and the money involved and the opportunities for propinquity. Oh, no, that's natural enough. I mean the way they're written about. I'm rather old-fashioned, you know, and I feel that that really shouldn't be allowed.'

'It's news,' said Dermot Craddock, 'and some pretty nasty things can be said in the way of fair comment.'

'I know,' said Miss Marple. 'It makes me sometimes very angry. I expect you think it's silly of me reading all these. But one does so badly want to be *in* things and of course sitting here in the house I can't really know as much about things as I would like to.'

'That's just what I thought,' said Dermot Craddock, 'and that's why I've come to tell you about them.'

'But, my dear boy, excuse me, would your superiors really approve of that?'

'I don't see why not,' said Dermot. 'Here,' he added, 'I have a list. A list of people who were there on that landing during the short time of Heather Badcock's arrival until her death. We've eliminated a lot of people, perhaps precipitately, but I don't think so. We've eliminated the mayor and his wife and Alderman somebody and his wife and a great many of the locals, though we've kept in the husband. If I remember rightly you were always very suspicious of husbands.'

'They are often the obvious suspects,' said Miss Marple, apologetically, 'and the obvious is so often right.'

'I couldn't agree with you more,' said Craddock.

'But which husband, my dear boy, are you referring to?'

'Which one do you think?' asked Dermot. He eyed her sharply.

Miss Marple looked at him.

'Jason Rudd?' she asked.

'Ah!' said Craddock. 'Your mind works just as mine does. I don't think it was Arthur Badcock, because you see, I don't think that Heather Badcock was meant to be killed. I think the intended victim was Marina Gregg.'

'That would seem almost certain, wouldn't it?' said Miss Marple.

'And so,' said Craddock, 'as we both agree on that, the field widens. To tell you who was there on that day, what they saw or said they saw, and where they were or said they were, is only a thing you could have observed for yourself if you'd been there. So my superiors, as you call them, couldn't possibly object to my discussing that with you, could they?'

'That's very nicely put, my dear boy,' said Miss Marple.

'I'll give you a little précis of what I was told and then we'll come to the list.'

He gave a brief résumé of what he had heard, and then he produced his list.

'It must be one of these,' he said. 'My godfather, Sir Henry Clithering, told me that you once had a club here. You called it the Tuesday Night Club. You all dined with each other in turn and then someone would tell a story—a story of some real life happening which had ended in mystery. A mystery of which only the teller of the tale knew the answer. And every time, so my godfather told me, you guessed right. So I thought I'd come along and see if you'd do a bit of guessing for me this morning.'

'I think that is rather a frivolous way of putting it,' said Miss Marple, reproving, 'but there is one question I should like to ask.'

'Yes?'

'What about the children?'

'The children? There's only one. An imbecile child in a sanatorium in America. Is that what you mean?'

'No,' said Miss Marple, 'that's not what I mean. It's very sad of course. One of those tragedies that seem to happen and there's no one to blame for it. No, I meant the children that I've seen mentioned in some article here.' She tapped the papers in front of her. 'Children that Marina Gregg adopted. Two boys, I think, and a girl. In one case a mother with a lot of children and very little money to bring them up in this country, wrote to her, and asked if she couldn't take a child. There was a lot of very silly false sentiment written about that. About the mother's unselfishness and the wonderful home and education and future the child was going to have. I can't find out much about the other two. One I think was a foreign refugee and the other was some American child. Marina Gregg adopted them at different times. I'd like to know what's happened to them.'

Dermot Craddock looked at her curiously. 'It's odd that you should think of that,' he said. 'I did just vaguely wonder about those children myself. But how do you connect them up?'

'Well,' said Miss Marple, 'as far as I can hear or find out, they're not living with her now, are they?'

'I expect they were provided for,' said Craddock. 'In fact, I think that the adoption laws would insist on that. There was probably money settled on them in trust.'

'So when she got—tired of them,' said Miss Marple with a very faint pause before the word 'tired', 'they were dismissed! After being brought up in luxury with every advantage. Is that it?'

'Probably,' said Craddock. 'I don't know exactly.' He continued to look at her curiously.

'Children feel things, you know,' said Miss Marple, nodding her head. 'They feel things more than the people around them ever imagine. The sense of hurt, of being rejected, of not belonging. It's a thing that you don't get over just because of advantages. Education is no substitute for it, or comfortable living, or an assured income, or a start in a profession. It's the sort of thing that might rankle.'

'Yes. But all the same, isn't it rather far-fetched to think that—well, what exactly do you think?'

'I haven't got as far as that,' said Miss Marple. 'I just wondered where they were now and how old they would be now? Grown up, I should imagine, from what I've read here.'

'I could find out, I suppose,' said Dermot Craddock slowly.

'Oh, I don't want to bother you in any way, or even to suggest that my little idea's worthwhile at all.'

'There's no harm,' said Dermot Craddock, 'in having that checked up on.' He made a note in his little book. 'Now do you want to look at my little list?'

'I don't really think I should be able to do anything useful about that. You see, I wouldn't know who the people were.'

'Oh, I could give you a running commentary,' said Craddock. 'Here we are. *Jason Rudd, husband,* (husbands always highly suspicious). Everyone says that Jason Rudd adores her. That is suspicious in itself, don't you think?'

'Not necessarily,' said Miss Marple with dignity.

'He's been very active in trying to conceal the fact that his wife was the object of attack. He hasn't hinted any suspicion of such a thing to the police. I don't know why he thinks we're such asses as not to think of it for ourselves. We've considered it from the first. But anyway, that's his story. He was afraid that knowledge of that fact might get to his wife's ears and that she'd go into a panic about it.'

'Is she the sort of woman who goes into panics?'

'Yes, she's neurasthenic, throws temperaments, has nervous breakdowns, gets in states.'

'That might not mean any lack of courage,' Miss Marple objected.

'On the other hand,' said Craddock, 'if she knows quite well that she was the object of attack, it's also possible that she may know who did it.'

'You mean she knows who did it—but does not want to disclose the fact?'

'I just say it's a possibility, and if so, one rather wonders why not? It looks as though the motive, the root of the matter, was something she didn't want to come to her husband's ear.'

'That is certainly an interesting thought,' said Miss Marple.

'Here are a few more names. The secretary, Ella Zielinsky. An extremely competent and efficient young woman.'

'In love with the husband, do you think?' asked Miss Marple.

'I should think definitely,' answered Craddock, 'but why should you think so?'

'Well, it so often happens,' said Miss Marple. 'And therefore not very fond of poor Marina Gregg, I expect?'

'Therefore possible motive for murder,' said Craddock.

'A lot of secretaries and employees are in love with their employers' husbands,' said Miss Marple, 'but very, very few of them try to poison them.'

'Well, we must allow for exceptions,' said Craddock. 'Then there were two local and one London photographer, and two members of the Press. None of them seems likely but we will follow them up. There was the woman who was formerly married to Marina Gregg's second or third husband. She didn't like it when Marina Gregg took her husband away. Still, that's about eleven or twelve years ago. It seems unlikely that she'd make a visit here at this juncture on purpose to poison Marina because of that. Then there's a man called Ardwyck Fenn. He was once a very close friend of Marina Gregg's. He hasn't seen her for years. He was not known to be in this part of the world and it was a great surprise when he turned up on this occasion.'

Agatha Christie

'She would be startled then when she saw him?'

'Presumably yes.'

'Startled—and possibly frightened.'

'"*The doom has come upon me*,"' said Craddock. 'That's the idea. Then there was young Hailey Preston dodging about that day, doing his stuff. Talks a good deal but definitely heard nothing, saw nothing and knew nothing. Almost too anxious to say so. Does anything there ring a bell?'

'Not exactly,' said Miss Marple. 'Plenty of interesting possibilities. But I'd still like to know a little more about the children.'

He looked at her curiously. 'You've got quite a bee in your bonnet about that, haven't you?' he said. 'All right, I'll find out.'

CHAPTER 13

'I suppose it couldn't possibly have been the mayor?' said Inspector Cornish wistfully.

He tapped the paper with the list of names on it with his pencil. Dermot Craddock grinned.

'Wishful thinking?' he asked.

'You could certainly call it that,' said Cornish. 'Pompous, canting old hypocrite!' he went on. 'Everybody's got it in for him. Throws his weight about, ultra sanctimonious, *and* neck deep in graft for years past!'

'Can't you ever bring it home to him?'

'No,' said Cornish. 'He's too slick for that. He's always just on the right side of the law.'

'It's tempting, I agree,' said Dermot Craddock, 'but I think you'll have to banish that rosy picture from your mind, Frank.'

'I know, I know,' said Cornish. 'He's a possible, but a wildly improbable. Who else have we got?'

Both men studied the list again. There were still eight names on it.

'We're pretty well agreed,' said Craddock, 'that there's

nobody missed out from here?' There was a faint question in his voice. Cornish answered it.

'I think you can be pretty sure that's the lot. After Mrs Bantry came the vicar, and after that the Badcocks. There were then eight people on the stairs. The mayor and his wife, Joshua Grice and wife from Lower Farm. Donald McNeil of the Much Benham *Herald & Argus*. Ardwyck Fenn, USA, Miss Lola Brewster, USA, Moving Picture Star. There you are. In addition there was an arty photographer from London with a camera set up on the angle of the stairs. If, as you suggest, this Mrs Bantry's story of Marina Gregg having a "frozen look" was occasioned by someone she saw on the stairs, you've got to take your pick among that lot. Mayor regretfully out. Grices out—never been away from St Mary Mead I should say. That leaves four. Local journalist unlikely, photographer girl had been there for half an hour already, so why should Marina react so late in the day? What does that leave?'

'Sinister strangers from America,' said Craddock with a faint smile.

'You've said it.'

'They're our best suspects by far, I agree,' said Craddock. 'They turned up unexpectedly. Ardwyck Fenn was an old flame of Marina's whom she had not seen for years. Lola Brewster was once married to Marina Gregg's third husband, who got a divorce from her in order to marry Marina. It was not, I gather, a very amicable divorce.'

'I'd put her down as Suspect Number One,' said Cornish.

'Would you, Frank? After a lapse of about fifteen years or so, and having remarried twice herself since then?'

Cornish said that you never knew with women. Dermot accepted that as a general dictum, but remarked that it seemed odd to him to say the least of it.

'But you agree that it lies between them?'

'Possibly. But I don't like it very much. What about the hired help who were serving the drinks?'

'Discounting the "frozen look" we've heard so much about? Well, we've checked up in a general way. Local catering firm from Market Basing had the job—for the fête, I mean. Actually in the house, there was the butler, Giuseppe, in charge; and two local girls from the studios canteen. I know both of them. Not over bright, but harmless.'

'Pushing it back at me, are you? I'll go and have a word with the reporter chap. He might have seen something helpful. Then to London. Ardwyck Fenn, Lola Brewster—and the photographer girl—what's her name?—Margot Bence. She also might have seen something.'

Cornish nodded. 'Lola Brewster is my best bet,' he said. He looked curiously at Craddock. 'You don't seem as sold on her as I am.'

'I'm thinking of the difficulties,' said Dermot slowly.

'Difficulties?'

'Of putting poison into Marina's glass without anybody seeing her.'

'Well, that's the same for everybody, isn't it? It was a mad thing to do.'

'Agreed it was a mad thing to do, but it would be a madder thing for someone like Lola Brewster than for anybody else.'

'Why?' asked Cornish.

'Because she was a guest of some importance. She's a somebody, a big name. Everyone would be looking at her.'

'True enough,' Cornish admitted.

'The locals would nudge each other and whisper and stare, and after Marina Gregg and Jason Rudd greeted her she'd have been passed on for the secretaries to look after. It wouldn't be easy, Frank. However adroit you were, you couldn't be sure *someone* wouldn't see you. That's the snag there, and it's a big snag.'

'As I say, isn't that snag the same for everybody?'

'No,' said Craddock. 'Oh no. Far from it. Take the butler now, Giuseppe. He's busy with the drinks and glasses, with pouring things out, with handing them. He could put a pinch or a tablet or two of Calmo in a glass easily enough.'

'Giuseppe?' Frank Cornish reflected. 'Do you think he did?'

'No reason to believe so,' said Craddock, 'but we might find a reason. A nice solid bit of motive, that is to say. Yes, he could have done it. Or one of the catering staff could have done it—unfortunately they weren't on the spot—a pity.'

'Someone might have managed to get himself or herself deliberately planted in the firm for the purpose.'

'You mean it might have been as premeditated as all that?'

'We don't know anything about it yet,' said Craddock, vexedly. 'We absolutely don't know the first thing about it. Not until we can prise what we want to know out of Marina Gregg, or out of her husband. They *must* know or suspect—but they're not telling. And we don't know yet *why* they're not telling. We've a long way to go.'

He paused and then resumed: 'Discounting the "frozen look" which may have been pure coincidence, there are other people who could have done it fairly easily. The secretary woman, Ella Zielinsky. She was also busy with glasses, with handing things to people. Nobody would be watching *her* with any particular interest. The same applies to that willow wand of a young man—I've forgotten his name. Hailey—Hailey Preston? That's right. There would have been a good opportunity for either of them. In fact if either of them *had* wanted to do away with Marina Gregg it would have been far safer to do so on a public occasion.'

'Anyone else?'

'Well, there's always the husband,' said Craddock.

'Back to husbands again,' said Cornish, with a faint smile. 'We thought it was that poor devil, Badcock, before we realised that Marina was the intended victim. Now we've transferred our suspicions to Jason Rudd. He seems devoted enough though, I must say.'

'He has the reputation of being so,' said Craddock, 'but one never knows.'

'If he wanted to get rid of her, wouldn't divorce be much easier?'

'It would be far more usual,' agreed Dermot, 'but there may be a lot of ins and outs to this business that we don't know yet.'

The telephone rang. Cornish took up the receiver.

'What? Yes? Put them through. Yes, he's here.' He listened for a moment then put his hand over the receiver and looked at Dermot. 'Miss Marina Gregg,' he said, 'is feeling very much better. She is quite ready to be interviewed.'

'I'd better hurry along,' said Dermot Craddock, 'before she changes her mind.'

At Gossington Hall Dermot Craddock was received by Ella Zielinsky. She was, as usual, brisk and efficient.

'Miss Gregg is waiting for you, Mr Craddock,' she said.

Dermot looked at her with some interest. From the beginning he had found Ella Zielinsky an intriguing personality. He had said to himself, 'A poker face if I ever saw one.' She had answered any questions he had asked with the utmost readiness. She had shown no signs of keeping anything back, but what she really thought or felt or even knew about the business, he still had no idea. There seemed to be no chink in the armour of her bright efficiency. She might know more than she said she did; she might know a good deal. The only thing he was sure of—and he had to admit to himself that he had no reasons to adduce for that surety—was that she was in love with Jason Rudd. It was, as he had said, an occupational disease of secretaries. It probably meant nothing. But the fact did at least suggest a motive and he was sure, quite sure, that she was concealing something. It might be love, it might be hate. It might, quite simply, be guilt. She might have taken her opportunity that afternoon, or she might have deliberately planned what she was going to do. He could see her in the part quite easily, as far as the execution of it went. Her swift but unhurried movements, moving here and there, looking after guests, handing glasses to one or another, taking glasses away, her eyes marking the spot where Marina had put

148

her glass down on the table. And then, perhaps at the very moment when Marina had been greeting the arrivals from the States, with surprise and joyous cries and everybody's eyes turned towards their meeting, she could have quietly and unobtrusively dropped the fatal dose into that glass. It would require audacity, nerve, swiftness. She would have had all those. Whatever she had done, she would not have looked guilty whilst she was doing it. It would have been a simple, brilliant crime, a crime that could hardly fail to be successful. But chance had ruled otherwise. In the rather crowded floorspace someone had joggled Heather Badcock's arm. Her drink had been spilt, and Marina, with her natural impulsive grace, had quickly proffered her own glass, standing there untouched. And so the wrong woman had died.

A lot of pure theory, and probably hooey at that, said Dermot Craddock to himself at the same time as he was making polite remarks to Ella Zielinsky.

'One thing I wanted to ask you, Miss Zielinsky. The catering was done by a Market Basing firm, I understand?'

'Yes.'

'Why was that particular firm chosen?'

'I really don't know,' said Ella. 'That doesn't lie amongst my duties. I know Mr Rudd thought it would be more tactful to employ somebody local rather than to employ a firm from London. The whole thing was really quite a small affair from our point of view.'

'Quite.' He watched her as she stood frowning a little and looking down. A good forehead, a determined chin, a figure which could look quite voluptuous if it was allowed to do so, a hard mouth, an acquisitive mouth. The eyes? He looked at them in surprise. The lids were reddened. He wondered. Had she been crying? It looked like it. And yet he could have sworn she was not the type of young woman to cry. She looked up at him, and as though she read his thoughts, she took out her handkerchief and blew her nose heartily.

'You've got a cold,' he said.

'Not a cold. Hay-fever. It's an allergy of some kind, really. I always get at it this time of year.'

There was a low buzz. There were two phones in the room, one on the table and one on another table in the corner. It was the latter one that was beginning to buzz. Ella Zielinsky went over to it and picked up the receiver.

'Yes,' she said, 'he's here. I'll bring him up at once.' She put the receiver down again. 'Marina's ready for you,' she said.

Marina Gregg received Craddock in a room on the first floor, which was obviously her own private sitting-room opening out of her bedroom. After the accounts of her prostration and her nervous state, Dermot Craddock had expected to find a fluttering invalid. But although Marina was half reclining on a sofa her voice was vigorous and her eyes were bright. She had very little make-up on, but in spite of this she did not look her age, and he was struck very forcibly by the subdued radiance of her beauty. It was the exquisite line of cheek and jawbone, the way the hair fell loosely and naturally to frame her face. The long sea-green eyes, the pencilled eyebrows, owing something to art but more to nature, and the warmth and sweetness of her smile, all had a subtle magic. She said:

'Chief-Inspector Craddock? I've been behaving disgracefully. I do apologize. I just let myself go to pieces after this awful thing. I could have snapped out of it but I didn't. I'm ashamed of myself.' The smile came, rueful, sweet, turning up the corners of the mouth. She extended a hand and he took it.

'It was only natural,' he said, 'that you should feel upset.'

'Well, everyone was upset,' said Marina. 'I'd no business to make out it was worse for me than anyone else.'

'Hadn't you?'

She looked at him for a minute and then nodded. 'Yes,' she said, 'you're very perceptive. Yes, I had.' She looked down and with one long forefinger gently stroked the arm of the sofa. It was a gesture he had noticed in one of her films. It was a meaningless gesture, yet it seemed fraught with significance. It had a kind of musing gentleness.

'I'm a coward,' she said, her eyes still cast down. 'Somebody wanted to kill me and I didn't want to die.'

'Why do you think someone wanted to kill you?'

Her eyes opened wide. 'Because it was my glass—*my* drink—that had been tampered with. It was just a mistake that that poor stupid woman got it. That's what's so horrible and so tragic. Besides—'

'Yes, Miss Gregg?'

She seemed a little uncertain about saying more.

'You had other reasons perhaps for believing that you were the intended victim?'

151

She nodded.

'What reasons, Miss Gregg?'

She paused a minute longer before saying, 'Jason says I must tell you all about it.'

'You've confided in him then?'

'Yes . . . I didn't want to at first—but Dr Gilchrist put it to me that I must. And then I found that he thought so too. He'd thought it all along but—it's rather funny really'—a rueful smile curled her lips again—'he didn't want to alarm me by telling me. Really!' Marina sat up with a sudden vigorous movement. 'Darling Jinks! Does he think I'm a complete fool?'

'You haven't told me yet, Miss Gregg, why you should think anyone wanted to kill you.'

She was silent for a moment and then with a sudden brusque gesture, she stretched out for her handbag, opened it, took out a piece of paper and thrust it into his hand. He read it. Typed on it was one line of writing.

Don't think you'll escape next time.

Craddock said sharply, 'When did you get this?'

'It was on my dressing-table when I came back from the bath.'

'So someone in the house—'

'Not necessarily. Someone could have climbed up the balcony outside my window and pushed it through there. I think they meant it to frighten me still more, but actually it didn't. I just felt furiously angry and sent word to you to come and see me.'

Dermot Craddock smiled. 'Possibly a rather unexpected result for whoever sent it. Is this the first kind of message like that you've had?'

Again Marina hesitated. Then she said, 'No, it isn't.'

'Will you tell me about any others?'

'It was three weeks ago, when we first came here. It came to the studio, not here. It was quite ridiculous. It was just a message. Not typewritten that time. In capital letters. It said, "*Prepare to die*."' She laughed. There was perhaps a very faint tinge of hysteria in the laugh. The mirth was genuine enough. 'It was so silly,' she said. 'Of course one often gets crank messages, threats, things like that. I thought it was probably religious you know. Someone who didn't approve of film actresses. I just tore it up and threw it into the waste-paper basket.'

'Did you tell anyone about it, Miss Gregg?'

Marina shook her head. 'No, I never said a word to anyone. As a matter of fact, we were having a bit of worry at the moment about the scene we were shooting. I just couldn't have thought of anything but that at the moment. Anyway, as I say, I thought it was either a silly joke or one of those religious cranks who write and disapprove of play-acting and things like that.'

'And after that, was there another?'

'Yes. On the day of the fête. One of the gardeners brought it to me, I think. He said someone had left a note for me and was there any answer? I thought perhaps it had to do with the arrangements. I just tore it open. It said "*Today will be your last day on earth*." I just crumpled it up and said, "No answer." Then I called the man back and asked him who gave it to him. He said it was a man with spectacles on a bicycle. Well, I mean, what could you think about that? I thought it was more silliness. I didn't think—I didn't think for a moment, it was a real genuine threat.'

'Where's that note now, Miss Gregg?'

'I've no idea. I was wearing one of those coloured Italian silk coats and I think, as far as I remember, that I crumpled it up and shoved it into the pocket of it. But it's not there now. It probably fell out.'

'And you've no idea who wrote these silly notes, Miss Gregg? Who inspired them? Not even now?'

Her eyes opened widely. There was a kind of innocent wonder in them that he took note of. He admired it, but he did not believe in it.

'How can I tell? How can I possibly tell?'

'I think you might have quite a good idea, Miss Gregg.'

'I haven't. I assure you I haven't.'

'You're a very famous person,' said Dermot. 'You've had great successes. Successes in your profession, and personal successes, too. Men have fallen in love with you, wanted to marry you, have married you. Women have been jealous and envied you. Men have been in love with you and been rebuffed by you. It's a pretty wide field, I agree, but I should think you must have *some* idea who could have written these notes.'

'It could have been anybody.'

'No, Miss Gregg, it couldn't have been *anybody*. It could possibly have been one of quite a lot of people. It could be someone quite humble, a dresser, an electrician, a servant; or it could be someone among the ranks of your friends, or so-called friends. But you must have some idea. Some name, more than one name, perhaps, to suggest.'

The door opened and Jason Rudd came in. Marina turned to him. She swept out an arm appealingly.

'Jinks, darling, Mr Craddock is insisting that I must know who wrote those horrid notes. And I don't. You know I don't. Neither of us knows. We haven't got the least idea.'

'Very urgent about that,' thought Craddock. 'Very urgent. Is Marina Gregg afraid of what her husband might say?'

Jason Rudd, his eyes dark with fatigue and the scowl on his face deeper than usual, came over to join them. He took Marina's hand in his.

'I know it sounds unbelievable to you, Inspector,' he said, 'but honestly neither Marina nor I have any idea about this business.'

'So you're in the happy position of having no enemies, is that it?' The irony was manifest in Dermot's voice.

Jason Rudd flushed a little. 'Enemies? That's a very biblical word, Inspector. In that sense, I can assure you I can think of no enemies. People who dislike one, would like to get the better of one, would do a mean turn to one if they could, in malice and uncharitableness, yes. But it's a long step from that to putting an overdose of poison in a drink.'

'Just now, in speaking to your wife, I asked her who could have written or inspired those letters. She said she didn't know. But when we come to the actual action, it narrows it down. *Somebody actually put the poison in that glass*. And that's a fairly limited field, you know.'

'I saw nothing,' said Jason Rudd.

'I certainly didn't,' said Marina. 'Well, I mean—if I had seen anyone putting anything in my glass, I wouldn't have drunk the stuff, would I?'

'I can't help believing, you know,' said Dermot Craddock gently, 'that you do know a little more than you're telling me.'

'It's not *true*,' said Marina. 'Tell him that that isn't true, Jason.'

'I assure you,' said Jason Rudd, 'that I am completely and absolutely at a loss. The whole thing's fantastic. I might believe it was a joke—a joke that had somehow gone wrong—that had proved dangerous, done by a person who never dreamt that it would be dangerous . . .'

There was a slight question in his voice, then he shook his head. 'No. I see that idea doesn't appeal to you.'

'There's one more thing I should like to ask you,' said Dermot Craddock. 'You remember Mr and Mrs Badcock's arrival, of course. They came immediately after the vicar. You greeted them, I understand, Miss Gregg, in the same charming way as you had received all your guests. But I am told by an eye-witness that immediately after greeting them you looked over Mrs Badcock's shoulder and that you saw something which seemed to alarm you. Is that true, and if so, what was it?'

Marina said quickly, 'Of course it isn't true. Alarm me—what should have alarmed me?'

'That's what we want to know,' said Dermot Craddock patiently. 'My witness is very insistent on the point, you know.'

156

'Who was your witness? What did he or she say she saw?'

'You were looking at the staircase,' said Dermot Craddock. 'There were people coming up the staircase. There was a journalist, there was Mr Grice and his wife, elderly residents in this place, there was Mr Ardwyck Fenn who had just arrived from the States and there was Miss Lola Brewster. Was it the sight of one of those people that upset you, Miss Gregg?'

'I tell you I wasn't upset.' She almost barked the words.

'And yet your attention wavered from greeting Mrs Badcock. She had said something to you which you left unanswered because you were staring past her at something else.'

Marina Gregg took hold on herself. She spoke quickly and convincingly.

'I can explain that, I really can. If you knew anything about acting you'd be able to understand quite easily. There comes a moment, even when you know a part well—in fact it usually happens when you *do* know a part well—when you go on with it mechanically. Smiling, making the proper movements and gestures, saying the words with the usual inflexions. But your mind isn't on it. And quite suddenly there's a horrible blank moment when you don't know where you are, where you've got to in the play, what your next lines are! Drying up, that's what we call it. Well, that's what happened to me. I'm not terribly strong, as my husband will tell you. I've had rather a strenuous time, and a good deal of nervous apprehension about this film. I wanted to make a success of this fête and to be nice and pleasant and welcoming to everybody. But one does say the same things over and over again, mechanically, to the people who are always saying the same things to you. You know, how they've always wanted to meet you. How they once saw you outside a theatre in San Francisco—or travelled in a plane with you. Something silly really, but one has to be nice about it and say things. Well, as I'm telling you, one does that automatically. One doesn't need to think what to say because one's said it so often before. Suddenly, I think, a wave of tiredness came over me. My brain went blank. Then I realized that Mrs Badcock had been telling me a long story which I hadn't really heard at all, and was now looking at me in an eager sort of way and that I hadn't answered her or said any of the proper things. It was just tiredness.'

'Just tiredness,' said Dermot Craddock slowly. 'You insist on that, Miss Gregg?'

'Yes, I do. I can't see why you don't believe me.'

Dermot Craddock turned towards Jason Rudd. 'Mr Rudd,' he said, 'I think you're more likely to understand my meaning than your wife is. I am concerned, very much concerned, for your wife's safety. There has been an attempt on her life, there have been threatening letters. That means, doesn't it, that there is someone who was here on the day of the fête and possibly is still here, someone in very close touch with this house and what goes on in it. That person, whoever it is, may be slightly insane. It's not just a question of threats. Threatened men live long, as they say. The same goes for women. But whoever it was didn't stop at threats. A deliberate attempt was made to poison Miss

Gregg. Don't you see in the whole nature of things, that the attempt is bound to be repeated? There's only one way to achieve safety. That is to give me all the clues you possibly can. I don't say that you *know* who that person is, but I think that you must be able to give a guess or to have a vague idea. Won't you tell me the truth? Or if, which is possible, you yourself do not know the truth, won't you urge your wife to do so? It's in the interests of her own safety that I'm asking you.'

Jason Rudd turned his head slowly. 'You hear what Inspector Craddock says, Marina,' he said. 'It's possible, as he says, that you may know something that I do not. If so, for God's sake, don't be foolish about it. If you've the least suspicion of *anyone*, tell it to us now.'

'But I haven't.' Her voice rose in a wail. 'You must believe me.'

'Who were you afraid of that day?' asked Dermot.

'I wasn't afraid of anyone.'

'Listen, Miss Gregg, of the people on the stairs or coming up it, there were two friends whom you were surprised to see, whom you had not seen for a long time and whom you did not expect to see that day. Mr Ardwyck Fenn and Miss Brewster. Had you any special emotions when you suddenly saw them coming up the stairs? You didn't know they were coming, did you?'

'No, we'd no idea they were even in England,' said Jason Rudd.

'I was delighted,' said Marina, 'absolutely delighted!'

'Delighted to see Miss Brewster?'

'Well—' She shot him a quick, faintly suspicious glance.

159

AgathaChristie

Craddock said, 'Lola Brewster was, I believe, originally married to your third husband Robert Truscott?'

'Yes, that's so.'

'He divorced her in order to marry you.'

'Oh, everyone knows about that,' said Marina Gregg impatiently. 'You needn't think it's anything you've found out. There was a bit of a rumpus at the time, but there wasn't any bad feeling about it in the end.'

'Did she make threats against you?'

'Well—in a way, yes. But, oh dear, I wish I could explain. No one takes those sort of threats *seriously*. It was at a party, she'd had a lot of drink. She might have taken a pot-shot at me with a pistol if she'd had one. But luckily she didn't. All that was *years* ago! None of these things last, these emotions! They don't, really they don't. That's true, isn't it, Jason?'

'I'd say it was true enough,' said Jason Rudd, 'and I can assure you, Mr Craddock, that Lola Brewster had no opportunity on the day of the fête of poisoning my wife's drink. I was close beside her most of the time. The idea that Lola would suddenly, after a long period of friendliness, come to England, and arrive at our house all prepared to poison my wife's drink—why the whole idea's absurd.'

'I appreciate your point of view,' said Craddock.

'It's not only that, it's a matter of *fact* as well. She was nowhere near Marina's glass.'

'And your other visitor—Ardwyck Fenn?'

There was, he thought, a very slight pause before Jason Rudd spoke.

'He's a very old friend of ours,' he said. 'We haven't seen

him for a good many years now, though we occasionally correspond. He's quite a big figure in American television.'

'Was he an old friend of yours too?' Dermot Craddock asked Marina.

Her breath came rather quickly as she replied. 'Yes, oh yes. He—he was quite a friend of mine always, but I've rather lost sight of him of late years.' Then with a sudden quick rush of words, she went on, 'If you think that I looked up and saw Ardwyck and was frightened of him, it's nonsense. It's absolute *nonsense*. Why should I be frightened of him, what reason would I have to be frightened of him? We were great friends. I was just very, very pleased when I suddenly saw him. It was a delightful surprise, as I told you. Yes, a delightful surprise.' She raised her head, looking at him, her face vivid and defiant.

'Thank you, Miss Gregg,' said Craddock quietly. 'If you should feel inclined at any moment to take me a little further into your confidence I should strongly advise you to do so.'

CHAPTER 14

Mrs Bantry was on her knees. A good day for hoeing. Nice dry soil. But hoeing wouldn't do everything. Thistles now, and dandelions. She dealt vigorously with these pests.

She rose to her feet, breathless but triumphant, and looked out over the hedge on to the road. She was faintly surprised to see the dark-haired secretary whose name she couldn't remember coming out of the public call box that was situated near the bus stop on the other side of the road.

What was her name now. It began with a B—or was it an R? No, *Zielinsky*, that was it. Mrs Bantry remembered just in time, as Ella crossed the road into the drive past the Lodge.

'Good morning, Miss Zielinsky,' she called in a friendly tone.

Ella Zielinsky jumped. It was not so much a jump, as a shy—the shy of a frightened horse. It surprised Mrs Bantry.

'Good morning,' said Ella, and added quickly: 'I came down to telephone. There's something wrong with our line today.'

Mrs Bantry felt more surprise. She wondered why Ella

Zielinsky bothered to explain her action. She responded civilly. 'How annoying for you. Do come in and telephone any time you want to.'

'Oh—thank you very much . . .' Ella was interrupted by a fit of sneezing.

'You've got hay-fever,' said Mrs Bantry with immediate diagnosis. 'Try weak bicarbonate of soda and water.'

'Oh, that's all right. I have some very good patent stuff in an atomizer. Thank you all the same.'

She sneezed again as she moved away, walking briskly up the drive.

Mrs Bantry looked after her. Then her eyes returned to her garden. She looked at it in a dissatisfied fashion. Not a weed to be seen anywhere.

'Othello's occupation's gone,' Mrs Bantry murmured to herself confusedly. 'I dare say I'm a nosy old woman but I would like to know if—'

A moment of irresolution and then Mrs Bantry yielded to temptation. She was going to be a nosy old woman and the hell with it! She strode indoors to the telephone, lifted the receiver and dialled it. A brisk transatlantic voice spoke.

'Gossington Hall.'

'This is Mrs Bantry, at the East Lodge.'

'Oh, good morning, Mrs Bantry. This is Hailey Preston. I met you on the day of the fête. What can I do for you?'

'I thought perhaps I could do something for you. If your telephone's out of order—'

His astonished voice interrupted her.

'Our telephone out of order? There's been nothing wrong with it. Why did you think so?'

163

'I must have made a mistake,' said Mrs Bantry. 'I don't always hear very well,' she explained unblushingly.

She put the receiver back, waited a minute, then dialled once more.

'Jane? Dolly here.'

'Yes, Dolly. What is it?'

'Well, it seems rather *odd*. The secretary woman was dialling from the public call box in the road. She took the trouble to explain to me quite unnecessarily that she was doing so because the line at Gossington Hall was out of order. But I've rung up there, and it *isn't* . . .'

She paused, and waited for intelligence to pronounce.

'Indeed,' said Miss Marple thoughtfully. 'Interesting.'

'For what reason, do you think?'

'Well, clearly, she didn't want to be overheard—'

'Exactly.'

'And there might be quite a number of reasons for that.'

'Yes.'

'Interesting,' said Miss Marple again.

Nobody could have been more ready to talk than Donald McNeil. He was an amiable red-headed young man. He greeted Dermot Craddock with pleasure and curiosity.

'How are you getting along,' he asked cheerfully, 'got any little special tit-bit for me?'

'Not as yet. Later perhaps.'

'Stalling as usual. You're all the same. Affable oysters! Haven't you come to the stage yet of inviting someone to come and "assist you in your inquiries"?'

'I've come to you,' said Dermot Craddock with a grin.

'Is there a nasty double entendre in that remark? Are you really suspicious that I murdered Heather Badcock and do you think I did it in mistake for Marina Gregg or that I meant to murder Heather Badcock all the time?'

'I haven't suggested anything,' said Craddock.

'No, no, you wouldn't do that, would you? You'd be very correct. All right. Let's go into it. I was there. I had opportunity but had I any motive? Ah, that's what you'd like to know. What was my motive?'

'I haven't been able to find one so far,' said Craddock.

'That's very gratifying. I feel safer.'

'I'm just interested in what you may have seen that day.'

'You've had that already. The local police had that straight away. It's humiliating. There I was on the scene of a murder. I practically *saw* the murder committed, must have done, and yet I've no idea who did it. I'm ashamed to confess that the first *I* knew about it was seeing the poor, dear woman sitting on a chair gasping for breath and then pegging out. Of course it made a very good eye-witness account. It was a good scoop for me—and all that. But I'll confess to you that I feel humiliated that I don't know more. I ought to know more. And you can't kid me that the dose was meant for Heather Badcock. She was a nice woman who talked too much, but nobody gets murdered for that—unless of course they give away secrets. But I don't think anybody would ever have told Heather Badcock a secret. She wasn't the kind of woman who'd have been interested in other people's secrets. My view of her is of a woman who invariably talked about *herself*.'

'That seems to be the generally accepted view,' agreed Craddock.

'So we come to the famous Marina Gregg. I'm sure there are lots of wonderful motives for murdering Marina. Envy and jealousy and love tangles—all the stuff of drama. But who did it? Someone with a screw loose, I presume. There! You've had my valuable opinion. Is that what you wanted?'

'Not that alone. I understand that you arrived and came up the stairs about the same time as the vicar and the mayor.'

'Quite correct. But that wasn't the first time I'd arrived. I'd been there earlier.'

'I didn't know that.'

'Yes. I was on a kind of roving commission, you know, going here and there. I had a photographer with me. I'd gone down to take a few local shots of the mayor arriving and throwing a hoopla and putting in a peg for buried treasure and that kind of thing. Then I went back up again, not so much on the job, as to get a drink or two. The drink was good.'

'I see. Now can you remember who else was on the staircase when you went up?'

'Margot Bence from London was there with her camera.'

'You know her well?'

'Oh I run against her quite often. She's a clever girl, who makes a success of her stuff. She takes all the fashionable things—First Nights, Gala Performances—specializes in photographs from unusual angles. Arty! She was in a corner of the half landing very well placed for taking anyone who came up and for taking the greetings going on at the top. Lola Brewster was just ahead of me on the stairs. Didn't know her at first. She's got a new rust-red hair-do. The very latest Fiji Islander type. Last time I saw her it was lank waves falling round her face and chin in a nice shade of auburn. There was a big dark man with her, American. I don't know who he was but he looked important.'

'Did you look at Marina Gregg herself at all as you were coming up?'

'Yes, of course I did.'

'She didn't look upset or as though she'd had a shock or was frightened?'

'It's odd you should say that. I *did* think for a moment or two she was going to faint.'

'I see,' said Craddock thoughtfully. 'Thanks. There's nothing else you'd like to tell me?'

McNeil gave him a wide innocent stare.

'What could there be?'

'I don't trust you,' said Craddock.

'But you seem quite sure I didn't do it. Disappointing. Suppose I turn out to be her first husband. Nobody knows who he was except that he was so insignificant that even his name's been forgotten.'

Dermot grinned.

'Married from your prep school?' he asked. 'Or possibly in rompers! I must hurry. I've got a train to catch.'

There was a neatly docketed pile of papers on Craddock's desk at New Scotland Yard. He gave a perfunctory glance through them, then threw a question over his shoulder.

'Where's Lola Brewster staying?'

'At the Savoy, sir. Suite 1800. She's expecting you.'

'And Ardwyck Fenn?'

'He's at the Dorchester. First floor, 190.'

'Good.'

He picked up some cablegrams and read through them again before shoving them into his pocket. He smiled a moment to himself over the last one. 'Don't say I don't do my stuff, Aunt Jane,' he murmured under his breath.

He went out and made his way to the Savoy.

In Lola Brewster's suite Lola went out of her way to welcome him effusively. With the report he had just read in his mind, he studied her carefully. Quite a beauty still, he thought, in a lush kind of way, what you might call a trifle over-blown, perhaps, but they still liked them that way. A completely different type, of course, from Marina Gregg. The amenities over, Lola pushed back her Fiji Islander hair, drew her generous lipsticked mouth into a provocative pout, and flickering blue eyelids over wide brown eyes, said:

'Have you come to ask me a lot more horrible questions? Like that local inspector did.'

'I hope they won't be too horrible, Miss Brewster.'

'Oh, but I'm sure they will be, and I'm sure the whole thing must have been some terrible mistake.'

'Do you really think so?'

'Yes. It's all such nonsense. Do you really mean that someone tried to poison Marina? Who on earth would poison Marina? She's an absolute sweetie, you know. Everybody loves her.'

'Including you?'

'I've always been devoted to Marina.'

'Oh come now, Miss Brewster, wasn't there a little trouble about eleven or twelve years ago?'

'Oh that.' Lola waved it away. 'I was terribly nervy and distraught, and Rob and I had been having the most frightful quarrels. We were neither of us normal at the moment. Marina just fell wildly in love with him and rushed him off his feet, the poor pet.'

'And you minded very much?'

'Well, I thought I did, Inspector. Of course I see now it was one of the best things that ever happened for me. I was really worried about the *children*, you know. Breaking up our home. I'm afraid I'd already realized that Rob and I were incompatible. I expect you know I got married to Eddie Groves as soon as the divorce went through? I think really I'd been in love with him for a long time, but of course I didn't want to break up my marriage, because of the children. It's so important, isn't it, that children should have a *home*?'

'Yet people say that actually you were terribly upset.'

'Oh, people always say things,' said Lola vaguely.

'You said quite a lot, didn't you, Miss Brewster? You went about threatening to shoot Marina Gregg, or so I understand.'

'I've told you one *says* things. One's *supposed* to say things like that. Of course I wouldn't really shoot *anyone*.'

'In spite of taking a pot-shot at Eddie Groves some few years later?'

'Oh, that was because we'd had an argument,' said Lola. 'I lost my temper.'

'I have it on very good authority, Miss Brewster, that you said—and these are your exact words or so I'm told,' (he read from a note-book)—"That bitch needn't think she'll get away with it. If I don't shoot her now I'll wait and get her in some other way. I don't care how long I wait, years if need be, but I'll get even with her in the end."'

'Oh, I'm sure I never said anything of the kind,' Lola laughed.

'I'm sure, Miss Brewster, that you did.'

'People exaggerate so.' A charming smile broke over her face. 'I was just mad at the moment, you know,' she murmured confidentially. 'One says all sorts of things when one's mad with people. But you don't really think I'd wait fourteen years and come across to England, and look up Marina and drop some deadly poison into her cocktail glass within three minutes of seeing her again?'

Dermot Craddock didn't really think so. It seemed to him wildly improbable. He merely said:

'I'm only pointing out to you, Miss Brewster, that there had been threats in the past and that Marina Gregg was certainly startled and frightened to see someone who came up the stairs that day. Naturally one feels that that someone must have been you.'

'But darling Marina was delighted to see me! She kissed me and exclaimed how wonderful it was. Oh really, Inspector, I do think you're being very, very silly.'

'In fact, you were all one big happy family?'

'Well, that's really much more true than all the things you've been thinking.'

'And you've no ideas that could help us in any way? No ideas who might have killed her?'

'I tell you nobody would have wanted to kill Marina. She's a very silly woman anyway. Always making terrible fusses about her health, and changing her mind and wanting this, that and the other, and when she's got it being dissatisfied with it! I can't think why people are as fond of her as they are. Jason's always been absolutely mad about her. What that man has to put up with! But there it is. Everybody puts up with Marina, puts themselves out for her. Then she gives them a sad, sweet smile and thanks them! And apparently that makes them feel that all the trouble is worthwhile. I really don't know how she does it. You'd better put the idea that somebody wanted to kill her right out of your head.'

'I should like to,' said Dermot Craddock. 'Unfortunately I can't put it out of my head because, you see, it happened.'

'What do you mean, *it happened*, nobody has killed Marina, have they?'

'No. But the attempt was made.'

'I don't believe it for a moment! I expect whoever it was meant to kill the other woman all the time—the one who *was* killed. I expect someone comes into money when she dies.'

'She hadn't any money, Miss Brewster.'

'Oh well, there was some other reason. Anyway, I shouldn't worry about Marina if I were you. Marina is *always* all right!'

'Is she? She doesn't look a very happy woman to me.'

'Oh, that's because she makes such a song and dance

about everything. Unhappy love affairs. Not being able to have any children.'

'She adopted some children, didn't she?' said Dermot with a lively remembrance of Miss Marple's urgent voice.

'I believe she did once. It wasn't a great success I believe. She does these impulsive things and then wishes she hadn't.'

'What happened to the children she adopted?'

'I've no idea. They just sort of vanished after a bit. She got tired of them, I suppose, like everything else.'

'I see,' said Dermot Craddock.

Next—the Dorchester. Suite 190.

'Well, Chief-Inspector—' Ardwyck Fenn looked down at the card in his hand.

'Craddock.'

'What can I do for you?'

'I hope you won't mind if I ask you a few questions.'

'Not at all. It's this business at Much Benham. No— what's the actual name, St Mary Mead?'

'Yes. That's right. Gossington Hall.'

'Can't think what Jason Rudd wanted to buy a place like that for. Plenty of good Georgian houses in England— or even Queen Anne. Gossington Hall is a purely Victorian mansion. Where's the attraction in that, I wonder?'

'Oh, there's some attraction—for some people, that is, in Victorian stability.'

'Stability? Well, perhaps you've got something there. Marina, I suppose, had a feeling for stability. It's a thing she never had herself, poor girl, so I suppose that's why she always covets it. Perhaps this place will satisfy her for a bit.'

'You know her well, Mr Fenn?'

Ardwyck Fenn shrugged his shoulders.

'Well? I don't know that I'd say that. I've known her over a long period of years. Known her off and on, that is to say.'

Craddock looked at him appraisingly. A dark man, heavily built, shrewd eyes behind thick glasses, heavy jowl and chin, Ardwyck Fenn went on:

'The idea is, I gather, from what I read in the newspapers, that this Mrs Whatever-her-name-was, was poisoned by mistake. That the dose was intended for Marina. Is that right?'

'Yes. That's it. The dose was in Marina Gregg's cocktail. Mrs Badcock spilt hers and Marina handed over her drink to her.'

'Well that seems pretty conclusive. I really can't think, though, who would want to poison Marina. Especially as Lynette Brown wasn't there.'

'Lynette Brown?' Craddock looked slightly at sea.

Ardwyck Fenn smiled. 'If Marina breaks this contract, throws up the part—Lynette will get it and it would mean a good deal to Lynette to get it. But for all that, I don't imagine she'd send some emissary along with poison. Much too melodramatic an idea.'

'It seems a little far-fetched,' said Dermot dryly.

'Ah, you'd be surprised what women will do when they're ambitious,' said Ardwyck Fenn. 'Mind you, death mayn't have been intended. It may have been just to give her a fright—Enough to knock her out but not to finish her.'

Craddock shook his head. 'It wasn't a borderline dose,' he said.

'People make mistakes in doses, quite big ones.'

'Is this really your theory?'

'Oh no, it isn't. It was only a suggestion. I've no theory. I was only an innocent bystander.'

'Was Marina Gregg very surprised to see you?'

'Yes, it was a complete surprise to her.' He laughed amusedly. 'Just couldn't believe her eyes when she saw me coming up the stairs. She gave me a very nice welcome, I must say.'

'You hadn't seen her for a long time?'

'Not for four or five years, I should say.'

'And some years before that there was a time when you and she were very close friends, I believe?'

'Are you insinuating anything in particular by that remark, Inspector Craddock?'

There was very little change in the voice but there was something there that had not been there before. A hint of steel, of menace. Dermot felt suddenly that this man would be a very ruthless opponent.

'It would be as well, I think,' said Ardwyck Fenn, 'that you said exactly what you do mean.'

'I'm quite prepared to do so, Mr Fenn. I have to inquire into the past relations of everyone who was there on that day with Marina Gregg. It seems to have been a matter of common gossip that at the time I have just referred to, you were wildly in love with Marina Gregg.'

Ardwyck Fenn shrugged his shoulders.

'One has these infatuations, Inspector. Fortunately, they pass.'

174

'It is said that she encouraged you and that later she turned you down and that you resented the fact.'

'It is said—it is said! I suppose you read all that in *Confidential*?'

'It has been told me by quite well informed and sensible people.'

Ardwyck Fenn threw back his head, showing the bull-like line of his neck.

'I had a yen for her at one time, yes,' he admitted. 'She was a beautiful and attractive woman and still is. To say that I ever threatened her is going a little far. I'm never pleased to be thwarted, Chief-Inspector, and most people who thwart me tend to be sorry that they have done so. But that principle applies mainly in my business life.'

'You did, I believe, use your influence to have her dropped from a picture that she was making?'

Fenn shrugged his shoulders.

'She was unsuitable for the role. There was conflict between her and the director. I had money in that picture and I had no intention of jeopardizing it. It was, I assure you, purely a business transaction.'

'But perhaps Marina Gregg did not think so?'

'Oh, naturally she did not think so. She would always think that anything like that was personal.'

'She actually told certain friends of hers that she was afraid of you, I believe?'

'Did she? How childish. I expect she enjoyed the sensation.'

'You think there was no need for her to be afraid of you?'

'Of course not. Whatever personal disappointment I might have had, I soon put it behind me. I've always gone on the principle that where women are concerned there are as good fish in the sea as ever came out of it.'

'A very satisfactory way to go through life, Mr Fenn.'

'Yes, I think it is.'

'You have a wide knowledge of the moving picture world?'

'I have financial interests in it.'

'And therefore you are bound to know a lot about it?'

'Perhaps.'

'You are a man whose judgement would be worth listening to. Can you suggest to me any person who is likely to have such a deep grudge against Marina Gregg that they would be willing to do away with her?'

'Probably a dozen,' said Ardwyck Fenn, 'that is to say, if they hadn't got to do anything about it personally. If it was a mere matter of pressing a button in a wall, I dare say there'd be a lot of willing fingers.'

'You were there that day. You saw her and talked to her. Do you think that amongst any of the people who were around you in that brief space of time—from when you arrived to the moment when Heather Badcock died—do you think that amongst them you can suggest—only suggest, mind you, I'm asking you for nothing more than a guess—anyone who might poison Marina Gregg?'

'I wouldn't like to say,' said Ardwyck Fenn.

'That means that you have some idea?'

'It means that I have nothing to say on that subject. And that, Chief-Inspector Craddock, is all you'll get out of me.'

CHAPTER 15

Dermot Craddock looked down at the last name and address he had written down in his note-book. The telephone number had been rung twice for him but there had been no response. He tried it now once more. He shrugged his shoulders, got up and decided to go and see for himself.

Margot Bence's studio was in a cul-de-sac off the Tottenham Court Road. Beyond the name on a plate on the side of a door, there was little to identify it, and certainly no form of advertising. Craddock groped his way to the first floor. There was a large notice here painted in black on a white board. 'Margot Bence, Personality Photographer. Please enter.'

Craddock entered. There was a small waiting-room but nobody in charge of it. He stood there hesitating, then cleared his throat in a loud and theatrical manner. Since that drew no attention he raised his voice.

'Anybody here?'

He heard a flap of slippers behind a velvet curtain, the curtain was pushed aside and a young man with exuberant hair and a pink and white face, peered round it.

'Terribly sorry, my dear,' he said. 'I didn't hear you. I had an absolutely new idea and I was just trying it out.'

He pushed the velvet curtain farther aside and Craddock followed him into an inner room. This proved to be unexpectedly large. It was clearly the working studio. There were cameras, lights, arc-lights, piles of drapery, screens on wheels.

'Such a mess,' said the young man, who was almost as willowy as Hailey Preston. 'But one finds it very hard to work, I think, unless one *does* get into a mess. Now what were you wanting to see us about?'

'I wanted to see Miss Margot Bence.'

'Ah, Margot. Now what a pity. If you'd been half an hour earlier you'd have found her here. She's gone off to produce some photographs of models for *Fashion Dream*. You should have rung up, you know, to make an appointment. Margot's terribly busy these days.'

'I did ring up. There was no reply.'

'Of course,' said the young man. 'We took the receiver off. I remember now. It disturbed us.' He smoothed down a kind of lilac smock that he was wearing. 'Can I do anything for you? Make an appointment? I do a lot of Margot's business arrangements for her. You wanted to arrange for some photography somewhere? Private or business?'

'From that point of view, neither,' said Dermot Craddock. He handed his card to the young man.

'How perfectly rapturous,' said the young man. 'CID! I believe, you know, I've seen pictures of you. Are you one of the Big Four or the Big Five, or is it perhaps the Big Six nowadays? There's so much crime about, they'd have

178

to increase the numbers, wouldn't they? Oh dear, is that disrespectful? I'm afraid it is. I didn't mean to be disrespectful at all. Now, what do you want Margot for—not to arrest her, I hope.'

'I just wanted to ask her one or two questions.'

'She doesn't do indecent photographs or anything like that,' said the young man anxiously. 'I hope nobody's been telling you any stories of that kind because it isn't true. Margot's very artistic. She does a lot of stage work and studio work. But her studies are terribly, terribly pure— almost prudish, I'd say.'

'I can tell you quite simply why I want to speak to Miss Bence,' said Dermot. 'She was recently an eye-witness of a crime that took place near Much Benham, at a village called St Mary Mead.'

'Oh, my dear, of *course*! I know about *that*. Margot came back and told me all about it. Hemlock in the cocktails, wasn't it? Something of that kind. So *bleak* it sounded! But all mixed up with the St John Ambulance which doesn't seem so bleak, does it? But haven't you already asked Margot questions about that—or was it somebody else?'

'One always finds there are more questions, as the case goes on,' said Dermot.

'You mean it develops. Yes, I can quite see that. Murder develops. Yes, like a photograph, isn't it?'

'It's very much like a photograph really,' said Dermot. 'Quite a good comparison of yours.'

'Well, it's very nice of you to say so, I'm sure. Now about Margot. Would you like to get hold of her right away?'

'If you can help me to do so, yes.'

'Well, at the moment,' said the young man, consulting his watch, 'at the moment she'll be outside Keats' house at Hampstead Heath. My car's outside. Shall I run you up there?'

'That would be very kind of you, Mr—?'

'Jethroe,' said the young man, 'Johnny Jethroe.'

As they went down the stairs Dermot asked:

'Why Keats' house?'

'Well, you know we don't pose fashion photographs in the studio any more. We like them to seem natural, blown about by the wind. And if possible some rather unlikely background. You know, an Ascot frock against Wandsworth Prison, or a frivolous suit outside a poet's house.'

Mr Jethroe drove rapidly but skilfully up Tottenham Court Road, through Camden Town and finally to the neighbourhood of Hampstead Heath. On the pavement near Keats' house a pretty little scene was being enacted. A slim girl, wearing diaphanous organdie, was standing clutching an immense black hat. On her knees, a little way behind her, a second girl was holding the first girl's skirt well pulled back so that it clung around her knees and legs. In a deep hoarse voice a girl with a camera was directing operations.

'For goodness' sake, Jane, get your *behind* down. It's showing behind her right knee. Get down *flatter*. That's it. No, more to the left. That's right. Now you're masked by the bush. That'll do. Hold it. We'll have one more. Both hands on the back of the hat this time. Head up. Good— now turn round, Elsie. Bend over. More. Bend! *Bend*, you've got to pick up that cigarette case. That's right. That's *heaven*!

Got it! Now move over to the left. Same pose, only just turn your head over your shoulder. So.'

'I can't see what you want to go taking photographs of my behind for,' said the girl called Elsie rather sulkily.

'It's a lovely behind, dear. It looks smashing,' said the photographer. 'And when you turn your head your chin comes up like the rising moon over a mountain. I don't think we need bother with any more.'

'Hi—Margot,' said Mr Jethroe.

She turned her head. 'Oh, it's you. What are you doing here?'

'I brought someone along to see you. Chief-Inspector Craddock, CID.'

The girl's eyes turned swiftly on to Dermot. He thought they had a wary, searching look but that, as he well knew, was nothing extraordinary. It was a fairly common reaction to detective-inspectors. She was a thin girl, all elbows and angles, but was an interesting shape for all that. A heavy curtain of black hair fell down either side of her face. She looked dirty as well as sallow and not particularly prepossessing, to his eyes. But he acknowledged that there was character there. She raised her eyebrows which were slightly raised by art already and remarked:

'And what can I do for you, Detective-Inspector Craddock?'

'How do you do, Miss Bence. I wanted to ask you if you would be so kind as to answer a few questions about that very unfortuante business at Gossington Hall, near Much Benham. You went there, if I remember, to take some photographs.'

181

The girl nodded. 'Of course. I remember quite well.' She shot him a quick searching look. 'I didn't see you there. Surely it was somebody else. Inspector—Inspector—'

'Inspector Cornish?' said Dermot.

'That's right.'

'We were called in later.'

'You're from Scotland Yard?'

'Yes.'

'You butted in and took over from the local people. Is that it?'

'Well, it isn't quite a question of butting in, you know. It's up to the Chief Constable of the County to decide whether he wants to keep it in his own hands or whether he thinks it'll be better handled by us.'

'What makes him decide?'

'It very often turns on whether the case has a local background or whether it's a more—universal one. Sometimes, perhaps, an international one.'

'And he decided, did he, that this was an international one?'

'Transatlantic, perhaps, would be a better word.'

'They've been hinting that in the papers, haven't they? Hinting that the killer, whoever he was, was out to get Marina Gregg and got some wretched local woman by mistake. Is that true or is it a bit of publicity for their film?'

'I'm afraid there isn't much doubt about it, Miss Bence.'

'What do you want to ask me? Have I got to come to Scotland Yard?'

He shook his head. 'Not unless you like. We'll go back to your studio if you prefer.'

182

'All right, let's do that. My car's just up the street.'

She walked rapidly along the footpath. Dermot went with her. Jethroe called after them.

'So long, darling, I won't butt in. I'm sure you and the Inspector are going to talk big secrets.' He joined the two models on the pavement and began an animated discussion with them.

Margot got into the car, unlocked the door on the other side, and Dermot Craddock got in beside her. She said nothing at all during the drive back to Tottenham Court Road. She turned down the cul-de-sac and at the bottom of it drove through an open doorway.

'Got my own parking place here,' she remarked. 'It's a furniture depository place really, but they rent me a bit of space. Parking a car is one of the big headaches in London, as you probably know only too well, though I don't suppose you deal with traffic, do you?'

'No, that's not one of my troubles.'

'I should think murder would be infinitely preferable,' said Margot Bence.

She led the way back to the studio, motioned him to a chair, offered him a cigarette and sank down on the large pouffe opposite him. From behind the curtain of dark hair she looked at him in a sombre questioning way.

'Shoot, stranger,' she said.

'You were taking photographs on the occasion of this death, I understand.'

'Yes.'

'You'd been engaged professionally?'

'Yes. They wanted someone to do a few specialized

shots. I do quite a lot of that stuff. I do some work for film studios sometimes, but this time I was just taking photographs of the fête, and afterwards a few shots of special people being greeted by Marina Gregg and Jason Rudd. Local notabilities or other personalities. That sort of thing.'

'Yes. I understand that. You had your camera on the stairs, I understand?'

'A part of the time, yes. I got a very good angle from there. You get people coming up the stairs below you and you could swivel round and get Marina shaking hands with them. You could get a lot of different angles without having to move much.'

'I know, of course, that you answered some questions at the time as to whether you'd seen anything unusual, anything that might be helpful. They were general questions.'

'Have you got more specialized ones?'

'A little more specialized, I think. You had a good view of Marina Gregg from where you were standing?'

She nodded. 'Excellent.'

'And of Jason Rudd?'

'Occasionally. But he was moving about more. Drinks and things and introducing people to one another. The locals to the celebrities. That kind of thing, I should imagine. I didn't see this Mrs Baddeley—'

'Badcock.'

'Sorry, Badcock. I didn't see her drink the fatal draught or anything like that. In fact I don't think I really know which she was.'

'Do you remember the arrival of the mayor?'

'Oh, yes. I remember the mayor all right. He had on his chain and his robes of office. I got one of him coming up the stairs—a close-up—rather a cruel profile, and then I got him shaking hands with Marina.'

'Then you can fix that time at least in your mind. Mrs Badcock and her husband came up the stairs to Marina Gregg immediately in front of him.'

She shook her head. 'Sorry. I still don't remember her.'

'That doesn't matter so much. I presume that you had a pretty good view of Marina Gregg and that you had your eyes on her and were pointing the camera at her fairly often.'

'Quite right. Most of the time. I'd wait till I got just the right moment.'

'Do you know a man called Ardwyck Fenn by sight?'

'Oh yes. I know him well enough. Television network—films too.'

'Did you take a photograph of him?'

'Yes. I got him coming up with Lola Brewster.'

'That would be just after the mayor?'

She thought a minute then agreed. 'Yes, about then.'

'Did you notice that about that time Marina Gregg seemed to feel suddenly ill? Did you notice any unusual expression on her face?'

Margot Bence leant forward, opened a cigarette box and took out a cigarette. She lit it. Although she had not answered Dermot did not press her. He waited, wondering what it was she was turning over in her mind. She said at last, abruptly:

'Why do you ask me that?'

'Because it's a question to which I am very anxious to have an answer—a reliable answer.'

'Do you think my answer's likely to be reliable?'

'Yes I do, as a matter of fact. You must have the habit of watching people's faces very closely, waiting for certain expressions, certain propitious moments.'

She nodded her head.

'Did you see anything of that kind?'

'Somebody else saw it too, did they?'

'Yes. More than one person, but it's been described rather differently.'

'How did the other people describe it?'

'One person has told me that she was taken faint.'

Margot Bence shook her head slowly.

'Someone else said that she was startled.' He paused a moment then went on, 'And somebody else describes her as having a frozen look on her face.'

'Frozen,' said Margot Bence thoughtfully.

'Do you agree to that last statement?'

'I don't know. Perhaps.'

'It was put rather more fancifully still,' said Dermot. 'In the words of the late poet, Tennyson. "The mirror crack'd from side to side; 'The doom has come upon me,' cried the Lady of Shalott."'

'There wasn't any mirror,' said Margot Bence, 'but if there had been it might have cracked.' She got up abruptly. 'Wait,' she said. 'I'll do something better than describe it to you. I'll show you.'

She pushed aside the curtain at the far end and

disappeared for some moments. He could hear her uttering impatient mutterings under her breath.

'What hell it is,' she said as she emerged again, 'one never can find things when one wants them. I've got it now though.'

She came across to him and put a glossy print into his hand. He looked down at it. It was a very good photograph of Marina Gregg. Her hand was clasped in the hand of a woman standing in front of her, and therefore with her back to the camera. But Marina Gregg was not looking at the woman. Her eyes stared not quite into the camera but slightly obliquely to the left. The interesting thing to Dermot Craddock was that the face expressed nothing whatever. There was no fear on it, no pain. The woman portrayed there was staring at *something*, something she saw, and the emotion it aroused in her was so great that she was physically unable to express it by any kind of facial expression. Dermot Craddock had seen such a look once on a man's face, a man who a second later had been shot dead . . .

'Satisfied?' asked Margot Bence.

Craddock gave a deep sigh. 'Yes, thank you. It's hard, you know, to make up one's mind if witnesses are exaggerating, if they are imagining they see things. But that's not so in this case. There *was* something to see and she saw it.' He asked, 'Can I keep this picture?'

'Oh, yes you can have the print. I've got the negative.'

'You didn't send it to the Press?'

Margot Bence shook her head.

'I rather wonder why you didn't. After all, it's rather a

dramatic photograph. Some paper might have paid a good price for it.'

'I wouldn't care to do that,' said Margot Bence. 'If you look into somebody's soul by accident, you feel a bit embarrassed about cashing in.'

'Did you know Marina Gregg at all?'

'No.'

'You come from the States, don't you?'

'I was born in England. I was trained in America though. I came over here, oh, about three years ago.'

Dermot Craddock nodded. He had known the answers to his questions. They had been waiting for him among the other lists of information on his office table. The girl seemed straightforward enough. He asked:

'Where did you train?'

'Reingarden Studios. I was with Andrew Quilp for a time. He taught me a lot.'

'Reingarden Studios and Andrew Quilp.' Dermot Craddock was suddenly alert. The names struck a chord of remembrance.

'You lived in Seven Springs, didn't you?'

She looked amused.

'You seem to know a lot about me. Have you been checking up?'

'You're a very well-known photographer, Miss Bence. There have been articles written about you, you know. Why did you come to England?'

She shrugged her shoulders.

'Oh, I like a change. Besides, as I tell you, I was born in England although I went to the States as a child.'

'Quite a young child, I think.'

'Five years old, if you're interested.'

'I am interested. I think, Miss Bence, you could tell me a little more than you have done.'

Her face hardened. She stared at him.

'What do you mean by that?'

Dermot Craddock looked at her and risked it. It wasn't much to go on. Reingarden Studios and Andrew Quilp and the name of one town. But he felt rather as if old Miss Marple were at his shoulder egging him on.

'I think you knew Marina Gregg better than you say.'

She laughed. 'Prove it. You're imagining things.'

'Am I? I don't think I am. And it *could* be proved, you know, with a little time and care. Come now, Miss Bence, hadn't you better admit the truth? Admit that Marina Gregg adopted you as a child and that you lived with her for four years.'

She drew her breath in sharply with a hiss.

'You nosy bastard!' she said.

It startled him a little, it was such a contrast to her former manner. She got up, shaking her black head of hair.

'All right, all right, it's true enough! Yes. Marina Gregg took me over to America with her. My mother had eight kids. She lived in a slum somewhere. She was one of hundreds of people, I suppose, who write to any film actress that they happen to see or hear about, spilling a hard luck story, begging her to adopt the child a mother couldn't give advantages to. Oh, it's such a sickening business, all of it.'

'There were three of you,' said Dermot. 'Three children adopted at different times from different places.'

'That's right. Me and Rod and Angus. Angus was older than I was, Rod was practically a baby. We had a wonderful life. Oh, a wonderful life! All the advantages!' Her voice rose mockingly. 'Clothes and cars and a wonderful house to live in and people to look after us, good schooling and teaching, and delicious food. Everything piled on! And she herself, our "Mom". "Mom" in inverted commas, playing her part, crooning over us, being photographed with us! Ah, such a pretty sentimental picture.'

'But she really wanted children,' said Dermot Craddock. 'That was real enough, wasn't it? It wasn't just a publicity stunt.'

'Oh, perhaps. Yes, I think that was true. She wanted children. But she didn't want *us*! Not really. It was just a glorious bit of play-acting. "*My family.*" "*So lovely to have a family of my own.*" And Izzy let her do it. He ought to have known better.'

'Izzy was Isidore Wright?'

'Yes, her third husband or her fourth, I forget which. He was a wonderful man really. He understood her, I think, and he was worried sometimes about us. He was kind to us, but he didn't pretend to be a father. He didn't feel like a father. He only cared really about his own writing. I've read some of his things since. They're sordid and rather cruel, but they're powerful. I think people will call him a great writer one day.'

'And this went on until when?'

Margot Bence's smile curved suddenly. 'Until she got sick

of that particular bit of play-acting. No, that's not quite true . . . She found she was going to have a child of her own.'

She laughed with sudden bitterness. 'Then we'd had it! We weren't wanted any more. We'd done very well as little stopgaps, but she didn't care a damn about us really, not a damn. Oh, she pensioned us off very prettily. With a home and a foster-mother and money for our education and a nice little sum to start us off in the world. Nobody can say that she didn't behave correctly and handsomely. But she'd never wanted *us*—all she wanted was a child of her own.'

'You can't blame her for that,' said Dermot gently.

'I don't blame her for wanting a child of her own, no! But what about us? She took us away from our own parents, from the place where we belonged. My mother sold me for a mess of pottage, if you like, but she didn't sell me for advantage to herself. She sold me because she was a damn' silly woman who thought I'd get "advantages" and "education" and have a wonderful life. She thought she was doing the best for me. Best for me? If she only knew.'

'You're still very bitter, I see.'

'No, I'm not bitter now. I've got over that. I'm bitter because I'm remembering, because I've gone back to those days. We were all pretty bitter.'

'All of you?'

'Well, not Rod. Rod never cared about anything. Besides he was rather small. But Angus felt like I did, only I think he was more revengeful. He said that when he was grown up he would go and kill that baby she was going to have.'

'You knew about the baby?'

'Oh, of course I knew. And everyone knows what happened. She went crazy with rapture about having it and then when it was born it was an idiot! Serve her right. Idiot or no idiot, she didn't want *us* back again.'

'You hate her very much?'

'Why shouldn't I hate her? She did the worst thing to me that anyone can do to anyone else. Let them believe that they're loved and wanted and then show them that it's all a sham.'

'What happened to your two—I'll call them brothers, for the sake of convenience.'

'Oh, we all drifted apart later. Rod's farming somewhere in the Middle West. He's got a happy nature, and always had. Angus? I don't know. I lost sight of him.'

'Did he continue to feel regretful?'

'I shouldn't think so,' said Margot. 'It's not the sort of thing you can go on feeling. The last time I saw him, he said he was going on the stage. I don't know whether he did.'

'*You*'ve remembered, though,' said Dermot.

'Yes. I've remembered,' said Margot Bence.

'Was Marina Gregg surprised to see you on that day or did she make the arrangements for your photography on purpose to please you?'

'She?' The girl smiled scornfully. 'She knew nothing about the arrangements. I was curious to see her, so I did a bit of lobbying to get the job. As I say I've got some influence with studio people. I wanted to see what she looked like nowadays.' She stroked the surface of the table. 'She didn't even recognize me. What do you think of that? I was with her for four years. From five years old to nine and she didn't recognize me.'

'Children change,' said Dermot Craddock, 'they change so much that you'd hardly know them. I have a niece I met the other day and I assure you I'd have passed her in the street.'

'Are you saying that to make me feel better? I don't care really. Oh, what the hell, let's be honest. I do care. I did. She had a magic, you know. Marina! A wonderful calamitous magic that took hold of you. You can hate a person and still mind.'

'You didn't tell her who you were?'

She shook her head. 'No, I didn't tell her. That's the last thing I'd do.'

'Did you try and poison her, Miss Bence?'

Her mood changed. She got up and laughed.

'What ridiculous questions you do ask! But I suppose you have to. It's part of your job. No. I can assure you I didn't kill her.'

'That isn't what I asked you, Miss Bence.'

She looked at him, frowning, puzzled.

'Marina Gregg,' he said, 'is still alive.'

'For how long?'

'What do you mean by that?'

'Don't you think it's likely, Inspector, that someone will try again, and this time—this time, perhaps—they'll succeed?'

'Precautions will be taken.'

'Oh, I'm sure they will. The adoring husband will look

after her, won't he, and make sure that no harm comes to her?'

He was listening carefully to the mockery in her voice.

'What did you mean when you said you didn't ask me that?' she said, harking back suddenly.

'I asked you if you tried to kill her. You replied that you didn't kill her. That's true enough, but *someone* died, *someone* was killed.'

'You mean I tried to kill Marina and instead I killed Mrs What's-her-name. If you'd like me to make it quite clear, I *didn't* try to poison Marina and I *didn't* poison Mrs Badcock.'

'But you know perhaps who did?'

'I don't know anything, Inspector, I assure you.'

'But you have some idea?'

'Oh, one always has ideas.' She smiled at him, a mocking smile. 'Among so many people it might be, mightn't it, the black-haired robot of a secretary, the elegant Hailey Preston, servants, maids, a masseur, the hairdresser, someone at the studios, so many people—*and one of them mightn't be what he or she pretended to be.*'

Then as he took an unconscious step towards her she shook her head vehemently.

'Relax, Inspector,' she said. 'I'm only teasing you. *Somebody's* out for Marina's blood, but who it is I've no idea. Really. I've no idea at all.'

CHAPTER 16

At No. 16 Aubrey Close, young Mrs Baker was talking to her husband. Jim Baker, a big good-looking blond giant of a man, was intent on assembling a model construction unit.

'Neighbours!' said Cherry. She gave a toss of her black curly head. 'Neighbours!' she said with venom.

She carefully lifted the frying pan from the stove, then neatly shot its contents on to two plates, one rather fuller than the other. She placed the fuller one before her husband.

'Mixed grill,' she announced.

Jim looked up and sniffed appreciatively.

'That's something like,' he said. 'What is today? My birthday?'

'You have to be well nourished,' said Cherry.

She was looking very pretty in a cerise and white striped apron with little frills on it. Jim Baker shifted the component parts of a strato-cruiser to make room for his meal. He grinned at his wife and asked:

'Who says so?'

'My Miss Marple for one!' said Cherry. 'And if it comes to that,' she added, sitting down opposite Jim and pulling her plate towards her, 'I should say *she* could do with a bit more solid nourishment herself. That old cat of a White Knight of hers, gives her nothing but carbohydrates. It's all she can think of! A "nice custard", a "nice bread and butter pudding", a "nice macaroni cheese". Squashy puddings with pink sauce. And gas, gas, gas, all day. Talks her head off, she does.'

'Oh well,' said Jim vaguely, 'it's invalid diet, I suppose.'

'Invalid diet!' said Cherry and snorted. 'Miss Marple isn't an invalid—she's just *old*. Always interfering, too.'

'Who, Miss Marple?'

'No. That Miss Knight. Telling me how to do things! She even tries to tell me how to cook! I know a lot more about cooking than she does.'

'You're tops for cooking, Cherry,' said Jim appreciatively.

'There's something *to* cooking,' said Cherry, 'something you can get your teeth into.'

Jim laughed. 'I'm getting my teeth into this all right. Why did your Miss Marple say that I needed nourishing? Did she think I looked run-down, the other day when I came in to fix that bathroom shelf?'

Cherry laughed. 'I'll tell you what she said to me. She said, "You've got a handsome husband, my dear. A *very* handsome husband." Sounds like one of those period books they read aloud on the telly.'

'I hope you agreed with her?' said Jim with a grin.

'I said you were all right.'

'All right indeed! That's a nice lukewarm way of talking.'

'And then she said "You must take care of your husband, my dear. Be sure you *feed* him properly. Men need plenty of good meat meals, well cooked."'

'Hear, hear!'

'And she told me to be sure and prepare fresh food for you and not to buy ready-made pies and things and slip them in the oven to warm up. Not that I do that often,' added Cherry virtuously.

'You can't do it too seldom for me,' said Jim. 'They don't taste a bit the same.'

'So long as you notice what you eat,' said Cherry, 'and aren't so taken up with those strato-cruisers and things you're always building. And don't tell me you bought that set as a Christmas present for your nephew Michael. You bought it so that you could play with it yourself.'

'He's not quite old enough for it yet,' said Jim apologetically.

'And I suppose you're going on dithering about with it all the evening. What about some music? Did you get that new record you were talking about?'

'Yes, I did. Tchaikovsky 1812.'

'That's the loud one with the battle, isn't it?' said Cherry. She made a face. 'Our Mrs Hartwell won't half like that! Neighbours! I'm fed up with neighbours. Always grousing and complaining. I don't know which is the worst. The Hartwells or the Barnabys. The Hartwells start rapping on the wall as early as twenty to eleven sometimes. It's a bit thick! After all even the telly and the BBC go on later than that. Why *shouldn't* we have a bit of music if we like? And always asking us to turn it down low.'

'You can't turn these things down low,' said Jim with authority. 'You don't get the *tone* unless you've got the volume. Everyone knows that. It's absolutely recognized in musical circles. And what about their cat—always coming over into our garden, digging up the beds, just when I've got it nice.'

'I tell you what, Jim. I'm fed up with this place.'

'You didn't mind your neighbours up in Huddersfield,' remarked Jim.

'It wasn't the same there,' said Cherry. 'I mean, you're all independent there. If you're in trouble, somebody'd give you a hand and you'd give a hand to them. But you don't interfere. There's something about a new estate like this that makes people look sideways at their neighbours. Because we're all new I suppose. The amount of back-biting and tale-telling and writing to the council and one thing and another round here beats me! People in real towns are too busy for it.'

'You may have something there, my girl.'

'D'you like it here, Jim?'

'The job's all right. And after all, this is a brand new house. I wish there was a bit more room in it so that I could spread myself a bit more. It would be fine if I could have a workshop.'

'I thought it was lovely at first,' said Cherry, 'but now I'm not so sure. The house is all right and I love the blue paint and the bathroom's nice, but I don't like the people and the *feeling* round here. Did I tell you that Lily Price and that Harry of hers have broken off? It was a funny business that day in that house they went to look over.

198

You know when she more or less fell out of the window. She said Harry just stood there like a stuck pig.'

'I'm glad she's broken off with him. He's a no-good if I ever saw one,' said Jim.

'No good marrying a chap just because a baby's on the way,' said Cherry. 'He didn't want to marry her, you know. He's not a very nice fellow. Miss Marple said he wasn't,' she added thoughtfully. 'She spoke to Lily about him. Lily thought she was crackers.'

'Miss Marple? I didn't know she'd ever seen him?'

'Oh yes, she was round here walking the day she fell down and Mrs Badcock picked her up and took her into her house. Do you think Arthur and Mrs Bain will make a match of it?'

Jim frowned as he picked up a bit of strato-cruiser and consulted the instructional diagram.

'I do wish you'd listen when I'm talking,' said Cherry.

'What did you say?'

'Arthur Badcock and Mary Bain.'

'For the Lord's sake, Cherry, his wife's only just dead! You women! I've heard he's in a terrible state of nerves still—jumps if you speak to him.'

'I wonder why . . . I shouldn't have thought he'd take it that way, would you?'

'Can you clear off this end of the table a bit?' said Jim, relinquishing even a passing interest in the affairs of his neighbours. 'Just so that I can spread some of these pieces out a bit.'

Cherry heaved an exasperated sigh.

'To get any attention round here, you have to be a super

jet, or a turbo prop,' she said bitterly. 'You and your constructional models!'

She piled the tray with the remains of supper and carried it over to the sink. She decided not to wash up, a necessity of daily life she always put off as long as possible. Instead, she piled everything into the sink, haphazard, slipped on a corduroy jacket and went out of the house, pausing to call over her shoulder:

'I'm just going to slip along to see Gladys Dixon. I want to borrow one of her *Vogue* patterns.'

'All right, old girl.' Jim bent over his model.

Casting a venomous look at her next-door neighbour's front door as she passed, Cherry went round the corner into Blenheim Close and stopped at No. 16. The door was open and Cherry tapped on it and went into the hall calling out:

'Is Gladdy about?'

'Is that you, Cherry?' Mrs Dixon looked out of the kitchen. 'She's upstairs in her room, dressmaking.'

'Right. I'll go up.'

Cherry went upstairs to a small bedroom in which Gladys, a plump girl with a plain face, was kneeling on the floor, her cheeks flushed, and several pins in her mouth, tacking up a paper pattern.

'Hallo, Cherry. Look, I got a lovely bit of stuff at Harper's sale at Much Benham. I'm going to do that cross-over pattern with frills again, the one I did in Terylene before.'

'That'll be nice,' said Cherry.

Gladys rose to her feet, panting a little.

'Got indigestion now,' she said.

'You oughtn't to do dressmaking right after supper,' said Cherry, 'bending over like that.'

'I suppose I ought to slim a bit,' said Gladys. She sat down on the bed.

'Any news from the studios?' asked Cherry, always avid for film news.

'Nothing much. There's a lot of talk still. Marina Gregg came back on the set yesterday—and she created something frightful.'

'What about?'

'She didn't like the taste of her coffee. You know, they have coffee in the middle of the morning. She took one sip and said there was something wrong with it. Which was nonsense, of course. There couldn't have been. It comes in a jug straight from the canteen. Of course I always put hers in a special china cup, rather posh—different from the others—but it's the same coffee. So there couldn't have been anything wrong with it, could there?'

'Nerves, I suppose,' said Cherry. 'What happened?'

'Oh, nothing. Mr Rudd just calmed everyone down. He's wonderful that way. He took the coffee from her and poured it down the sink.'

'That seems to be rather stupid,' said Cherry slowly.

'Why—what do you mean?'

'Well, if there *was* anything wrong with it—now nobody will ever know.'

'Do you think there really might have been?' asked Gladys looking alarmed.

'Well—' Cherry shrugged her shoulders, '—there was

201

something wrong with her cocktail the day of the fête, wasn't there, so why not the coffee? If at first you don't succeed, try, try, try again.'

Gladys shivered.

'I don't half like it, Cherry,' she said. 'Somebody's got it in for her all right. She's had more letters, you know, threatening her—and there was that bust business the other day.'

'What bust business?'

'A marble bust. On the set. It's a corner of a room in some Austrian palace or other. Funny name like Shotbrown. Pictures and china and marble busts. This one was up on a bracket—suppose it hadn't been pushed back enough. Anway, a heavy lorry went past out in the road and jarred it off—right on to the chair where Marina sits for her big scene with Count Somebody-or-other. Smashed to smithereens! Lucky they weren't shooting at the time. Mr Rudd, he said not to say a word to her, and he put another chair there, and when she came yesterday and asked why the chair had been changed, he said the other chair was the wrong period, and this gave a better angle for the camera. But he didn't half like it—I can tell you that.'

The two girls looked at each other.

'It's exciting in a way,' said Cherry slowly. 'And yet—it isn't . . .'

'I think I'm going to give up working in the canteen at the studios,' said Gladys.

'Why? Nobody wants to poison you or drop marble busts on your head!'

'No. But it's not always the person who's meant to get done in who gets done in. It may be someone else. Like Heather Badcock that day.'

'True enough,' said Cherry.

'You know,' said Gladys, 'I've been thinking. I was at the Hall that day, helping. I was quite close to them at the time.'

'When Heather died?'

'No, when she spilt the cocktail. All down her dress. A lovely dress it was, too, royal blue nylon taffeta. She'd got it quite new for the occasion. And it was funny.'

'What was funny?'

'I didn't think anything of it at the time. But it does seem funny when I think it over.'

Cherry looked at her expectantly. She accepted the adjective 'funny' in the sense that it was meant. It was not intended humorously.

'For goodness' sake, what was funny?' she demanded.

'I'm almost sure she did it on purpose.'

'Spilt the cocktail on purpose?'

'Yes. And I do think that was funny, don't you?'

'On a brand new dress? I don't believe it.'

'I wonder now,' said Gladys, 'what Arthur Badcock will do with all Heather's clothes. That dress would clean all right. Or I could take out half a breadth, it's a lovely full skirt. Do you think Arthur Badcock would think it very awful of me if I wanted to buy it off him? It would need hardly any alteration—and it's lovely stuff.'

'You wouldn't—' Cherry hesitated '—mind?'

'Mind what?'

'Well—having a dress that a woman had died in—I mean died that way . . .'

Gladys stared at her.

'I hadn't thought of that,' she admitted. She considered for a moment or two. Then she cheered up.

'I can't see that it really matters,' she said. 'After all, every time you buy something second-hand, somebody's usually worn it who has died, haven't they?'

'Yes. But it's not quite the same.'

'I think you're being fanciful,' said Gladys. 'It's a lovely bright shade of blue, and really expensive stuff. About that funny business,' she continued thoughtfully, 'I think I'll go up to the hall tomorrow morning on my way to work and have a word with Mr Giuseppe about it.'

'Is he the Italian butler?'

'Yes. He's awfully handsome. Flashing eyes. He's got a terrible temper. When we go and help there, he chivvies us girls something terrible.' She giggled. 'But none of us really mind. He can be awfully nice sometimes . . . Anyway, I might just tell him about it, and ask him what I ought to do.'

'I don't see that you've got anything to tell,' said Cherry.

'Well, it was funny,' said Gladys, defiantly clinging to her favourite adjective.

'*I* think,' said Cherry, 'that you just want an excuse to go and talk to Mr Giuseppe—and you'd better be careful, my girl. You know what these wops are like! Affiliation orders all over the place. Hot-blooded and passionate, that's what these Italians are.'

Gladys sighed ecstatically.

Cherry looked at her friend's fat slightly spotty face and

decided that her warnings were unnecessary. Mr Giuseppe, she thought, would have better fish to fry elsewhere.

'Aha!' said Dr Haydock, 'unravelling, I see.'

He looked from Miss Marple to a pile of fluffy white fleecy wool.

'You advised me to try unravelling if I couldn't knit,' said Miss Marple.

'You seem to have been very thorough about it.'

'I made a mistake in the pattern right at the beginning. That made the whole thing go out of proportion, so I've had to unravel it all. It's a very elaborate pattern, you see.'

'What are elaborate patterns to you? Nothing at all.'

'I ought really, I suppose, with my bad eyesight, to stick to plain knitting.'

'You'd find that very boring. Well, I'm flattered that you took my advice.'

'Don't I always take your advice, Doctor Haydock?'

'You do when it suits you,' said Dr Haydock.

'Tell me, Doctor, was it really knitting you had in mind when you gave me that advice?'

He met the twinkle in her eyes and twinkled back at her.

'How are you getting on with unravelling the murder?' he asked.

'I'm afraid my faculties aren't quite what they were,' said Miss Marple, shaking her head with a sigh.

'Nonsense,' said Dr Haydock. 'Don't tell me you haven't formed *some* conclusions.'

'Of course I have formed conclusions. Very definite ones.'

'Such as?' asked Haydock inquiringly.

'If the cocktail glass was tampered with that day—and I don't see quite how that could have been done—'

'Might have had the stuff ready in an eye-dropper,' suggested Haydock.

'You are so professional,' said Miss Marple admiringly. 'But even then it seems to me so very peculiar that nobody saw it happen.'

'Murder should not only be done, but be *seen* to be done! Is that it?'

'You know exactly what I mean,' said Miss Marple.

'That was a chance the murderer had to take,' said Haydock.

'Oh quite so. I'm not disputing *that* for a moment. But there were, I have found by inquiry and adding up the persons, at least eighteen to twenty people on the spot. It seems to me that amongst twenty people *somebody* must have seen that action occur.'

Haydock nodded. 'One would think so, certainly. But obviously no one did.'

'I wonder,' said Miss Marple thoughtfully.

'What have you got in mind exactly?'

'Well, there are three possibilities. I'm assuming that at least one person *would* have seen something. One out of twenty. I think it's only reasonable to assume that.'

'I think you're begging the question,' said Haydock, 'and I can see looming ahead one of those terrible exercises in probability where six men have white hats and six men have black and you have to work it out by mathematics how likely it is that the hats will get mixed up and in what proportion. If you start thinking about things like that you would go round the bend. Let me assure you of that!'

'I wasn't thinking of anything like that,' said Miss Marple. 'I was just thinking of what is likely—'

'Yes,' said Haydock thoughtfully, 'you're very good at that. You always have been.'

'It *is* likely, you know,' said Miss Marple, 'that out of twenty people one at least should be an observant one.'

'I give in,' said Haydock. 'Let's have the three possibilities.'

'I'm afraid I'll have to put them rather sketchily,' said Miss Marple. 'I haven't quite thought it out. Inspector Craddock, and probably Frank Cornish before him, will have questioned everybody who was there so the natural thing would be that whoever saw anything of the kind would have said so at once.'

'Is that one of the possibilities?'

'No, of course it isn't,' said Miss Marple, 'because it hasn't happened. What you have to account for is if one person *did* see something why didn't that person say so?'

'I'm listening.'

'Possibility One,' said Miss Marple, her cheeks going pink with animation. 'The person who saw it didn't realize what they had seen. That would mean, of course, that it would have to be rather a stupid person. Someone, let us say, who can use their eyes but not their brain. The sort of person who, if you asked them. "Did you see anyone put anything in Marina Gregg's glass?" would answer, "Oh, no," but if you said "Did you see anyone put their hand over the top of Marina Gregg's glass?" would say "Oh, yes, of course I did."'

Haydock laughed. 'I admit,' he said, 'that one never quite allows for the moron in our midst. All right, I grant you Possibility One. The moron saw it, the moron didn't grasp what the action meant. And the second possibility?'

'This one's very far-fetched, but I do think it *is* just a possibility. It might have been a person whose action in putting something in a glass was natural.'

'Wait, wait, explain that a little more clearly.'

'It seems to me nowadays,' said Miss Marple, 'that people are always adding things to what they eat and drink. In my young days it was considered to be very bad manners to take medicines with one's meals. It was on a par with blowing your nose at the dinner table. It just wasn't *done*. If you *had* to take pills or capsules, or a spoonful of something, you went out of the room to do so. That's not the case now. When staying with my nephew Raymond, I observed some of his guests seemed to arrive with quite a quantity of little bottles of pills and tablets. They take them with food, or before food, or after food. They keep aspirins and such things in their handbags and take them the whole time—with cups of tea or with their after-dinner coffee. You understand what I mean?'

'Oh, yes,' said Dr Haydock, 'I've got your meaning now and it's interesting. You mean that someone—' He stopped. 'Let me have it in your own words.'

'I meant,' said Miss Marple, 'that it would be quite possible, audacious but possible, for someone to pick up that glass which as soon as it was in his or her hand, of course, would be assumed to be his or her own drink and to add whatever was added quite *openly*. In that case, you see, people wouldn't think twice of it.'

'He—or she—couldn't be sure of that, though,' Haydock pointed out.

'No,' agreed Miss Marple, 'it would be a gamble, a risk—but it *could* happen. And then,' she went on, 'there's the third possibility.'

'Possibility One, a moron,' said the doctor. 'Possibility Two, a gambler—what's Possibility Three?'

'Somebody saw what happened, and has held their tongue deliberately.'

Haydock frowned. 'For what reason?' he asked. 'Are you suggesting blackmail? If so—'

'If so,' said Miss Marple, 'it's a very dangerous thing to do.'

'Yes, indeed.' He looked sharply at the placid old lady with the white fleecy garment on her lap. 'Is the third possibility the one you consider the most probable one?'

'No,' said Miss Marple, 'I wouldn't go so far as that. I have, at the moment, insufficient grounds. Unless,' she added carefully, 'someone else gets killed.'

'Do you think someone else is going to get killed?'

'I hope not,' said Miss Marple. 'I trust and pray not. But it so often happens, Doctor Haydock. That's the sad and frightening thing. It so often happens.'

CHAPTER 17

Ella put down the telephone receiver, smiled to herself and came out of the public telephone box. She was pleased with herself.

'Chief-Inspector God Almighty Craddock!' she said to herself. 'I'm twice as good as he is at the job. Variations on the theme of: "Fly, all is discovered!"'

She pictured to herself with a good deal of pleasure the reactions recently suffered by the person at the other end of the line. That faint menacing whisper coming through the receiver. '*I saw you . . .*'

She laughed silently, the corners of her mouth curving up in a feline cruel line. A student of psychology might have watched her with some interest. Never until the last few days had she had this feeling of power. She was hardly aware herself of how much the heady intoxication of it affected her . . .

'Damn that old woman,' thought Ella. She could feel Mrs Bantry's eyes following her as she walked up the drive.

A phrase came into her head for no particular reason.

The pitcher goes to the well once too often . . .

Nonsense. Nobody could suspect that it was she who had whispered those menacing words . . .

She sneezed.

'Damn this hay-fever,' said Ella Zielinsky.

When she came into her office, Jason Rudd was standing by the window.

He wheeled round.

'I couldn't think where you were.'

'I had to go and speak to the gardener. There were—' she broke off as she caught sight of his face.

She asked sharply: 'What is it?'

His eyes seemed set deeper in his face than ever. All the gaiety of the clown was gone. This was a man under strain. She had seen him under strain before but never looking like this.

She said again: 'What is it?'

He held a sheet of paper out to her. 'It's the analysis of that coffee. The coffee that Marina complained about and wouldn't drink.'

'You sent it to be analysed?' She was startled. 'But you poured it away down the sink. I saw you.'

His wide mouth curled up in a smile. 'I'm pretty good at sleight of hand, Ella,' he said. 'You didn't know that, did you? Yes, I poured most of it away but I kept a little and I took it along to be analysed.'

She looked down at the paper in her hand.

'*Arsenic*.' She sounded incredulous.

'Yes, arsenic.'

'So Marina was right about it tasting bitter?'

'She wasn't right about that. Arsenic has no taste. But her instinct was quite right.'

'And we thought she was just being hysterical!'

'She is hysterical! Who wouldn't be? She has a woman drop dead at her feet practically. She gets threatening notes—one after another—there's not been anything today, has there?'

Ella shook her head.

'Who plants the damned things? Oh well, I suppose it's easy enough—all these open windows. Anyone could slip in.'

'You mean we ought to keep the house barred and locked? But it's such hot weather. There's a man posted in the grounds, after all.'

'Yes, and I don't want to frighten her more than she's frightened already. Threatening notes don't matter two hoots. But arsenic, Ella, arsenic's different . . .'

'Nobody could tamper with food here in the house.'

'Couldn't they, Ella? Couldn't they?'

'Not without being seen. No unauthorized person—'

He interrupted.

'People will do things for money, Ella.'

'Hardly murder!'

'Even that. And they mightn't realize it *was* murder . . . The servants . . .'

'I'm sure the servants are all right.'

'Giuseppe now. I doubt if I'd trust Giuseppe very far if it came to the question of money . . . He's been with us some time, of course, but—'

'Must you torture yourself like this, Jason?'

He flung himself down in the chair. He leaned forward, his long arms hanging down between his knees.

'What to do?' he said slowly and softly. 'My God, what to do?'

Ella did not speak. She sat there watching him.

'She was happy here,' said Jason. He was speaking more to himself than to Ella. He stared down between his knees at the carpet. If he had looked up, the expression on her face might perhaps have surprised him.

'She was happy,' he said again. 'She hoped to be happy and she *was* happy. She was saying so that day, the day Mrs What's-her-name—'

'Bantry?'

'Yes. The day Mrs Bantry came to tea. She said it was "so peaceful". She said that at last she'd found a place where she could settle down and be happy and feel secure. My goodness, secure!'

'Happy ever after?' Ella's voice held a slight tone of irony. 'Yes, put like that, it sounds just like a fairy story.'

'At any rate she believed it.'

'But you didn't,' said Ella. 'You never thought it *would* be like that?'

Jason Rudd smiled. 'No. I didn't go the whole hog. But I did think that for a while, a year—two years—there might be a period of calm and content. It might have made a new woman of her. It might have given her confidence in herself. She can be happy, you know. When she is happy she's like a child. Just like a child. And now—*this* had to happen to her.'

Ella moved restlessly. 'Things have to happen to all of us,' she said brusquely. 'That's the way life is. You just have

213

to take it. Some of us can, some of us can't. She's the kind
that can't.'

She sneezed.

'Your hay-fever bad again?'

'Yes. By the way, Giuseppe's gone to London.'

Jason looked faintly surprised.

'To London? Why?'

'Some kind of family trouble. He's got relations in Soho,
and one of them's desperately ill. He went to Marina about
it and she said it was all right, so I gave him the day off.
He'll be back sometime tonight. You don't mind, do you?'

'No,' said Jason, 'I don't mind . . .'

He got up and walked up and down.

'If I could take her away . . . now . . . at once.'

'Scrap the picture? But just think—'

His voice rose.

'I can't think of anything but Marina. Don't you understand? She's in danger. That's all I can think about.'

She opened her mouth impulsively, then closed it.

She gave another muffled sneeze and rose.

'I'd better get my atomizer.'

She left the room and went to her bedroom, a word
echoing in her mind.

Marina . . . Marina . . . Marina . . . Always Marina . . .

Fury rose up in her. She stilled it. She went into the
bathroom and picked up the spray she used.

She inserted the nozzle into one nostril and squeezed.

The warning came a second too late . . . Her brain
recognized the unfamiliar odour of bitter almonds . . . but
not in time to paralyse the squeezing fingers.

CHAPTER 18

Frank Cornish replaced the receiver.

'Miss Brewster is out of London for the day,' he announced.

'Is she now?' said Craddock.

'Do you think she—'

'I don't know. I shouldn't think so, but I don't know. Ardwyck Fenn?'

'Out. I left word for him to ring you. And Margot Bence, Personality Photographer, has got an assignment somewhere in the country. Her pansy partner didn't know where—or said he didn't. And the butler's hooked it to London.'

'I wonder,' said Craddock thoughtfully, 'if the butler has hooked it for good. I always suspect dying relatives. Why was he suddenly anxious to go to London today?'

'He could have put the cyanide in the atomizer easily enough before he left.'

'Anybody could.'

'But I think he's indicated. It could hardly be someone from outside.'

'Oh, yes, it could. You'd have to judge your moment. You could leave a car in one of the side drives, wait until

215

everyone is in the dining-room, say, and slip in through a window and upstairs. The shrubberies come close up to the house.'

'Damn' risky.'

'This murderer doesn't mind taking risks, you know. That's been apparent all along.'

'We've had a man on duty in the grounds.'

'I know. One man wasn't enough. So long as it was a question of these anonymous letters I didn't feel so much urgency. Marina Gregg herself is being well guarded. It never occurred to me that anyone else was in danger. I—'

The telephone rang. Cornish took the call.

'It's the Dorchester. Mr Ardwyck Fenn is on the line.'

He proffered the receiver to Craddock who took it.

'Mr Fenn? This is Craddock here.'

'Ah, yes. I heard you had rung me. I have been out all day.'

'I am sorry to tell you, Mr Fenn, that Miss Zielinsky died this morning—of cyanide poisoning.'

'Indeed? I am shocked to hear it. An accident? Or not an accident?'

'Not an accident. Prussic acid had been put in an atomizer she was in the habit of using.'

'I see. Yes, I see . . .' There was a short pause. 'And why, may I ask, should you ring me about this distressing occurrence?'

'You knew Miss Zielinsky, Mr Fenn?'

'Certainly I knew her. I have known her for some years. But she was not an intimate friend.'

'We hoped that you could, perhaps, assist us?'

'In what way?'

'We wondered if you could suggest any motive for her death. She is a stranger in this country. We know very little about her friends and associates and the circumstances of her life.'

'I would suggest that Jason Rudd is the person to question about that.'

'Naturally. We have done so. But there might be an off-chance that you might know something about her that he does not.'

'I'm afraid that is not so. I know next to nothing about Ella Zielinsky except that she was a most capable young woman, and first-class at her job. About her private life I know nothing at all.'

'So you have no suggestions to make?'

Craddock was ready for the decisive negative, but to his surprise it did not come. Instead there was a pause. He could hear Ardwyck Fenn breathing rather heavily at the other end.

'Are you still there, Chief-Inspector?'

'Yes, Mr Fenn. I'm here.'

'I have decided to tell you something that may be of assistance to you. When you hear what it is, you will realize that I have every reason to keep it to myself. But I judge that in the end that might be unwise. The facts are these. A couple of days ago I received a telephone call. A voice spoke to me in a whisper. It said—I am quoting now—*I saw you . . . I saw you put the tablets in the glass . . . You didn't know there had been an eye-witness, did you? That's all for now—very soon you will be told what you have to do.*'

Craddock uttered an ejaculation of astonishment.

'Surprising, was it not, Mr Craddock? I will assure you categorically that the accusation was entirely unfounded. I did *not* put tablets in anybody's glass. I defy anyone to prove that I did. The suggestion is utterly absurd. But it would seem, would it not, that Miss Zielinsky was embarking on blackmail.'

'You recognized her voice?'

'You cannot recognize a whisper. But it was Ella Zielinsky all right.'

'How do you know?'

'The whisperer sneezed heavily before ringing off. I knew that Miss Zielinsky suffered from hay-fever.'

'And you think—what?'

'I think that Miss Zielinsky got hold of the wrong person at her first attempt. It seems to me possible that she was more successful later. Blackmail can be a dangerous game.'

Craddock pulled himself together.

'I must thank you for your statement, Mr Fenn. As a matter of form, I shall have to check upon your movements today.'

'Naturally. My chauffeur will be able to give you precise information.'

Craddock rang off and repeated what Fenn had said. Cornish whistled.

'Either that lets him out completely. Or else—'

'Or else it's a magnificent piece of bluff. It could be. He's the kind of man who has the nerve for it. If there's the least chance that Ella Zielinsky left a record of her suspicions, then this taking of the bull by the horns is a magnificent bluff.'

'And his alibi?'

'We've come across some very good faked alibis in our time,' said Craddock. 'He could afford to pay a good sum for one.'

It was past midnight when Giuseppe returned to Gossington. He took a taxi from Much Benham, as the last train on the branch line to St Mary Mead had gone.

He was in very good spirits. He paid off the taxi at the gate, and took a short cut through the shrubbery. He opened the back door with his key. The house was dark and silent. Giuseppe shut and bolted the door. As he turned to the stair which led to his own comfortable suite of bed and bath, he noticed that there was a draught. A window open somewhere, perhaps. He decided not to bother. He went upstairs smiling and fitted a key into his door. He always kept his suite locked. As he turned the key and pushed the door open, he felt the pressure of a hard round ring in his back. A voice said, 'Put your hands up and don't scream.'

Giuseppe threw his hands up quickly. He was taking no chances. Actually there was no chance to take.

The trigger was pressed—once—twice.

Giuseppe fell forward . . .

Bianca lifted her head from her pillow.

Was that a shot . . . She was almost sure she had heard a shot . . . She waited some minutes. Then she decided she had been mistaken and lay down again.

CHAPTER 19

'It's too dreadful,' said Miss Knight. She put down her parcels and gasped for breath.

'Something has happened?' asked Miss Marple.

'I really don't like to tell you about it, dear, I really don't. It might be a shock to you.'

'If you don't tell me,' said Miss Marple, 'somebody else will.'

'Dear, dear, that's true enough,' said Miss Knight. 'Yes, that's terribly true. Everybody talks too much, they say. And I'm sure there's a lot in that. I never repeat anything myself. Very careful I am.'

'You were saying,' said Miss Marple, 'that something rather terrible had happened?'

'It really quite bowled me over,' said Miss Knight. 'Are you sure you don't feel the draught from that window, dear?'

'I like a little fresh air,' said Miss Marple.

'Ah, but we mustn't catch cold, must we?' said Miss Knight archly. 'I'll tell you what. I'll just pop out and make you a nice egg-nog. We'd like that, wouldn't we?'

'I don't know whether *you* would like it,' said Miss Marple. '*I* should be delighted for you to have it if you would like it.'

'Now, now,' said Miss Knight, shaking her finger, 'so fond of our joke, aren't we?'

'But you were going to tell me something,' said Miss Marple.

'Well, you mustn't worry about it,' said Miss Knight, 'and you mustn't let it make you nervous in any way, because I'm sure it's nothing to do with *us*. But with all these American gangsters and things like that, well I suppose it's nothing to be surprised about.'

'Somebody else has been killed,' said Miss Marple, 'is that it?'

'Oh, that's very sharp of you, dear. I don't know what should put such a thing into your head.'

'As a matter of fact,' said Miss Marple thoughtfully, 'I've been expecting it.'

'Oh, really!' exclaimed Miss Knight.

'Somebody always sees something,' said Miss Marple, 'only sometimes it takes a little while for them to realize what it is they have seen. Who is it who's dead?'

'The Italian butler. He was shot last night.'

'I see,' said Miss Marple thoughtfully. 'Yes, very likely, of course, but I should have thought that he'd have realized before now the importance of what he saw—'

'Really!' exclaimed Miss Knight. 'You talk as though you knew all about it. Why should he have been killed?'

'I expect,' said Miss Marple, thoughtfully, 'that he tried to blackmail somebody.'

221

'He went to London yesterday, they say.'

'Did he now,' said Miss Marple, 'that's very interesting, and suggestive too, I think.'

Miss Knight departed to the kitchen intent on the concoction of nourishing beverages. Miss Marple remained sitting thoughtfully till disturbed by the loud aggressive humming of the vacuum cleaner, assisted by Cherry's voice singing the latest favourite ditty of the moment, 'I Said to You and You Said to Me'.

Miss Knight popped her head round the kitchen door.

'Not quite so much noise, please, Cherry,' she said. 'You don't want to disturb Miss Marple, do you? You mustn't be thoughtless, you know.'

She shut the kitchen door again as Cherry remarked, either to herself or the world at large, 'And who said you could call me Cherry, you old jelly-bag?' The vacuum continued to whine while Cherry sang in a more subdued voice. Miss Marple called in a high clear voice:

'Cherry, come here a minute.'

Cherry switched off the vacuum and opened the drawing-room door.

'I didn't mean to disturb you by singing, Miss Marple.'

'Your singing is much pleasanter than the horrid noise that vacuum makes,' said Miss Marple, 'but I know one has to go with the times. It would be no use on earth asking any of you young people to use the dustpan and brush in the old-fashioned way.'

'What, get down on my knees with a dustpan and brush?' Cherry registered alarm and surprise.

'Quite unheard of, I know,' said Miss Marple. 'Come in

and shut the door. I called you because I wanted to talk to you.'

Cherry obeyed and came towards Miss Marple looking inquiringly at her.

'We've not much time,' said Miss Marple. 'That old— Miss Knight I mean—will come in any moment with an egg drink of some kind.'

'Good for you, I expect. It'll pep you up,' said Cherry encouragingly.

'Had you heard,' asked Miss Marple, 'that the butler at Gossington Hall was shot last night?'

'What, the wop?' demanded Cherry.

'Yes. His name is Giuseppe, I understand.'

'No,' said Cherry, 'I hadn't heard *that*. I heard that Mr Rudd's secretary had a heart attack yesterday, and somebody said she was actually dead—but I suspect that was just a rumour. Who told you about the butler?'

'Miss Knight came back and told me.'

'Of course I haven't seen anyone to speak to this morning,' said Cherry, 'not before coming along here. I expect the news has only just got round. Was he bumped off?' she demanded.

'That seems to be assumed,' said Miss Marple, 'whether rightly or wrongly I don't quite know.'

'This is a wonderful place for talk,' said Cherry. 'I wonder if Gladys got to see him or not,' she added thoughtfully.

'Gladys?'

'Oh, a sort of friend of mine. She lives a few doors away. Works in the canteen at the studios.'

'And she talked to you about Giuseppe?'

'Well, there was something that struck her as a bit funny and she was going to ask him what he thought about it. But if you ask me it was just an excuse—she's a bit sweet on him. Of course he's quite handsome and Italians do have a way with them—I told her to be careful about him, though. You know what Italians are.'

'He went to London yesterday,' said Miss Marple, 'and only returned in the evening, I understand.'

'I wonder if she managed to get to see him before he went?'

'Why did she want to see him, Cherry?'

'It was just something which she felt was a bit funny,' said Cherry.

Miss Marple looked at her inquiringly. She was able to take the word 'funny' at the valuation it usually had for the Gladyses of the neighbourhood.

'She was one of the girls who helped at the party there,' explained Cherry. 'The day of the fête. You know, when Mrs Badcock got hers.'

'Yes?' Miss Marple was looking more alert than ever, much as a fox terrier might look at a waiting rat-hole.

'And there was something that she saw that struck her as a bit funny.'

'Why didn't she go to the police about it?'

'Well, she didn't really think it meant anything, you see,' explained Cherry. 'Anyway she thought she'd better ask Mr Giuseppe first.'

'What was it that she saw that day?'

'Frankly,' said Cherry, 'what she told me seemed nonsense! I've wondered, perhaps, if she was just putting me off—and what she was going to see Mr Giuseppe about was something quite different.'

'What *did* she say?' Miss Marple was patient and pursuing.

Cherry frowned. 'She was talking about Mrs Badcock and the cocktail and she said she was quite near her at the time. And she said she did it herself.'

'Did what herself?'

'Spilt her cocktail all down her dress, and ruined it.'

'You mean it was clumsiness?'

'No, not clumsiness. Gladys said she did it on *purpose*— that she *meant* to do it. Well, I mean, that doesn't make sense, does it, however you look at it?'

Miss Marple shook her head, perplexed. 'No,' she said. 'Certainly not—no, I can't see any sense in that.'

'She'd got on a new dress too,' said Cherry. 'That's how the subject came up. Gladys wondered whether she'd be able to buy it. Said it ought to clean all right but she didn't like to go and ask Mr Badcock herself. She's very good at dressmaking, Gladys is, and she said it was lovely stuff. Royal blue artificial taffeta; and she said even if the stuff *was* ruined where the cocktail stained it, she could take out a seam—half a breadth say—because it was one of those full skirts.'

Miss Marple considered this dressmaking problem for a moment and then set it aside.

'But you think your friend Gladys might have been keeping something back?'

'Well, I just wondered because I don't see if that's all she saw—Heather Badcock deliberately spilling her cocktail over herself—I don't see that there'd be anything to ask Mr Giuseppe *about*, do you?'

'No, I don't,' said Miss Marple. She sighed. 'But it's always interesting when one doesn't see,' she added. 'If you don't see what a thing means you must be looking at it wrong way round, unless of course you haven't got full information. Which is probably the case here.' She sighed. 'It's a pity she didn't go straight to the police.'

The door opened and Miss Knight bustled in holding a tall tumbler with a delicious pale yellow froth on top.

'Now here you are, dear,' she said, 'a nice little treat. We're going to enjoy this.'

She pulled forward a little table and placed it beside her employer. Then she turned a glance on Cherry. 'The vacuum cleaner,' she said coldly, 'is left in a most difficult position in the hall. I nearly fell over it. *Anyone* might have an accident.'

'Righty-ho,' said Cherry. 'I'd better get on with things.' She left the room.

'Really,' said Miss Knight, 'that Mrs Baker! I'm continually having to speak to her about something or other. Leaving vacuum cleaners all over the place and coming in here chattering to you when you want to be quiet.'

'I called her in,' said Miss Marple. 'I wanted to speak to her.'

'Well, I hope you mentioned the way the beds are made,' said Miss Knight. 'I was quite shocked when I came to turn down your bed last night. I had to make it all over again.'

'That was very kind of you,' said Miss Marple.

226

'Oh, I never grudge being helpful,' said Miss Knight. 'That's why I'm here, isn't it. To make a certain person we know as comfortable and happy as possible. Oh dear, dear,' she added, 'you've pulled out a lot of your knitting again.'

Miss Marple leaned back and closed her eyes. 'I'm going to have a little rest,' she said. 'Put the glass here—thank you. And please don't come in and disturb me for at least three-quarters of an hour.'

'Indeed I won't, dear,' said Miss Knight. 'And I'll tell that Mrs Baker to be very quiet.'

She bustled out purposefully.

The good-looking young American glanced round him in a puzzled way.

The ramifications of the housing estate perplexed him.

He addressed himself politely to an old lady with white hair and pink cheeks who seemed to be the only human being in sight.

'Excuse me, ma'am, but could you tell me where to find Blenheim Close?'

The old lady considered him for a moment. He had just begun to wonder if she was deaf, and had prepared himself to repeat his demand in a louder voice, when she spoke.

'Along here to the right, then turn left, second to the right again, and straight on. What number do you want?'

'No. 16.' He consulted a small piece of paper. 'Gladys Dixon.'

'That's right,' said the old lady. 'But I believe she works

at the Hellingforth Studios. In the canteen. You'll find her there if you want her.'

'She didn't turn up this morning,' explained the young man. 'I want to get hold of her to come up to Gossington Hall. We're very shorthanded there today.'

'Of course,' said the old lady. 'The butler was shot last night, wasn't he?'

The young man was slightly staggered by this reply.

'I guess news gets round pretty quickly in these parts,' he said.

'It does indeed,' said the old lady. 'Mr Rudd's secretary died of some kind of seizure yesterday, too, I understand.' She shook her head. 'Terrible. Quite terrible. What are we coming to?'

CHAPTER 20

A little later in the day yet another visitor found his way to 16 Blenheim Close. Detective-Sergeant William (Tom) Tiddler.

In reply to his sharp knock on the smart yellow painted door, it was opened to him by a girl of about fifteen. She had long straggly fair hair and was wearing tight black pants and an orange sweater.

'Miss Gladys Dixon live here?'

'You want Gladys? You're unlucky. She isn't here.'

'Where is she? Out for the evening?'

'No. She's gone away. Bit of a holiday like.'

'Where's she gone to?'

'That's telling,' said the girl.

Tom Tiddler smiled at her in his most ingratiating manner. 'May I come in? Is your mother at home?'

'Mum's out at work. She won't be in until half past seven. But she can't tell you any more than I can. Gladys has gone off for a holiday.'

'Oh, I see. When did she go?'

'This morning. All of a sudden like. Said she'd got the chance of a free trip.'

'Perhaps you wouldn't mind giving me her address.'

The fair-haired girl shook her head. 'Haven't got an address,' she said. 'Gladys said she'd send us her address as soon as she knew where she was going to stay. As like as not she won't though,' she added. 'Last summer she went to Newquay and never sent us as much as a postcard. She's slack that way and besides, she says, why do mothers have to bother all the time?'

'Did somebody stand her this holiday?'

'Must have,' said the girl. 'She's pretty hard up at the moment. Went to the sales last week.'

'And you've no idea at all who gave her this trip or—er—paid for her going there?'

The fair girl bristled suddenly.

'Now don't get any wrong ideas. Our Gladys isn't that sort. She and her boyfriend may like to go to the same place for holidays in August, but there's nothing wrong about it. She pays for herself. So don't you get ideas, mister.'

Tiddler said meekly that he wouldn't get ideas but he would like the address if Gladys Dixon should send a postcard.

He returned to the station with the result of his various inquiries. From the studios, he had learnt that Gladys Dixon had rung up that day and said she wouldn't be able to come to work for about a week. He had also learned some other things.

'No end of a shemozzle there's been there lately,' he said. 'Marina Gregg's been having hysterics most days. Said some coffee she was given was poisoned. Said it tasted bitter. Awful state of nerves she was in. Her husband took it and threw it down the sink and told her not to make so much fuss.'

'Yes?' said Craddock. It seemed plain there was more to come.

'But word went round as Mr Rudd didn't throw it all away. He kept some and had it analysed and it *was* poison.'

'It sounds to me,' said Craddock, 'very unlikely. I'll have to ask him about that.'

Jason Rudd was nervous, irritable.

'Surely, Inspector Craddock,' he said, 'I was only doing what I had a perfect right to do.'

'If you suspected anything was wrong with that coffee, Mr Rudd, it would have been much better if you'd turned it over to us.'

'The truth of it is that I didn't suspect for a moment that anything was wrong with it.'

'In spite of your wife saying that it tasted odd?'

'Oh, that!' A faintly rueful smile came to Rudd's face. 'Ever since the date of the fête everything that my wife has eaten or drunk has tasted odd. What with that and the threatening notes that have been coming—'

'There have been more of them?'

'Two more. One through the window down there. The other one was slipped in the letter-box. Here they are if you would like to see them.'

Craddock looked. They were printed, as the first one had been. One ran:

It won't be long now. Prepare yourself.

The other had a rough drawing of a skull and crossbones and below it was written: *This means you, Marina.*

Craddock's eyebrows rose.

'Very childish,' he said.

'Meaning you discount them as dangerous?'

'Not at all,' said Craddock. 'A murderer's mind usually is childish. You've really no idea at all, Mr Rudd, who sent these?'

'Not the least,' said Jason. 'I can't help feeling it's more like a macabre joke than anything else. It seemed to me perhaps—' he hesitated.

'Yes, Mr Rudd?'

'It could be somebody local, perhaps, who—who had been excited by the poisoning on the day of the fête. Someone perhaps, who has a grudge against the acting profession. There are rural pockets where acting is considered to be one of the devil's weapons.'

'Meaning that you think Miss Gregg is not actually threatened? But what about this business of the coffee?'

'I don't even know how you got to hear about that,' said Rudd with some annoyance.

Craddock shook his head.

'Everyone's talked about that. It always comes to one's ears sooner or later. But you should have come to us. Even when you got the result of the analysis you didn't let us know, did you?'

'No,' said Jason. 'No, I didn't. But I had other things to think about. Poor Ella's death for one thing. And now this business of Giuseppe. Inspector Craddock, when can I get my wife away from here? She's half frantic.'

'I can understand that. But there will be the inquests to attend.'

'You do realize that her life is still in danger?'

'I hope not. Every precaution will be taken—'

'Every precaution! I've heard that before, I think . . . I must get her away from here, Craddock. I *must*.'

Marina was lying on the chaise-longue in her bedroom, her eyes closed. She looked grey with strain and fatigue.

Her husband stood there for a moment looking at her. Her eyes opened.

'Was that that Craddock man?'

'Yes.'

'What did he come about? Ella?'

'Ella—and Giuseppe.'

Marina frowned.

'Giuseppe? Have they found out who shot him?'

'Not yet.'

'It's all a nightmare . . . Did he say we could go away?'

'He said—not yet.'

'Why not? We must. Didn't you make him see that I can't go on waiting day after day for someone to kill me. It's fantastic.'

'Every precaution will be taken.'

'They said that before. Did it stop Ella being killed?

Or Giuseppe? Don't you see, they'll get me in the end . . .
There was something in my coffee that day at the studio.
I'm sure there was . . . if only you hadn't poured it away!
If we'd kept it, we could have had it analysed or whatever
you call it. We'd have known for sure . . .'

'Would it have made you happier to know for sure?'

She stared at him, the pupils of her eyes widely dilated.

'I don't see what you mean. If they'd known for sure
that someone was trying to poison me, they'd have let us
leave here, they'd have let us get away.'

'Not necessarily.'

'But I can't go on like this! I can't . . . I can't . . . You
must help me, Jason. You must do *something*. I'm frightened. I'm so terribly frightened . . . There's an enemy here.
And I don't know who it is . . . It might be anyone—anyone.
At the studios—or here in the house. Someone who hates
me—but why? . . . Why? . . . Someone who wants me dead
. . . But who is it? Who is it? I thought—I was almost
sure—it was Ella. But now—'

'You thought it was Ella?' Jason sounded astonished.
'But why?'

'Because she hated me—oh yes she did. Don't men ever
see these things? She was madly in love with you. I don't
believe you had the least idea of it. But it can't be Ella,
because Ella's dead. Oh, Jinks, Jinks—do help me—get me
away from here—let me go somewhere safe . . . safe . . .'

She sprang up and walked rapidly up and down, turning
and twisting her hands.

The director in Jason was full of admiration for those
passionate, tortured movements. I must remember them,

234

he thought. For Hedda Gabler, perhaps? Then, with a shock, he remembered that it was his wife he was watching.

He went to her and put his arms around her.

'It's all right, Marina—all right. I'll look after you.'

'We must go away from this hateful house—at once. I hate this house—hate it.'

'Listen, we can't go away immediately.'

'Why not? Why *not*?'

'Because,' said Rudd, 'deaths cause complications . . . and there's something else to consider. Will running away do any good?'

'Of course it will. We'll get away from this person who hates me.'

'If there's anyone who hates you that much, they could follow you easily enough.'

'You mean—you mean—I shall *never* get away? I shall never be safe again?'

'Darling—it will be all right. I'll look after you. I'll keep you safe.'

She clung to him.

'Will you, Jinks? Will you see that nothing happens to me?'

She sagged against him, and he laid her down gently on the chaise-longue.

'Oh, I'm a coward,' she murmured, 'a coward . . . if I knew *who* it was—and why? . . . Get me my pills—the yellow ones—not the brown. I must have something to calm me.'

'Don't take too many, for God's sake, Marina.'

'All right—all right . . . Sometimes they don't have any effect any more . . .' She looked up in his face.

She smiled, a tender exquisite smile.

'You'll take care of me, Jinks? Swear you'll take care of me . . .'

'Always,' said Jason Rudd. 'To the bitter end.'

Her eyes opened wide.

'You looked so—so odd when you said that.'

'Did I? How did I look?'

'I can't explain. Like—like a clown laughing at something terribly sad, that no one else has seen . . .'

CHAPTER 21

It was a tired and depressed Inspector Craddock who came to see Miss Marple the following day.

'Sit down and be comfortable,' she said. 'I can see you've had a very hard time.'

'I don't like to be defeated,' said Inspector Craddock. 'Two murders within twenty-four hours. Ah well, I'm poorer at my job than I thought I was. Give me a nice cup of tea, Aunt Jane, with some thin bread and butter and soothe me with your earliest remembrances of St Mary Mead.'

Miss Marple clicked with her tongue in a sympathetic manner.

'Now it's no good talking like that, my dear boy, and I don't think bread and butter is *at all* what you want. Gentlemen, when they've had a disappointment, want something stronger than tea.'

As usual, Miss Marple said the word 'gentlemen' in the way of someone describing a foreign species.

'I should advise a good stiff whisky and soda,' she said.

'Would you really, Aunt Jane? Well, I won't say no.'

'And I shall get it for you myself,' said Miss Marple, rising to her feet.

'Oh, no, don't do that. Let me. Or what about Miss What's-her-name?'

'We don't want Miss Knight fussing about in here,' said Miss Marple. 'She won't be bringing my tea for another twenty minutes so that gives us a little peace and quiet. Clever of you to come to the window and not through the front door. Now we can have a nice quiet little time by ourselves.'

She went to a corner cupboard, opened it and produced a bottle, a syphon of soda and a glass.

'You are full of surprises,' said Dermot Craddock. 'I'd no idea that's what you kept in your corner cupboard. Are you quite sure you're not a secret drinker, Aunt Jane?'

'Now, now,' Miss Marple admonished him. 'I have never been an advocate of teetotalism. A little strong drink is always advisable on the premises in case there is a shock or an accident. Invaluable at such times. Or, of course, if a gentleman should arrive suddenly. There!' said Miss Marple, handing him her remedy with an air of quiet triumph. 'And you don't need to joke any more. Just sit quietly there and relax.'

'Wonderful wives there must have been in your young days,' said Dermot Craddock.

'I'm sure, my dear boy, you would find the young lady of the type you refer to as a very inadequate helpmeet nowadays. Young ladies were not encouraged to be intellectual and very few of them had university degrees or any kind of academic distinction.'

'There are things that are preferable to academic distinctions,' said Dermot. 'One of them is knowing when a man wants a whisky and soda and giving it to him.'

Miss Marple smiled at him affectionately.

'Come,' she said, 'tell me all about it. Or as much as you are allowed to tell me.'

'I think you probably know as much as I do. And very likely you have something up your sleeve. How about your dogsbody, your dear Miss Knight? What about her having committed the crime?'

'Now why should Miss Knight have done such a thing?' demanded Miss Marple, surprised.

'Because she's the most unlikely person,' said Dermot. 'It so often seems to hold good when you produce your answer.'

'Not at all,' said Miss Marple with spirit. 'I have said over and over again, not only to you, my dear Dermot—if I may call you so—that it is always the *obvious* person who has done the crime. One thinks so often of the wife or the husband and so very often it *is* the wife or the husband.'

'Meaning Jason Rudd?' He shook his head. 'That man adores Marina Gregg.'

'I was speaking generally,' said Miss Marple, with dignity. 'First we had Mrs Badcock apparently murdered. One asked oneself who could have done such a thing and the first answer would naturally be the husband. So one had to examine that possibility. Then we decided that the real object of the crime was Marina Gregg and there again we have to look for the person most intimately connected with

Marina Gregg, starting as I say with the husband. Because there is no doubt about it that husbands do, very frequently, want to make away with their wives, though sometimes, of course, they only *wish* to make away with their wives and do not actually do so. But I agree with you, my dear boy, that Jason Rudd really cares with all his heart for Marina Gregg. It *might* be very clever acting, though I can hardly believe that. And one certainly cannot see a motive of any kind for his doing away with her. If he wanted to marry somebody else there could, I should say, be nothing more simple. Divorce, if I may say so, seems second nature to film stars. A practical advantage does not seem to arise either. He is not a poor man by any means. He has his own career, and is, I understand, most successful in it. So we must go farther afield. But it certainly is difficult. Yes, very difficult.'

'Yes,' said Craddock, 'it must hold particular difficulties for you because of course this film world is entirely new to you. You don't know the local scandals and animosities and all the rest of it.'

'I know a little more than you may think,' said Miss Marple. 'I have studied very closely various numbers of *Confidential*, *Film Life*, *Film Talk* and *Film Topics*.'

Dermot Craddock laughed. He couldn't help it.

'I must say,' he said, 'it tickles me to see you sitting there and telling me what your course of literature has been.'

'I found it very interesting,' said Miss Marple. 'They're not particularly well written, if I may say so. But it really is disappointing in a way that it is all so much the same as it used to be in my young days. *Modern Society* and

240

Tit Bits and all the rest of them. A lot of gossip. A lot of scandal. A great preoccupation with who is in love with whom, and all the rest of it. Really, you know, practically exactly the same sort of thing goes on in St Mary Mead. And in the Development too. Human nature, I mean, is just the same everywhere. One comes back, I think, to the question of who could have been likely to want to kill Marina Gregg, to want to so much that having failed once they sent threatening letters and made repeated attempts to do so. Someone perhaps a little—' very gently she tapped her forehead.

'Yes,' said Craddock, 'that certainly seems indicated. And of course it doesn't always show.'

'Oh, I know,' agreed Miss Marple, fervently. 'Old Mrs Pike's second boy, Alfred, *seemed* perfectly rational and normal. Almost painfully prosaic, if you know what I mean, but actually, it seems, he had the most abnormal psychology, or so I understand. Really positively dangerous. He seems quite happy and contented, so Mrs Pike told me, now that he is in Fairways Mental Home. They understand him there, and the doctors think him a most interesting case. That of course pleases him very much. Yes, it all ended quite happily, but she had one or two very near escapes.'

Craddock revolved in his mind the possibility of a parallel between someone in Marina Gregg's entourage and Mrs Pike's second son.

'The Italian butler,' continued Miss Marple, 'the one who was killed. He went to London, I understand, on the day of his death. Does anyone know what he did there—if you are allowed to tell me, that is,' she added conscientiously.

'He arrived in London at eleven-thirty in the morning,' said Craddock, 'and what he did in London nobody knows until at a quarter to two he visited his bank and made a deposit of five hundred pounds in cash. I may say that there was no confirmation of his story that he went to London to visit an ill relative or a relative who had got into trouble. None of his relatives there had seen him.'

Miss Marple nodded her head appreciatively.

'Five hundred pounds,' she said. 'Yes, that's quite an interesting sum, isn't it? I should imagine it would be the first instalment of a good many other sums, wouldn't you?'

'It looks that way,' said Craddock.

'It was probably all the ready money the person he was threatening could raise. He may even have pretended to be satisfied with that or he may have accepted it as a down payment and the victim may have promised to raise further sums in the immediate future. It seems to knock out the idea that Marina Gregg's killer could have been someone in humble circumstances who had a private vendetta against her. It would also knock out, I should say, the idea of someone who'd obtained work as a studio helper or attendant or a servant or a gardener. Unless'—Miss Marple pointed out—'such a person may have been the active agent whereas the employing agent may not have been in the neighbourhood. Hence the visit to London.'

'Exactly. We have in London Ardwyck Fenn, Lola Brewster and Margot Bence. All three were present at the party. All three of them could have met Giuseppe at an arranged meeting-place somewhere in London between the hours of eleven and a quarter to two. Ardwyck Fenn was out of his office during those hours. Lola Brewster had left her suite to go shopping. Margot Bence was not in her studio. By the way—'

'Yes?' said Miss Marple. 'Have you something to tell me?'

'You asked me,' said Dermot, 'about the children. The children that Marina Gregg adopted before she knew she could have a child of her own.'

'Yes I did.'

Craddock told her what he had learned.

'Margot Bence,' said Miss Marple softly. 'I had a feeling, you know, that it had something to do with children . . .'

'I can't believe that after all these years—'

'I know, I know. One never can. But do you really, my dear Dermot, know very much about children? Think back to your own childhood. Can't you remember some incident, some happening that caused you grief, or a passion quite incommensurate with its real importance? Some sorrow or passionate resentment that has really never been equalled since? There was such a clever book, you know, written by that brilliant writer, Mr Richard Hughes. I forget the name of it but it was about some children who had been through a hurricane. Oh yes—the hurricane in Jamaica. What made a vivid impression on them was their cat rushing madly through the house. It was the only thing they remembered. But the whole of the horror and excitement and fear that they had experienced was bound up in that one incident.'

'It's odd you should say that,' said Craddock thoughtfully.

'Why, has it made you remember something?'

'I was thinking of when my mother died. I was five I

think. Five or six. I was having dinner in the nursery, jam roll pudding. I was very fond of jam roll pudding. One of the servants came in and said to my nursery governess, "Isn't it awful? There's been an accident and Mrs Craddock has been killed." . . . Whenever I think of my mother's death, d'you know what I see?'

'What?'

'A plate with jam roll pudding on it, and I'm staring at it. Staring at it and I can see as well now as then, how the jam oozed out of it at one side. I didn't cry or say anything. I remember just sitting there as though I'd been frozen stiff, staring at the pudding. And d'you know, even now if I see in a shop or a restaurant or in anyone's house a portion of jam roll pudding, a whole wave of horror and misery and despair comes over me. Sometimes for a moment I don't remember *why*. Does that seem very crazy to you?'

'No,' said Miss Marple, 'it seems entirely natural. It's very interesting, that. It's given me a sort of idea . . .'

The door opened and Miss Knight appeared bearing the tea tray.

'Dear, dear,' she exclaimed, 'and so we've got a visitor, have we? How very nice. How do you do, Inspector Craddock. I'll just fetch another cup.'

'Don't bother,' Dermot called after her. 'I've had a drink instead.'

Miss Knight popped her head back round the door.

'I wonder—could you just come here a minute, Mr Craddock?'

Dermot joined her in the hall. She went to the dining-room and shut the door.

'You will be careful, won't you?' she said.

'Careful? In what way, Miss Knight?'

'Our old dear in there. You know, she's so interested in everything but it's not very good for her to get excited over murders and nasty things like that. We don't want her to brood and have bad dreams. She's very old and frail, and she really must lead a very sheltered life. She always has, you know. I'm sure all this talk of murders and gangsters and things like that is very, very bad for her.'

Dermot looked at her with faint amusement.

'I don't think,' he said gently, 'that anything that you or I could say about murders is likely unduly to excite or shock Miss Marple. I can assure you, my dear Miss Knight, that Miss Marple can contemplate murder and sudden death and indeed crime of all kinds with the utmost equanimity.'

He went back to the drawing-room, and Miss Knight, clucking a little in an indignant manner, followed him. She talked briskly during tea with an emphasis on political news in the paper and the most cheerful subjects she could think of. When she finally removed the tea tray and shut the door behind her, Miss Marple drew a deep breath.

'At last we've got some peace,' she said. 'I hope I shan't murder that woman some day. Now listen, Dermot, there are some things I want to know.'

'Yes? What are they?'

'I want to go over very carefully what happened on the

day of the fête. Mrs Bantry has arrived, and the vicar shortly after her. Then come Mr and Mrs Badcock, and on the stairs at that time were the mayor and his wife, this man Ardwyck Fenn, Lola Brewster, a reporter from the *Herald & Argus* of Much Benham, and this photographer girl, Margot Bence. Margot Bence, you said, had her camera at an angle on the stairs, and was taking photographs of the proceedings. Have you seen any of those photographs?'

'Actually I brought one to show you.'

He took from his pocket an unmounted print. Miss Marple looked at it steadfastly. It showed Marina Gregg with Jason Rudd a little behind her to one side, Arthur Badcock, his hand to his face, looking slightly embarrassed, was standing back, whilst his wife had Marina Gregg's hand in hers and was looking up at her and talking. Marina was not looking at Mrs Badcock. She was staring over her head looking, it seemed, full into the camera, or possibly just slightly to the left of it.

'*Very* interesting,' said Miss Marple. 'I've had descriptions, you know, of what this look was on her face. A frozen look. Yes, that describes it quite well. A look of doom. I'm not really so sure about that. It's more a kind of paralysis of feeling rather than apprehension of doom. Don't you think so? I wouldn't say it was actually fear, would you, although fear of course might take you that way. It might paralyse you. But I don't think it was fear. I think rather that it was *shock*. Dermot, my dear boy, I want you to tell me, if you've got notes of it, what exactly Heather Badcock said to Marina Gregg on that occasion.

I know roughly the gist of it, of course, but how near can you get to the actual *words*. I suppose you had accounts of it from different people.'

Dermot nodded.

'Yes. Let me see. Your friend, Mrs Bantry, then Jason Rudd and I think Arthur Badcock. As you say they varied a little in wording, but the gist of them was the same.'

'I know. It's the variations that I want. I think it might help us.'

'I don't see how,' said Dermot, 'though perhaps you do. Your friend, Mrs Bantry, was probably the most definite on the point. As far as I remember—wait—I carry a good many of my jottings around with me.'

He took out a small note-book from his pocket, looked through it to refresh his memory.

'I haven't got the exact words here,' he said, 'but I made a rough note. Apparently Mrs Badcock was very cheerful, rather arch, and delighted with herself. She said something like "I can't tell you how wonderful this is for me. You won't remember but years ago in Bermuda—I got up from bed when I had chicken pox and came along to see you and you gave me an autograph and it's one of the proudest days of my life which I have never forgotten."'

'I see,' said Miss Marple, 'she mentioned the place but not the date, did she?'

'Yes.'

'And what did Rudd say?'

'Jason Rudd? He said that Mrs Badcock told his wife that she'd got up from bed when she had the 'flu and had come to meet Marina and she still had her autograph. It was a shorter account than your friend's but the gist of it was the same.'

'Did he mention the time and place?'

'No. I don't think he did. I think he said roughly that it was some ten or twelve years ago.'

'I see. And what about Mr Badcock?'

'Mr Badcock said that Heather was extremely excited and anxious to meet Marina Gregg, that she was a great fan of Marina Gregg's and that she'd told him that once when she was ill as a girl she managed to get up and meet Miss Gregg and get her autograph. He didn't go into any close particulars, as it was evidently in the days before he was married to his wife. He impressed me as not thinking the incident of much importance.'

'I see,' said Miss Marple. 'Yes, I see . . .'

'And what do you see?' asked Craddock.

'Not quite as much as I'd like to yet,' said Miss Marple, honestly, 'but I have a sort of feeling if I only knew why she'd ruined her new dress—'

'Who—Mrs Badcock?'

'Yes. It seems to me such a very odd thing—such an inexplicable one unless—of course—Dear me, I think I must be *very* stupid!'

Miss Knight opened the door and entered, switching the light on as she did so.

'I think we want a little light in here,' she said brightly.

'Yes,' said Miss Marple, 'you are so right, Miss Knight. That is exactly what we did want. A little light. I think, you know, that at last we've got it.'

The tête-à-tête seemed ended and Craddock rose to his feet.

'There only remains one thing,' he said, 'and that is for you to tell me just what particular memory from your own past is agitating your mind now.'

'Everyone always teases me about that,' said Miss Marple, 'but I must say that I was reminded just for a moment of the Lauristons' parlourmaid.'

'The Lauristons' parlourmaid?' Craddock looked completely mystified.

'She had, of course, to take messages on the telephone,' said Miss Marple, 'and she wasn't very good at it. She used to get the general *sense* right, if you know what I mean, but the way she wrote it down used to make quite nonsense of it sometimes. I suppose really, because her grammar was so bad. The result was that some very unfortunate incidents occurred. I remember one in particular. A Mr Burroughs, I think it was, rang up and said he had been to see Mr Elvaston about the fence being broken down but he said that the fence wasn't his business at all to repair. It was on the other side of the property and he said he would like to know if that was really the case before proceeding further as it would depend on whether he was liable or not and it was important for him to know the proper lie of the land before instructing solicitors. A very obscure message, as you see. It confused rather than enlightened.'

'If you're talking about parlourmaids,' said Miss Knight with a little laugh, 'that must have been a *very* long time ago. I've never heard of a parlourmaid for many years now.'

'It was a good many years ago,' said Miss Marple, 'but nevertheless human nature was very much the same then as it is now. Mistakes were made for very much the same reasons. Oh dear,' she added, 'I *am* thankful that that girl is safely in Bournemouth.'

'The girl? What girl?' asked Dermot.

'That girl who did dressmaking and went up to see Giuseppe that day. What was her name—Gladys something.'

'Gladys Dixon?'

'Yes, that's the name.'

'She's in *Bournemouth*, do you say? How on earth do you know that?'

'I know,' said Miss Marple, 'because I sent her there.'

'What?' Dermot stared at her. 'You? Why?'

'I went out to see her,' said Miss Marple, 'and I gave her some money and told her to take a holiday and not to write home.'

'Why on earth did you do that?'

'Because I didn't want her to be killed, of course,' said Miss Marple, and blinked at him placidly.

CHAPTER 22

'Such a sweet letter from Lady Conway,' Miss Knight said two days later as she deposited Miss Marple's breakfast tray. 'You remember my telling you about her? Just a little, you know—' she tapped her forehead—'wanders sometimes. And her memory's bad. Can't recognize her relations always and tells them to go away.'

'That might be shrewdness really,' said Miss Marple, 'rather than a loss of memory.'

'Now, now,' said Miss Knight, 'aren't we being naughty to make suggestions like that? She's spending the winter at the Belgrave Hotel at Llandudno. *Such* a nice residential hotel. Splendid grounds and a very nice glassed-in terrace. She's most anxious for me to come and join her there.' She sighed.

Miss Marple sat herself upright in bed.

'But please,' she said, 'if you are wanted—if you are needed there and would like to go—'

'No, no, I couldn't hear of it,' cried Miss Knight. 'Oh, no, I never meant anything like that. Why, what would Mr Raymond West say? He explained to me that being here might turn out to be a permanency. I should *never* dream of not fulfilling my obligations. I was only just mentioning the fact in passing, so don't worry, dear,' she added, patting Miss Marple on the shoulder. 'We're not going to be deserted! No, no, indeed we're not! We're going to be looked after and cosseted and made very happy and comfortable always.'

She went out of the room. Miss Marple sat with an air of determination, staring at her tray and failing to eat anything. Finally she picked up the receiver of the telephone and dialled with vigour.

'Dr Haydock?'

'Yes?'

'Jane Marple here.'

'And what's the matter with you? In need of my professional services?'

'No,' said Miss Marple. 'But I want to see you as soon as possible.'

When Dr Haydock came, he found Miss Marple still in bed waiting for him.

'You look the picture of health,' he complained.

'That is why I wanted to see you,' said Miss Marple. 'To tell you that I am perfectly well.'

'An unusual reason for sending for the doctor.'

'I'm quite strong, I'm quite fit, and it's absurd to have anybody living in the house. So long as someone comes every day and does the cleaning and all that I don't see any need at all for having someone living here permanently.'

'I dare say you don't, but I do,' said Dr Haydock.

'It seems to me you're turning into a regular old fuss-budget,' said Miss Marple unkindly.

'And don't call me names!' said Dr Haydock. 'You're a very healthy woman for your age; you were pulled down a bit by bronchitis which isn't good for the elderly. But to stay alone in a house at your age is a risk. Supposing you fall down the stairs one evening or fall out of bed or slip in the bath. There you'd lie and nobody'd know about it.'

'One can imagine anything,' said Miss Marple. 'Miss Knight might fall down the stairs and I'd fall over her rushing out to see what had happened.'

'It's no good your bullying me,' said Dr Haydock. 'You're an old lady and you've got to be looked after in a proper manner. If you don't like this woman you've got, change her and get somebody else.'

'That's not always so easy,' said Miss Marple.

'Find some old servant of yours, someone that you like, and who's lived with you before. I can see this old hen irritates you. She'd irritate me. There must be some old servant somewhere. That nephew of yours is one of the best-selling authors of the day. He'd make it worth her while if you found the right person.'

'Of course dear Raymond would do anything of that kind. He is most generous,' said Miss Marple. 'But it's not so easy to find the right person. Young people have their own lives to live, and so many of my faithful old servants, I am sorry to say, are dead.'

'Well, you're not dead,' said Dr Haydock, 'and you'll live a good deal longer if you take proper care of yourself.'

He rose to his feet.

'Well,' he said. 'No good my stopping here. You look as fit as a fiddle. I shan't waste time taking your blood pressure or feeling your pulse or asking you questions. You're thriving on all this local excitement, even if you can't get about to poke your nose in as much as you'd like to do. Goodbye, I've got to go now and do some real doctoring. Eight to ten cases of German measles, half a dozen whooping coughs, and a suspected scarlet fever as well as my regulars!'

Dr Haydock went out breezily—but Miss Marple was frowning . . . Something that he had said . . . what was it? Patients to see . . . the usual village ailments . . . village ailments? Miss Marple pushed her breakfast tray farther away with a purposeful gesture. Then she rang up Mrs Bantry.

'Dolly? Jane here. I want to ask you something. Now pay attention. Is it true that you told Inspector Craddock that Heather Badcock told Marina Gregg a long pointless story about how she had chicken pox and got up in spite of it to go and meet Marina and get her autograph?'

'That was it more or less.'

'*Chicken pox?*'

'Well, something like that. Mrs Allcock was talking to me about vodka at the time, so I wasn't really listening closely.'

'You're sure,' Miss Marple took a breath, 'that she didn't say whooping cough?'

'Whooping cough?' Mrs Bantry sounded astounded. 'Of course not. She wouldn't have had to powder her face and do it up for whooping cough.'

'I see—that's what you went by—her special mention of make-up?'

'Well, she laid stress on it—she wasn't the making-up kind. But I think you're right, it wasn't chicken pox . . . Nettlerash, perhaps.'

'You only say that,' said Miss Marple coldly, 'because you once had nettlerash yourself and couldn't go to a wedding. You're hopeless, Dolly, quite hopeless.'

She put the receiver down with a bang, cutting off Mrs Bantry's astonished protest of 'Really, Jane.'

Miss Marple made a ladylike noise of vexation like a cat sneezing to indicate profound disgust. Her mind reverted to the problem of her own domestic comfort. Faithful Florence? Could faithful Florence, that grenadier of a former parlourmaid be persuaded to leave her comfortable small house and come back to St Mary Mead to look after her erstwhile mistress? Faithful Florence had always been very devoted to her. But faithful Florence was very attached to her own little house. Miss Marple shook her head vexedly. A gay rat-tat-tat sounded at the door. On Miss Marple's calling 'Come in' Cherry entered.

'Come for your tray,' she said. 'Has anything happened? You're looking rather upset, aren't you?'

'I feel so helpless,' said Miss Marple. 'Old and helpless.'

'Don't worry,' said Cherry, picking up the tray. 'You're very far from helpless. You don't know the things I hear about you in this place! Why practically everybody in the Development knows about you now. All sorts of extra-ordinary things you've done. *They* don't think of you as the old and helpless kind. It's *she* puts it into your head.'

'She?'

Cherry gave a vigorous nod of her head backwards towards the door behind her.

'Pussy, pussy,' she said. 'Your Miss Knight. Don't you let her get you down.'

'She's very kind,' said Miss Marple, 'really *very* kind,' she added, in the tone of one who convinces herself.

'Care killed the cat, they say,' said Cherry. 'You don't want kindness rubbed into your skin, so to speak, do you?'

'Oh, well,' said Miss Marple sighing, 'I suppose we all have our troubles.'

'I should say we do,' said Cherry. 'I oughtn't to complain but I feel sometimes that if I live next door to Mrs Hartwell any longer there's going to be a regrettable incident. Sour-faced old cat, always gossiping and complaining. Jim's pretty fed up too. He had a first-class row with her last night. Just because we had The Messiah on a bit loud! You can't object to *The Messiah*, can you? I mean, it's religious.'

'Did she object?'

'She created something terrible,' said Cherry. 'Banged on the wall and shouted and one thing and another.'

'Do you have to have your music tuned in so loud?' asked Miss Marple.

'Jim likes it that way,' said Cherry. 'He says you don't get the tone unless you have full volume.'

'It might,' suggested Miss Marple, 'be a *little* trying for anyone if they *weren't* musical.'

'It's these houses being semi-detached,' said Cherry. 'Thin as anything, the walls. I'm not so keen really on all this new building, when you come to think of it. It looks all very prissy and nice but you can't express your personality without somebody being down on you like a ton of bricks.'

Miss Marple smiled at her.

'You've got a lot of personality to express, Cherry,' she said.

'D'you think so?' Cherry was pleased and she laughed. 'I wonder,' she began. Suddenly she looked embarrassed. She put down the tray and came back to the bed.

'I wonder if you'd think it cheek if I asked you something? I mean—you've only got to say "out of the question" and that's that.'

'Something you want me to do?'

'Not quite. It's those rooms over the kitchen. They're never used nowadays, are they?'

'No.'

'Used to be a gardener and wife there once, so I heard. But that's old stuff. What I wondered—what Jim and I wondered—is if we could have them. Come and live here, I mean.'

Miss Marple stared at her in astonishment.

'But your beautiful new house in the Development?'

'We're both fed up with it. We like gadgets, but you can have gadgets anywhere—get them on HP and there would be a nice lot of room here, especially if Jim could have the room over the stables. He'd fix it up like new, and he could have all his construction models there, and wouldn't have to clear them away all the time. And if we had our stereogram there too, you'd hardly hear it.'

'Are you really serious about this, Cherry?'

'Yes, I am. Jim and I, we've talked about it a lot. Jim

257

could fix things for you any time—you know, plumbing or a bit of carpentry, and I'd look after you every bit as well as your Miss Knight does. I know you think I'm a bit slap-dash—but I'd try and take trouble with the beds and the washing-up—and I'm getting quite a dab hand at cooking. Did Beef Stroganoff last night, it's quite easy, really.'

Miss Marple contemplated her.

Cherry was looking like an eager kitten—vitality and joy of life radiated from her. Miss Marple thought once more of faithful Florence. Faithful Florence would, of course, keep the house far better. (Miss Marple put no faith in Cherry's promise.) But she was at least sixty-five—perhaps more. And would she really want to be uprooted? She might accept that out of her very real devotion for Miss Marple. But did Miss Marple really want sacrifices made for her? Wasn't she already suffering from Miss Knight's conscientious devotion to duty?

Cherry, however inadequate her housework, *wanted* to come. And she had qualities that to Miss Marple at this moment seemed of supreme importance.

Warm-heartedness, vitality, and a deep interest in everything that was going on.

'I don't want, of course,' said Cherry, 'to go behind Miss Knight's back in any way.'

'Never mind about Miss Knight,' said Miss Marple, coming to a decision. 'She'll go off to someone called Lady Conway at a hotel in Llandudno—and enjoy herself thoroughly. We'll have to settle a lot of details, Cherry, and I shall want to talk to your husband—but if you really think you'd be happy . . .'

'It'll suit us down to the ground,' said Cherry. 'And you really can rely on me doing things properly. I'll even use the dustpan and brush if you like.'

Miss Marple laughed at this supreme offer.

Cherry picked up the breakfast tray again.

'I must get cracking. I got here late this morning—hearing about poor Arthur Badcock.'

'Arthur Badcock? What happened to him?'

'Haven't you heard? He's up at the police-station now,' said Cherry. 'They asked him if he'd come and "assist them with their inquiries" and you know what that always means.'

'When did this happen?' demanded Miss Marple.

'This morning,' said Cherry. 'I suppose,' she added, 'that it got out about his once having been married to Marina Gregg.'

'What!' Miss Marple sat up again. 'Arthur Badcock was once married to Marina Gregg?'

'That's the story,' said Cherry. 'Nobody had any idea of it. It was Mr Upshaw put it about. He's been to the States once or twice on business for his firm and so he knows a lot of gossip from over there. It was a long time ago, you know. Really before she'd begun her career. They were only married a year or two and then she won a film award and of course he wasn't good enough for her then, so they had one of these easy American divorces and he just faded out, as you might say. He's the fading out kind, Arthur Badcock. He wouldn't make a fuss. He changed his name and came back to England. It's all ever so long ago. You wouldn't think anything like that mattered nowadays, would you? Still, there it is. It's enough for the police to go on, I suppose.'

'Oh no,' said Miss Marple. 'Oh *no*. This mustn't happen. If I could only think what to do—Now, let me see.' She made a gesture to Cherry. 'Take the tray away, Cherry, and send Miss Knight up to me. I'm going to get up.'

Cherry obeyed. Miss Marple dressed herself with fingers that fumbled slightly. It irritated her when she found excitement of any kind affecting her. She was just hooking up her dress when Miss Knight entered.

'Did you want me? Cherry said—'

Miss Marple broke in incisively.

'Get Inch,' she said.

'I beg your pardon,' said Miss Knight, startled.

'Inch,' said Miss Marple, 'get Inch. Telephone for him to come at once.'

'Oh, oh I see. You mean the taxi people. But his name's Roberts, isn't it?'

'To me,' said Miss Marple, 'he is Inch and always will be. But anyway get him. He's to come here at once.'

'You want to go for a little drive?'

'Just get him, can you?' said Miss Marple. 'And hurry, please.'

Miss Knight looked at her doubtfully and proceeded to do as she was told.

'We are feeling all right, dear, aren't we?' she said anxiously.

'We are both feeling very well,' said Miss Marple, 'and I am feeling *particularly* well. Inertia does not suit me, and never has. A practical course of action, that is what I have been wanting for a long time.'

'Has that Mrs Baker been saying something that has upset you?'

'Nothing has upset me,' said Miss Marple. 'I feel particularly well. I am annoyed with myself for being stupid. But really, until I got a hint from Dr Haydock this morning—now I wonder if I remember rightly. Where is that medical book of mine?' She gestured Miss Knight aside and walked firmly down the stairs. She found the book she wanted on a shelf in the drawing-room. Taking it out she looked up the index, murmured, 'Page 210,' turned to the page in question, read for a few moments then nodded her head, satisfied.

'Most remarkable,' she said, 'most curious. I don't suppose anybody would ever have thought of it. I didn't myself, until the two things came together, so to speak.'

Then she shook her head, and a little line appeared between her eyes. 'If only there was *someone* . . .'

She went over in her mind the various accounts she had been given of that particular scene . . .

Her eyes widened in thought. There was someone—but would he, she wondered, be any good? One never knew with the vicar. He was quite unpredictable.

Nevertheless she went to the telephone and dialled.

'Good morning, Vicar, this is Miss Marple.'

'Oh, yes, Miss Marple—anything I can do for you?'

'I wonder if you could help me on a small point. It concerns the day of the fête when poor Mrs Badcock died. I believe you were standing quite near Miss Gregg when Mr and Mrs Badcock arrived.'

'Yes—yes—I was just before them, I think. Such a tragic day.'

'Yes, indeed. And I believe that Mrs Badcock was

recalling to Miss Gregg that they had met before in Bermuda. She had been ill in bed and had got up specially.'

'Yes, yes, I do remember.'

'And do you remember if Mrs Badcock mentioned the illness she was suffering from?'

'I think now—let me see—yes, it was measles—at least not real measles—German measles—a much less serious disease. Some people hardly feel ill at all with it. I remember my cousin Caroline . . .'

Miss Marple cut off reminiscences of Cousin Caroline by saying firmly: 'Thank you so much, Vicar,' and replacing the receiver.

There was an awed expression on her face. One of the great mysteries of St Mary Mead was what made the vicar remember certain things—only outstripped by the greater mystery of what the vicar could manage to forget!

'The taxi's here, dear,' said Miss Knight, bustling in. 'It's a very old one, and not too clean I should say. I don't really like you driving in a thing like that. You might pick up some germ or other.'

'Nonsense,' said Miss Marple. Setting her hat firmly on her head and buttoning up her summer coat, she went out to the waiting taxi.

'Good morning, Roberts,' she said.

'Good morning, Miss Marple. You're early this morning. Where do you want to go?'

'Gossington Hall, please,' said Miss Marple.

'I'd better come with you, hadn't I, dear?' said Miss Knight. 'It won't take a minute just to slip on outdoor shoes.'

'No, thank you,' said Miss Marple, firmly. 'I'm going by myself. Drive on, Inch. I mean Roberts.'

Mr Roberts drove on, merely remarking:

'Ah, Gossington Hall. Great changes there and everywhere nowadays. All that development. Never thought anything like that'd come to St Mary Mead.'

Upon arrival at Gossington Hall Miss Marple rang the bell and asked to see Mr Jason Rudd.

Giuseppe's successor, a rather shaky-looking elderly man, conveyed doubt.

'Mr Rudd,' he said, 'does not see anybody without an appointment, madam. And today especially—'

'I have no appointment,' said Miss Marple, 'but I will wait,' she added.

She stepped briskly past him into the hall and sat down on a hall chair.

'I'm afraid it will be quite impossible this morning, madam.'

'In that case,' said Miss Marple, 'I shall wait until this afternoon.'

Baffled, the new butler retired. Presently a young man came to Miss Marple. He had a pleasant manner and a cheerful, slightly American voice.

'I've seen you before,' said Miss Marple. 'In the Development. You asked me the way to Blenheim Close.'

Hailey Preston smiled good-naturedly. 'I guess you did your best, but you misdirected me badly.'

'Dear me, did I?' said Miss Marple. 'So many Closes, aren't there? Can I see Mr Rudd?'

'Why, now, that's too bad,' said Hailey Preston. 'Mr

Rudd's a busy man and he's—er—fully occupied this morning and really can't be disturbed.'

'I'm sure he's very busy,' said Miss Marple. 'I came here quite prepared to wait.'

'Why, I'd suggest now,' said Hailey Preston, 'that you should tell me what it is you want. I deal with all these things for Mr Rudd, you see. Everyone has to see me first.'

'I'm afraid,' said Miss Marple, 'that I want to see Mr Rudd himself. And,' she added, 'I shall wait here until I do.'

She settled herself more firmly in the large oak chair.

Hailey Preston hesitated, started to speak, finally turned away and went upstairs.

He returned with a large man in tweeds.

'This is Dr Gilchrist. Miss—er—'

'Miss Marple.'

'So you're Miss Marple,' said Dr Gilchrist. He looked at her with a good deal of interest.

Hailey Preston slipped away with celerity.

'I've heard about you,' said Dr Gilchrist. 'From Dr Haydock.'

'Dr Haydock is a very old friend of mine.'

'He certainly is. Now you want to see Mr Jason Rudd? Why?'

'It is necessary that I should,' said Miss Marple.

Dr Gilchrist's eyes appraised her.

'And you're camping here until you do?' he asked.

'Exactly.'

'You would, too,' said Dr Gilchrist. 'In that case I will give you a perfectly good reason why you cannot see Mr Rudd. His wife died last night in her sleep.'

'Dead!' exclaimed Miss Marple. 'How?'

'An overdose of sleeping stuff. We don't want the news to leak out to the Press for a few hours. So I'll ask you to keep this knowledge to yourself for the moment.'

'Of course. Was it an accident?'

'That is definitely my view,' said Gilchrist.

'But it could be suicide.'

'It could—but most unlikely.'

'Or someone could have given it to her?'

Gilchrist shrugged his shoulders.

'A most remote contingency. And a thing,' he added firmly, 'that would be quite impossible to prove.'

'I see,' said Miss Marple. She took a deep breath. 'I'm sorry, but it's more necessary than ever that I should see Mr Rudd.'

Gilchrist looked at her.

'Wait here,' he said.

CHAPTER 23

Jason Rudd looked up as Gilchrist entered.

'There's an old dame downstairs,' said the doctor; 'looks about a hundred. Wants to see you. Won't take no and says she'll wait. She'll wait till this afternoon, I gather, or she'll wait till this evening and she's quite capable, I should say, of spending the night here. She's got something she badly wants to say to you. I'd see her if I were you.'

Jason Rudd looked up from his desk. His face was white and strained.

'Is she mad?'

'No. Not in the least.'

'I don't see why I—Oh, all right—send her up. What does it matter?'

Gilchrist nodded, went out of the room and called to Hailey Preston.

'Mr Rudd can spare you a few minutes now, Miss Marple,' said Hailey Preston, appearing again by her side.

'Thank you. That's very kind of him,' said Miss Marple as she rose to her feet. 'Have you been with Mr Rudd long?' she asked.

'Why, I've worked with Mr Rudd for the last two and a half years. My job is public relations generally.'

'I see.' Miss Marple looked at him thoughtfully. 'You remind me very much,' she said, 'of someone I knew called Gerald French.'

'Indeed? What did Gerald French do?'

'Not very much,' said Miss Marple, 'but he was a very good talker.' She sighed. 'He had had an unfortunate past.'

'You don't say,' said Hailey Preston, slightly ill at ease. 'What kind of a past?'

'I won't repeat it,' said Miss Marple. 'He didn't like it talked about.'

Jason Rudd rose from his desk and looked with some surprise at the slender elderly lady who was advancing towards him.

'You wanted to see me?' he said. 'What can I do for you?'

'I am very sorry about your wife's death,' said Miss Marple. 'I can see it has been a great grief to you and I want you to believe that I should not intrude upon you now or offer you sympathy unless it was absolutely necessary. But there are things that need badly to be cleared up unless an innocent man is going to suffer.'

'An innocent man? I don't understand you.'

'Arthur Badcock,' said Miss Marple. 'He is with the police now, being questioned.'

'Questioned in connection with my wife's death? But that's absurd, absolutely absurd. He's never been near the place. He didn't even know her.'

'I think he knew her,' said Miss Marple. 'He was married to her once.'

'Arthur *Badcock*? But—he was—he was Heather Badcock's husband. Aren't you perhaps—' he spoke kindly and apologetically—'making a little mistake?'

'He was married to both of them,' said Miss Marple. 'He was married to your wife when she was very young, before she went into pictures.'

Jason Rudd shook his head.

'My wife was first married to a man called Alfred Beadle. He was in real estate. They were not suited and they parted almost immediately.'

'Then Alfred Beadle changed his name to Badcock,' said Miss Marple. 'He's in a real estate firm here. It's odd how some people never seem to like to change their job and want to go on doing the same thing. I expect really that's why Marina Gregg felt that he was no use to her. He couldn't have kept up with her.'

'What you've told me is most surprising.'

'I can assure you that I am not romancing or imagining things. What I am telling you is sober fact. These things get round very quickly in a village, you know, though they take a little longer,' she added, 'in reaching the Hall.'

'Well,' Jason Rudd stalled, uncertain what to say, then he accepted the position, 'and what do you want me to do for you, Miss Marple?' he asked.

'I want, if I may, to stand on the stairs at the spot where you and your wife received guests on the day of the fête.'

He shot a quick doubtful glance at her. Was this, after

all, just another sensation-seeker? But Miss Marple's face was grave and composed.

'Why certainly,' he said, 'if you want to do so. Come with me.'

He led her to the staircase head and paused in the hollowed-out bay at the top of it.

'You've made a good many changes in the house since the Bantrys were here,' said Miss Marple. 'I like this. Now, let me see. The tables would be about here, I suppose, and you and your wife would be standing—'

'My wife stood here.' Jason showed her the place. 'People came up the stairs, she shook hands with them and passed them on to me.'

'She stood here,' said Miss Marple.

She moved over and took her place where Marina Gregg had stood. She remained there quite quietly without moving. Jason Rudd watched her. He was perplexed but interested. She raised her right hand slightly as though shaking, looked down the stairs as though to see people coming up it. Then she looked straight ahead of her. On the wall half-way up the stairs was a large picture, a copy of an Italian Old Master. On either side of it were narrow windows, one giving out on the garden and the other giving on to the end of the stables and the weathercock. But Miss Marple looked at neither of these. Her eyes were fixed on the picture itself.

'Of course you always hear a thing right the first time,' she said. 'Mrs Bantry told me that your wife stared at the picture and her face "froze", as she put it.' She looked at the rich red and blue robes of the Madonna, a Madonna with her head slightly back, laughing up at the Holy Child that she was holding up in her arms. 'Giacomo Bellini's "Laughing Madonna",' she said. 'A religious picture, but also a painting of a happy mother with her child. Isn't that so, Mr Rudd?'

'I would say so, yes.'

'I understand now,' said Miss Marple. 'I understand quite well. The whole thing is really very simple, isn't it?' She looked at Jason Rudd.

'Simple?'

'I think you know how simple it is,' said Miss Marple. There was a peal on the bell below.

'I don't think,' said Jason Rudd, 'I quite understand.' He looked down the stairway. There was a sound of voices.

'I know that voice,' said Miss Marple. 'It's Inspector Craddock's voice, isn't it?'

'Yes, it seems to be Inspector Craddock.'

'He wants to see you, too. Would you mind very much if he joined us?'

'Not at all as far as I am concerned. Whether he will agree—'

'I think he will agree,' said Miss Marple. 'There's really not much time now to be lost, is there? We've got to the moment when we've got to understand just how everything happened.'

'I thought you said it was simple,' said Jason Rudd.

'It was so simple,' said Miss Marple, 'that one just couldn't see it.'

The decayed butler arrived at this moment up the stairs.

'Inspector Craddock is here, sir,' he said.

'Ask him to join us here, please,' said Jason Rudd.

The butler disappeared again and a moment or two later Dermot Craddock came up the stairs.

'You!' he said to Miss Marple, 'how did you get here?'

'I came in Inch,' said Miss Marple, producing the usual confused effect that that remark always caused.

From slightly behind her Jason Rudd rapped his forehead interrogatively. Dermot Craddock shook his head.

'I was saying to Mr Rudd,' said Miss Marple, '—has the butler gone away—'

Dermot Craddock cast a look down the stairs.

'Oh, yes,' he said, 'he's not listening. Sergeant Tiddler will see to that.'

'Then that is all right,' said Miss Marple. 'We could of course have gone into a room to talk, but I prefer it like this. Here we are on the spot where the thing happened, which makes it so much easier to understand.'

'You are talking,' said Jason Rudd, 'of the day of the fête here, the day when Heather Badcock was poisoned.'

'Yes,' said Miss Marple, 'and I'm saying that it is all very simple if one only looks at it in the proper way. It all began, you see, with Heather Badcock being the kind of person she was. It was inevitable, really, that something of that kind should happen some day to Heather.'

'I don't understand what you mean,' said Jason Rudd. 'I don't understand at all.'

'No, it has to be explained a little. You see, when my friend, Mrs Bantry who was here, described the scene to me, she quoted a poem that was a great favourite in my youth, a poem of dear Lord Tennyson's. "The Lady of Shalott".' She raised her voice a little.

> *'The mirror crack'd from side to side:*
> *"The curse is come upon me," cried*
> *The Lady of Shalott.*

'That's what Mrs Bantry saw, or thought she saw, though actually she misquoted and said "doom" instead of "curse"—perhaps a better word in the circumstances. She saw your wife speaking to Heather Badcock and heard Heather Badcock speaking to your wife and she saw this look of doom on your wife's face.'

'Haven't we been over that a great many times?' said Jason Rudd.

'Yes, but we shall have to go over it once more,' said Miss Marple. 'There was that expression on your wife's face and she was looking not at Heather Badcock but at that picture. At a picture of a laughing, happy mother holding up a happy child. The mistake was that though there *was* doom foreshadowed in Marina Gregg's face, it was not on *her* the doom would come. The doom was to come upon Heather. Heather was doomed from the first moment that she began talking and boasting of an incident in the past.'

'Could you make yourself a little clearer?' said Dermot Craddock.

Miss Marple turned to him.

'Of course I will. This is something that you know nothing about. You couldn't know about it, because nobody has told you what it was Heather Badcock actually said.'

'But they have,' protested Dermot. 'They've told me over and over again. Several people have told me.'

'Yes,' said Miss Marple, 'but you don't know because, you see, Heather Badcock didn't tell it to *you*.'

'She hardly could tell it to me seeing she was dead when I arrived here,' said Dermot.

'Quite so,' said Miss Marple. 'All you know is that she was ill but she got up from bed and came along to a celebration of some kind where she met Marina Gregg and spoke to her and asked for an autograph and was given one.'

'I know,' said Craddock with slight impatience. 'I've heard all that.'

'But you didn't hear the one operative phrase, because no one thought it was important,' said Miss Marple. 'Heather Badcock was ill in bed—with *German measles*.'

'German measles? What on earth has that got to do with it?'

'It's a very slight illness, really,' said Miss Marple. 'It hardly makes you feel ill at all. You have a rash which is easy to cover up with powder, and you have a little fever, but not very much. You feel quite well enough to go out and see people if you want to. And of course in repeating all this the fact that it was German measles didn't strike people particularly. Mrs Bantry, for instance, just said that Heather had been ill in bed and mentioned chicken pox and nettlerash. Mr Rudd here said that it was 'flu, but of course he did that on purpose. But I think myself that what

Heather Badcock said to Marina Gregg was that she had had German measles and got up from bed and went off to meet Marina. And that's really the answer to the whole thing, because, you see, German measles is extremely infectious. People catch it very easily. And there's one thing about it which you've got to remember. If a woman contracts it in the first four months of—' Miss Marple spoke the next word with a slight Victorian modesty '—of—er—pregnancy, it may have a terribly serious effect. It may cause an unborn child to be born blind or to be born mentally affected.'

She turned to Jason Rudd.

'I think I am correct in saying, Mr Rudd, that your wife had a child who was born mentally afflicted and that she has never really recovered from the shock. She had always wanted a child and when at last the child came, this was the tragedy that happened. A tragedy she has never forgotten, that she has not allowed herself to forget and which ate into her as a kind of deep sore, an obsession.'

'It's quite true,' said Jason Rudd. 'Marina developed German measles early on in her pregnancy and was told by the doctor that the mental affliction of her child was due to that cause. It was not a case of inherited insanity or anything of that kind. He was trying to be helpful but I don't think it helped her much. She never knew how, or when or from whom she had contracted the disease.'

'Quite so,' said Miss Marple, 'she never knew until one afternoon here when a perfectly strange woman came up those stairs and told her the fact—told her, what was more—with a great deal of pleasure! With an air of being proud of what she'd done! *She* thought she'd been resourceful and brave and shown a lot of spirit in getting up from her bed, covering her face with make-up, and going along to meet the actress on whom she had such a crush and obtaining her autograph. It's a thing she has boasted of all through her life. Heather Badcock meant no harm. She never did mean harm but there is no doubt that people like Heather Badcock (and like my old friend Alison Wilde), are capable of doing a lot of harm because they lack—not kindness, they have kindness—but any real consideration for the way their actions may affect other people. She thought always of what an action meant to *her*, never sparing a thought to what it might mean to somebody else.'

Miss Marple nodded her head gently.

'So she died, you see, for a simple reason out of her own past. You must imagine what that moment meant to Marina Gregg. I think Mr Rudd understands it very well. I think she had nursed all those years a kind of hatred for the unknown person who had been the cause of her tragedy. And here suddenly she meets that person face to face. And a person who is gay, jolly and pleased with herself. It was too much for her. If she had had time to think, to calm down, to be persuaded to relax—but she gave herself no time. Here was this woman who had destroyed her happiness and destroyed the sanity and health of her child. She wanted to punish her. She wanted to kill her. And unfortunately the means were to hand. She carried with her that well-known specific, Calmo. A somewhat dangerous drug because you had to be careful of the exact dosage. It was very easy to do. She put the stuff into her own glass. If by any chance anyone noticed what she was doing they were probably so used to her pepping herself up or soothing herself down in any handy liquid that they'd hardly notice it. It's possible that one person did see her, but I rather doubt it. I think that Miss Zielinsky did no more than guess. Marina Gregg put her glass down on the table and presently she managed to jog Heather Badcock's arm so that Heather Badcock spilt her own drink all down her new dress. And that's where the element of puzzle has come into the matter, owing to the fact that people cannot remember to use their pronouns properly.

'It reminds me so much of that parlourmaid I was telling you about,' she added to Dermot. 'I only had the account, you see, of what Gladys Dixon said to Cherry which simply was that she was worried about the ruin of Heather Badcock's dress with the cocktail spilt down it. What seemed so funny, she said, was that she did it on purpose. But the "she" that Gladys referred to was not Heather Badcock, it was Marina Gregg. As Gladys said: She did it on purpose! She jogged Heather's arm. Not by accident but because she *meant* to do so. We do know that she must have been standing very close to Heather because we have heard that she mopped up both Heather's dress and her own before pressing her cocktail on Heather. It was really,' said Miss Marple meditatively, 'a very perfect murder; because, you see, it was committed on the spur of the moment without pausing to think or reflect. She wanted Heather Badcock dead and a few minutes later Heather Badcock *was* dead. She didn't realize, perhaps, the seriousness of what she'd done and certainly not the danger of it until afterwards. But she realized it then. She was afraid, horribly afraid. Afraid that someone had seen her dope her own glass, that someone had seen her deliberately jog Heather's elbow, afraid that someone would accuse her of having poisoned Heather. She could see only one way out. To insist that the murder had been aimed at *her*, that *she* was the prospective victim. She tried that idea first on her doctor. She refused to let him tell her husband because I think she knew that her husband would not be deceived. She did fantastic things. She wrote notes to herself and arranged to find them in extraordinary places and at extraordinary moments. She doctored her own coffee at the studios one day. She did things that could really have been seen through fairly easily if one had happened to be thinking that way. They were seen through by one person.'

She looked at Jason Rudd.

'This is only a theory of yours,' said Jason Rudd.

'You can put it that way, if you like,' said Miss Marple, 'but you know quite well, don't you, Mr Rudd, that I'm speaking the truth. You know, because you knew from the first. You knew because you heard that mention of German measles. You knew and you were frantic to protect her. But you didn't realize how much you would have to protect her from. You didn't realize that it was not only a question of hushing up one death, the death of a woman whom you might say quite fairly had brought her death on herself. But there were other deaths—the death of Giuseppe, a blackmailer, it is true, but a human being. And the death of Ella Zielinsky of whom I expect you were fond. You were frantic to protect Marina and also to prevent her from doing more harm. All you wanted was to get her safely away somewhere. You tried to watch her all the time, to make sure that nothing more should happen.'

She paused, and then coming nearer to Jason Rudd, she laid a gentle hand on his arm.

'I am very sorry for you,' she said, 'very sorry. I do realize the agony you've been through. You cared for her so much, didn't you?'

Jason Rudd turned slightly away.

'That,' he said, 'is, I believe, common knowledge.'

'She was such a beautiful creature,' said Miss Marple gently. 'She had such a wonderful gift. She had a great power of love and hate but no stability. That's what's so sad for anyone, to be born with no stability. She couldn't let the past go and she could never see the future as it really was, only as she imagined it to be. She was a great actress and a beautiful and very unhappy woman. What a wonderful Mary, Queen of Scots she was! I shall never forget her.'

Sergeant Tiddler appeared suddenly on the stairs.

'Sir,' he said, 'can I speak to you a moment?'

Craddock turned.

'I'll be back,' he said to Jason Rudd, then he went towards the stairs.

'Remember,' Miss Marple called after him, 'poor Arthur Badcock had nothing to do with this. He came to the fête because he wanted to have a glimpse of the girl he had married long ago. I should say she didn't even recognize him. Did she?' she asked Jason Rudd.

Jason Rudd shook his head.

'I don't think so. She certainly never said anything to me. I don't think,' he added thoughtfully, 'she would recognize him.'

'Probably not,' said Miss Marple. 'Anyway,' she added, 'he's quite innocent of wanting to kill her or anything of that kind. Remember that,' she added to Dermot Craddock as he went down the stairs.

'He's not been in any real danger, I can assure you,' said Craddock, 'but of course when we found out that he had actually been Miss Marina Gregg's first husband we naturally had to question him on the point. Don't worry about him, Aunt Jane,' he added in a low murmur, then he hurried down the stairs.

Miss Marple turned to Jason Rudd. He was standing there like a man in a daze, his eyes far away.

'Would you allow me to see her?' said Miss Marple.

He considered her for a moment or two, then he nodded.

'Yes, you can see her. You seem to—understand her very well.'

He turned and Miss Marple followed him. He preceded her into the big bedroom and drew the curtains slightly aside.

Marina Gregg lay in the great white shell of the bed— her eyes closed, her hands folded.

So, Miss Marple thought, might the Lady of Shalott have lain in the boat that carried her down to Camelot. And there, standing musing, was a man with a rugged, ugly face, who might pass as a Lancelot of a later day.

Miss Marple said gently, 'It's very fortunate for her that

279

she—took an overdose. Death was really the only way of escape left to her. Yes—very fortunate she took that overdose—or—*was given it?*'

His eyes met hers, but he did not speak.

He said brokenly, 'She was—so lovely—and she had suffered so much.'

Miss Marple looked back against the still figure.

She quoted softly the last lines of the poem:

'He said: *"She has a lovely face;*
God in His mercy lend her grace,
The Lady of Shalott."'

Printed by RR Donnelley at Glasgow, UK